Greyladies

PORTRAIT OF SASKIA

Dorothy Emily Stevenson, born in Edinburgh in 1892, was very proud of her family tradition of engineering and writing; her great-grandfather, Robert Stevenson, designed the famous Bell Rock Lighthouse and many others around the Scottish coast, and her father was a first cousin of Robert Louis Stevenson. She herself started writing stories as a small child,

Her first novel, *Peter West*, was published in 1929, but she did not find fame until 1932 with the publication of *Mrs. Tim of the Regiment* based on her own experience as an army wife with her husband Captain James Peploe, whom she had married in 1916. She went on to write a total of 45 (published) novels, which sold over seven million copies and brought her worldwide fame.

The extent of her early writing is becoming more evident with the recent discovery of some boxes of unpublished manuscripts, including *The Fair Miss Fortune*, *Emily Dennistoun* and *Portrait of Saskia* in her granddaughter's attic.

The family moved to Moffat in the Scottish Borders in 1940, where she wrote her books in longhand, reclining on a sofa looking out over the Dumfriesshire hills.

She died in 1973.

BY THE SAME AUTHOR
published by Greyladies

The Fair Miss Fortune
Emily Dennistoun

PORTRAIT OF SASKIA

D. E. STEVENSON

Greyladies

Published by
Greyladies
an imprint of The Old Children's Bookshelf
175 Canongate, Edinburgh EH8 8BN

© The Estate of D. E. Stevenson
First published 2011
Design and layout © Shirley Neilson 2011
Foreword © Geraldine Hogg 2011
It is not our intention to breach any copyright. If we have
inadvertently done so, we will be happy to remedy this if the
appropriate copyright holder would contact us.

ISBN 978-1-907503-16-0

All rights reserved. No part of this publication may be
reproduced, stored in or introduced into a retrieval system, or
transmitted, in any form or by any means (electronic,
mechanical, photocopying, recording or otherwise) without the
prior written permission of the above copyright owners and the
above publisher of this book.

Set in Sylfaen / Perpetua
Printed and bound by the MPG Books Group,
Bodmin and Kings Lynn.

CONTENTS

Foreword	
Portrait of Saskia	3
The Murder of Alma Atherton	169
Where the Gentian Blooms	187
Moira	231
The Mulberry Coach	247
The Secret of the Black Rock	265

Foreword

I think it was in 2009 that Penny Kent first contacted me about a treasure trove of D. E. Stevenson manuscripts that had come to light. I had been reading and re-reading D. E. Stevenson novels since the late 1960s or early 1970s, so my joy at learning there were things that I'd never read or heard of before was as if all my birthdays and Christmases had come at once.

Penny asked me if various character names and locations were familiar to me from already published D. E. Stevenson novels. I was able to confirm that none of the ones she quoted were things I recognised, and stories were submitted to Greyladies for their judgement. I didn't see any of these manuscripts, therefore when "*The Fair Miss Fortune*" and "*Emily Dennistoun*" were released I had the fun of reading "brand new" D. E. Stevenson novels in print for the first time.

It was very hard for me to keep quiet about this. The only person that I talked to about it during this time was my husband, Dick. I was certain that the other members of The DESsies, the D. E. Stevenson email discussion group, would be equally ecstatic when they learnt that there were "new to all of us" stories which might be publishable. I hadn't been asked to keep this a secret but in my opinion it was up to either a member of the family or the publisher to break this exciting news to the rest of the world. Naturally when Shirley emailed the DESsie Group to let them know about the forthcoming publications there was rejoicing and eager anticipation on both sides of the Atlantic.

Perhaps I should explain how I got to know Penny. In

the 1990s I began to research D. E. Stevenson's life for my own interest and was astonished to discover that for many years she had lived in Moffat, and was buried there in the cemetery on the Edinburgh Road. This is a town that was familiar to me because a relative of my husband lived in Moffat. At the tourist information office in Moffat I was given the address of Wendy, one of D. E. Stevenson's grand-daughters who lives in the town. I wrote to Wendy when we returned home to Bedfordshire.

Wendy very kindly gave me the contact details for her mother, D. E. Stevenson's daughter, Rosemary, who lives in Hertfordshire. I got the impression that I was the first person researching D. E. Stevenson to contact the family, rather than researching the deservedly famous Lighthouse Engineer Stevensons. My husband and I visited Rosemary a few times, and later on we met another of Rosemary's daughters, Penny, who also lives in Hertfordshire.

Towards the end of 1999 I did a search on Google for "D. E. Stevenson" and came across a fascinating website, which led to me joining the DESsie discussion group in January 2000. Unlike many of the DESsies I'd always known that I wasn't the only person in the world who loved the books, because my late mother, one of my two sisters, and that sister's only daughter were also fans.

After the publication of "*The Fair Miss Fortune*" and "*Emily Dennistoun*" was arranged, Penny asked me if I'd like to look at some manuscripts and give her my opinion. I typed copies of two hand-written manuscripts that I had borrowed from Penny; one of the two being an untitled story that I felt could be titled either "*Kenneth Leslie*" after the hero of the story, or "*Portrait of Saskia*". This story was one of my favourites from the batch of unpublished work that Penny had so kindly loaned me, and I hope that other people will enjoy reading it as much as I did.

The other manuscript that I made a typed copy of, gave me a surprise as I was reading it. Towards the end of the story there were things that I recalled from a published D. E. Stevenson novel, and by chance it was the book that the email group were discussing at that time. I had to sit on my hands not to burst out with the fact that some of the events in *"Rochester's Wife"* published by Collins in 1940 had been recycled from an unpublished novel which D. E. Stevenson had called *"The Self Seekers"*. There were altered names, and a change of gender for one young character; Jinny Ann became Wattie, but there was enough word for word reuse for me to recognise certain scenes, between the two otherwise very different stories.

This made me think of how D. E. Stevenson had reworked *"The House of the Deer"*. This had originally been serialised in the *Glasgow Bulletin* newspaper in June – July 1936, and many years later was greatly revised and published in 1970 by Collins as a sequel to *"Gerald and Elizabeth"*. There were some sections of the story that were common to both versions but with enough alterations in other parts to make the two versions unlike each other.

Also among the short stories in the latest selection of manuscripts that I'd borrowed from Penny were two versions of a novella, *"Where the Gentian Blooms"*. The one in this book is a marriage of the two versions, as we felt that it had the more satisfying ending.

Geraldine Hogg, Bedfordshire 2011

PORTRAIT OF SASKIA

CHAPTER 1
Alan Seton Introduces Himself

SOME YEARS AGO I fell into a crevasse when I was climbing in the Swiss Alps. I ought to have been killed of course but I landed in a heap of snow and got off with an injured hip; the doctors did what they could for me but my right leg remained some three inches shorter than the left and the limp put an end to most of my activities. Fortunately I have a small income so I bought a flat in London and settled down to a quiet life.

I had enjoyed adventuring, but now I had to take my adventures second-hand so I looked for them amongst the people I met and became adept at putting two and two together and making a story of it. Anybody who says there is no adventure left in the modern world is walking about with his eyes and ears shut to what goes on around him.

This story is not about me, it is about Kenneth Leslie, a man young enough to be my son, and I have pieced it together from what he told me afterwards and from what other people told me. I got some of it from his friend Robert Couper and some from Anne Carr; Doctor Stott filled in a few of the gaps and Jim Slater gave me his account of the days fishing on the River Fleece. Colonel MacLean was too cautious to tell me much, but I got his angle on the affair from Wallace, and Mr. Ingram Whitehill gave me an extremely amusing account of the part he played.

At first I thought I would let the story stand just as it

was, and let the different people tell their own tales; but it was too muddled that way, so I decided to sit on a cloud like Jove and tell the story in proper sequence.

The whole thing began on a fine evening in April when I went out for a walk and sat down on my favourite bench in St James's Park. I often sat here and watched the people. Sometimes there were old men sitting upon the bench and smoking and sometimes there were young women with shopping baskets or babies in perambulators. I listened to them talking and managed to get a good deal of amusement out of it. On this particular evening there was nobody sitting upon the bench, so I sat down at one end of it and rested. It was getting dark but it was quite warm and there was a feeling of spring in the air. Presently two young people, a man and a girl, came along. They had a small black spaniel with them and when they sat down the spaniel sat down beside them and waited patiently.

By this time it was getting pretty dark so I could not see them clearly and perhaps that was why they did not bother about me — or perhaps it was because they were too taken up with their own affairs to bother whether a strange man sitting on a bench in the park overheard their conversation.

"We'd have plenty of money if I went on with my job," said the girl. It was a pretty voice but there was a complaining note in it and I formed the opinion that the argument had been going on for some time.

"But I've told you I don't want that," the young man replied.

"I know, but don't you see — "

"We could live on my salary."

"We couldn't."

"I think we could. Honestly Margaret, lots of people get married on less and manage all right."

"Pinching and scraping!" exclaimed the girl. "No nice clothes and no fun! Besides what would I do all day when you were at the office? I can't see the object of it."

"I've told you —"

"Oh, I know. You've told me a dozen times but I still can't see any sense in it. If I go on working for Mr. Ballintray we can have a nice flat and be comfortable."

The young man was silent for a few moments. Then he said, "I wouldn't mind so much if it was an ordinary job, in an office—"

"Well, I would!" cried the girl. "I'd hate a dull dreary job in an office. Besides I wouldn't get nearly so much money. Oh Ken, why can't you be sensible?"

"I am being sensible."

"You don't try to understand what I feel about it. You don't love me!"

"Of course I love you," he said. His voice was low and deep and very earnest. "It's just because I love you that I want you all to myself — and not working for that man."

"I like working for him!"

"That makes it worse."

"You're jealous, Ken."

"Not really," he said slowly. "I mean not jealous in the ordinary way — but I just couldn't bear it. All day long I would be thinking about you. It would make me miserable."

"Lots of girls go on with their work after they're

5

married."

"I know," he agreed.

"Well then, why shouldn't I? It's an interesting job and well-paid and we should be so much better off — so much more comfortable. Why should I give it up?"

"Because I ask you to give it up," he said.

"Oh goodness!" she cried. "I'm sick of this argument. Let's go and have supper."

They rose and walked on. They spaniel rose too; he came and sniffed my legs and wagged his tail, so I gave him a small piece of biscuit which I had in my pocket. He accepted it gratefully and allowed himself to be patted before trotting off after his friends.

It was nearly a week before I walked that way again and in the meantime I had thought about the two young people quite often. Both voices had sounded determined and I wondered which of them had won the day. I hoped that "Ken" had not given in, for I was old-fashioned and held the opinion that a man should support his wife by his own efforts . . . yes, I was on Ken's side.

When I approached the bench I saw the girl. She was sitting on the bench where she had sat before, but this time she was alone except for the spaniel. It was earlier and the skies were clear so there was light enough for me to see that she was very pretty with dark curly hair and a good profile. Obviously she was expecting or hoping for somebody to meet her for she looked up eagerly when she heard my footsteps on the path, but when she saw it was only a lame old man her shoulders drooped and she looked away. The spaniel was not disappointed; he rose and came towards me wagging his tail. Spaniels have long memories for people who have given them biscuits.

"Trusty seems to know you!" exclaimed his mistress in surprise.

"I like dogs," I told her. "Dogs know when people like them. May I give him a biscuit?"

"If you want to," she replied listlessly. "He's very greedy."

I sat down on the far end of the bench and gave Trusty his biscuit. "Spaniels enjoy food and petting," I said. "It's their nature so we mustn't blame them. Dogs act according to their nature and so do people for that matter."

She turned and looked at me. "Do you really believe that? Do you mean we shouldn't blame people for being selfish and — and unreasonable?"

"That depends on circumstances," I replied cautiously. Then suddenly I decided to give the young woman a fright. "For instance," I said thoughtfully as I caressed the silky ears of the spaniel. "Let's take an imaginary case. We'll suppose two young people are in love with each other and decide to get married. The young man is earning a small salary so the young woman thinks it would be a good plan to keep on her job and contribute to household expenses. But the young man doesn't agree; he wants to support his wife by his own efforts; he wants to have her to himself. He asks the girl to give up her job. Now the point is —"

"Who are you?" cried the girl in amazement.

"My name is Alan Seton."

"But who are you? I mean I've never seen you before."

"Just a useless old man with a lame leg," I told her.

7

"How did you know about Ken and me?"

"I happened to be sitting here on Monday night."

"You mean you listened to what we said?"

"I couldn't help listening," I replied, somewhat annoyed at her tone. "I was sitting on this bench and you came and sat down near me — and talked. Do you think I should have got up and gone away?"

"Then — it was just — just an accident," said the girl uncertainly. "You don't know Ken? You can't tell me where he's gone."

"Gone?"

"Ken has disappeared," said the girl in tragic tones.

There was nothing to say to that — or at least I could find nothing.

After a few moments she moved nearer to me. "Is it true?" she asked. "You aren't just playing a game with me, are you? Ken didn't send you here to — to find out if I had changed my mind?"

"I know nothing about him," I told her.

"We quarrelled," she said in a low voice. "We were having supper together in a restaurant and he was so selfish and unreasonable that I got up and went away. I thought he would ring me up and say he was sorry."

"But he didn't?"

"No, he didn't. I waited for two whole days and then I rang up the office where he works and asked to speak to him — and they said he had gone away."

"Perhaps he has got another job."

"But where?" said the girl miserably. "And why? They were annoyed at the office because he hadn't given a week's notice so they were unsympathetic about it. They just said they didn't know where he had gone. Then yesterday I went round to his flat — he shares it with a friend. I rang and knocked but nobody came. I've been there again tonight, knocking and ringing the bell, but the flat is empty, it's all shut up. Where can he have gone?"

"I've no idea," I said.

"But what am I to do? How can I find out? Do you think he has had some accident? Or do you think he has gone abroad? He used to talk about going to Canada. Oh, it's horrid of him to go off like that without telling me!"

By this time it was getting cold and had begun to rain so I suggested we should go to my flat, which is quite near the park, and continue our conversation in comfort. The girl hesitated but only for a moment. I suppose I look a respectable sort of person and she was desperate; she had to talk to somebody about her troubles.

When I had given her a glass of sherry we settled down comfortably with the spaniel lying stretched out upon the hearth-rug at our feet and she told me the whole story. Her name was Margaret Coke; she lived with her parents in Bromley and travelled to town daily; his name was Kenneth Leslie, he came from Aberdeen and except for a married sister who lived near Bristol he had no relations at all. They had met at a cocktail party about six months ago and had fallen in love.

"We got engaged just after Christmas," said Margaret. "It was marvellous. I took Ken home with me and he was a great success; Mummy and Daddy liked him and he liked them too. He's very good-looking, isn't he? So tall and strong, with his blue-grey eyes and thick brown hair, and he has such nice manners. It was all absolutely marvellous until we began to talk about the future . . . and then we — we disagreed. I want to go on with my job so that we can have a comfortable flat and plenty of money but Ken's idea is that I'm to give up my job and — and just be his wife. I thought that in time he would come round to my point of view but the more we argued about it the more stubborn he became. It was so silly. It made me angry. On Monday night I got quite desperate and I thought I would give him a fright — "

"A fright?" I echoed in surprise.

"Yes — well — I took off my ring."

"You mean you broke off your engagement?"

"Not really. It was just — I mean I only wanted him to be sensible, that's all. He's so sensible about most things, why couldn't he be sensible about this?"

"Perhaps because it was very important to him," I suggested.

"It's important to me, too."

"You can't have everything," I told her. "It seems to me you'll have to make up your mind what you want most."

"I want Ken," said Margaret, and she began to cry.

"Don't!" I exclaimed. "My dear girl, for goodness sake don't cry. We'll find him and everything will be all right."

"If only — I had someone — to help me!"

"I'll help you," I declared. "I'll do all I can. Give me the address of his flat and I'll go round tomorrow morning. Perhaps some of the neighbours will know where he has gone. I'll get his address and you can write to him."

10

CHAPTER 2
The Missing Advertisement

IT WAS NOT AS EASY as I had hoped to get news of Kenneth Leslie. I went round to his flat and hung about the building and questioned the neighbours but without any success. Nobody knew anything about the young man; nobody seemed to care. Every evening after her work Margaret came in to see me, to ask if there was any news and to spur me on.

To be honest I became a little tired of Margaret. My first impression had been that she was pretty and attractive — she was, of course — but the more I saw of her the less I liked her. There was a hard streak in Margaret and she was selfish. Although she had said she "wanted Ken" I realised that she wanted him on her own terms and was not prepared to take him on his.

"If only you could get his address," she kept saying, "then I could write to him. He has behaved very badly but I'll forgive him if he'll be sensible."

"Listen, Margaret," I said at last. "You'll have to give up your job if you want to marry Ken. That's obvious."

"But I like my job," she objected.

"What is your job?" I asked.

She told me. She was secretary to an author, Victor Ballintray, whose books sold in hundreds of thousands all over the world. I happened to know they were very

11

unsavoury books and the man himself had an unpleasant reputation.

"Of course they aren't *nice* books," admitted Margaret. "But that's nothing to do with me. I take his stuff down in shorthand and type it for him — it doesn't affect me one way or the other. He pays me very well and treats me like a human being. Some people treat you as if you were a piece of furniture."

I said nothing to this. It was no wonder that young Leslie had objected to Margaret's job.

"He's very kind," continued Margaret. "He gives me a comfortable room to work in and he doesn't mind me taking Trusty with me — and he's very sympathetic about Ken. He said this morning that we ought to tell the police about Ken in case there's been an accident."

"Oh no!" I exclaimed.

"Why not? Mr. Ballintray thinks we should. Ken may have been run over — or murdered — "

I thought this most unlikely. The young man had left his job and shut up his flat so the inference was that he had gone off on some business of his own.

"Wait and see," I said. "I expect that he'll write to you soon. He's probably waiting till he gets settled — "

"If I don't hear soon I shall go to the police," said Margaret.

I had intended to give up the search (I had wasted a lot of time over it already) but somehow the problem worried me and the next morning found me toiling up the stairs to Kenneth Leslie's flat. This was to be the last visit. If I could hear no news of him today I had decided to call it off.

When I reached the door it was slightly ajar so I pushed it open and walked in. A young man was sitting at the table having his breakfast; he looked up and said, "Hullo!"

Naturally I had expected to see Kenneth Leslie himself, but it was not he. It was a small man with flaming red hair and a freckled face.

"Hullo!" he said again, looking at me in surprise. "What do you want?"

I told him I wanted to see Kenneth Leslie.

"So do I," he replied. "The blighter has gone off with the key of the store-cupboard in his pocket and I can't get out the gin. We share this flat — and we share the gin. In fact we share most things."

"Do you know where he is?"

"Not a ghost of an idea. I just got back from Greece last night and Ken wasn't here. He left a letter for me but it's not very informative — just says I needn't expect to hear from him for two months. Excuse me if I go on with my breakfast, won't you?"

"Yes, of course."

"Sit down and talk to me. Tell me why you want to see Ken. By the way there's a girl called Margaret something or other who might know where he is."

"She doesn't — that's just the trouble," I said, and I sat down and told him my story.

"Umph," he said, munching a roll and nodding. "Can't say I'm surprised. Fact is I never liked that girl; she's not nearly good enough for Ken. And I'll tell you another thing: Ken was a bit fed-up with that office. He's an adventurous type and he hated being chained up to an

13

office stool. If you take my tip you'll leave things alone."

"Yes, I suppose I shall have to."

"I shan't stir a finger to find him — for that Margaret girl," added the red-haired young man firmly.

"No," I agreed. "But she keeps on badgering me and if I don't do something about it she'll go to the police."

"Good lord, she mustn't do that!"

"The only way I can prevent her is by trying to find him myself."

"Are you a relation — or what?" he enquired.

I could not help smiling. "I'm just an interfering old codger who's beginning to wish he hadn't interfered."

The young man had finished his breakfast by this time and he sat back and thought the matter over. At last he said, "There's just one clue. I wasn't going to say anything about it because I hate meddling in other fellows' affairs . . . but perhaps we'd better follow it up. But look here. Mr. — er —"

"Seton," I told him.

"Mr. Seton," said the young man, nodding. "Look here, I don't want that Margaret girl put on his track."

I hesitated.

"Take it or leave it," he said. "I'm sorry to be brutal but you see Ken may have done a bunk to escape from her clutches."

"Very well," I said. "If we find young Leslie I'll just tell her he's all right — nothing more. She'll be furious of course but it can't be helped.

He rose at once and went over to a desk in the corner of the room and produced a crumpled piece of newspaper.

14

"This is the famous clue," he said with a wide grin. "I found it when I was emptying the waste paper basket and I kept it just in case. As I said I don't believe in meddling but — well — you never know what will Ken do next. He's a sort of Don Quixote; there's a romantic streak in him. He reads adventure stories in his spare time —"

"And was chained to an office-stool."

"Exactly. When people like that cut loose it's apt to be a bit dangerous."

The paper which he handed me was an old copy of the *Daily Clarion* and there was a space in it where an advertisement had been cut out.

"You see," he said, pointing to the space. "Ken must have cut it out. It may mean nothing at all but my guess is he applied for the job, whatever it was, and probably got it. If you want to follow it up you could nip round to the *Clarion* office and have a look at the paper for that date."

I told him I would do so and asked if he would care to come along to my flat in the evening.

"You bet," he said cheerfully. "I want to know about Ken. By the way my name is Robert Couper but everybody calls me Copper. It's just one of those things."

We said goodbye.

The offices of the *Daily Clarion* are in Fleet Street. I went there at once and asked to see their files of back papers — there was no difficulty about that — and the moment my eyes fell upon the missing advertisement I knew we were on the right track; it was exactly the sort of advertisement which would appeal to young man of Quixotic temperament.

> Retired Army Office offers a large sum of money to a
> Young Man who wants Adventure. Must be of good
> appearance and free from dependants. Engagement
> for two months.

There was a box office number to apply to, and that stumped me for obviously I could not apply. Then I decided to see what I could do with the young woman behind the counter. I approached her with my best smile and asked if she could let me have the advertiser's name and address.

"It's against the rules," she replied. "No, I couldn't possibly. You can write to the box number and it will be forwarded, but as a matter of fact you'll be wasting your time if you do. The advertisement has been withdrawn which means the post is filled." She looked at me curiously and added, "Besides it says a young man of good appearance."

"I wasn't asking for myself," I assured her and came away. As far as I could see there was nothing more to be done.

Robert Couper dropped in at tea-time. I had not expected him to come so early and I had nothing very appetising to give him to eat. (Tea is a meal which I don't bother about when I am alone) but he seemed quite pleased with large slices of new bread, spread with butter and strawberry jam.

"What luck?" he enquired.

I showed him the advertisement, which I had copied out of the paper, and told him I had tried, and failed, to obtain the advertiser's name.

"That's Ken all right," he said. "It's just the sort of wild goose chase that would appeal to him — buried treasure or something."

I had thought of buried treasure too.

"I might be able to work that dame," he added thoughtfully. "At any rate I could have a go. What are you going to say to the Margaret girl? Have you thought?"

As a matter of fact I had been thinking of little else all day. "I don't know," I said. "And she'll be probably be here soon. She's made a habit of coming to see me when she gets off work."

"I'll stay and see her, shall I?"

"Yes, if you've time, Mr. Couper," I replied quickly.

He smiled. "All right, you leave her to me. You're too soft, that's what's the matter — and I wish you'd call me Copper, it sounds more friendly."

I was quite pleased to call him Copper for I liked him immensely and I liked him even more when we had had a little chat. He told me that he was a free-lance journalist and had been in Greece collecting material for a series of talks on the radio. He was alive and vivid and his description of his travels was extremely interesting; I had a feeling that the talks would be well worth listening to.

Neither of us was particularly pleased when Margaret arrived, but Copper greeted her politely and asked how she was getting on.

"You've heard about Ken?" she asked. "I mean I suppose Mr. Seton has told you. He's disappeared."

"Disappeared is rather a dramatic way of describing it," replied Copper, helping himself to another slice of new bread and plastering it with jam. "Ken was fed up with office life so he's taken another job."

"How do you know? Have you seen him? Did he leave a letter for you?"

"He left a letter for me," said Copper casually.

"Where has he gone?"

"He didn't say where he was going."

"How can we find out?"

"We can't find out," replied Copper. "Why should we try? If Ken had wanted us to know where he was going he would have left his address."

"But I want to know," she declared.

Copper did not make any comment. He continued to eat his horribly indigestible food with every appearance of enjoyment.

"We must find out," said Margaret. "Surely we can find out somehow. What did he say in his letter?"

Copper did not answer at once and then he said thoughtfully. "It seems funny to me."

"What seems funny?"

"Why didn't he tell you? I mean if you and Ken are engaged to be married — but I see you aren't wearing a ring."

"We had a — a sort of quarrel."

"Oh, that explains the matter."

"Not really. I mean it wasn't a serious quarrel. We just — but it's nothing to do with you."

"Nothing whatever," agreed Copper cheerfully.

There was a short silence.

"Why won't you help?" asked Margaret in a fretful tone. "I thought you and Ken were such friends. It's horrid of you not to care what's happened to him. Why don't you find out where he's gone?"

"I've told you why," said Copper patiently. "If Ken wants me to know where he's gone he'll tell me. If he wants you to know he'll tell you."

Margaret began to cry. Her tears had melted me, but Copper was made of sterner stuff.

"It looks as if you'd had it," he said brutally. "If you take my advice you'll call off the whole thing and leave Mr. Seton in peace."

She looked at me beseechingly, but I had had enough. "I think Copper is right," I said. "We've done all we can."

"You're both horrid," declared Margaret. She rose and added, "I shall go straight to the police."

"That will put the lid on it," said Copper with conviction.

"What do you mean?"

"Ken will be simply rabid — and I shan't blame him. If any of my friends put the police on my tracks I'd never speak to them again. But go ahead," said Copper cheerfully. "Do what you like. It isn't my funeral."

She looked at him doubtfully. "Perhaps I'd better wait."

"Do what you like," repeated Copper. "Don't ask me."

"Perhaps I'd better wait," repeated Margaret and she went away.

Copper smiled. "It was kinder to be cruel — honestly. I've noticed people of your generation are apt to be a bit soft."

"Yes, I daresay you're right," I said humbly.

19

CHAPTER 3
The Retired Army Officer

THE TRAIN DREW UP at a small wayside station in Cornwall and Kenneth Leslie got out. He stood looking about him with his suitcase in his hand. He had been travelling all day, changing at various places, and he felt very dirty and somewhat dazed; he was also rather unhappy. An elderly man, tall and upright with white hair and a bronzed complexion, emerged from the waiting-room and came towards him.

"Are you Kenneth Leslie?" he asked.

"Yes. I suppose you're Colonel MacLean."

"That's right," said the Colonel nodding and holding out his hand.

Ken was aware that he was being examined critically, but that was natural of course. All the same he wished he did not feel so crumpled and dirty. He put down his suitcase and shook hands with Colonel MacLean and then picked it up again and followed him down the platform. There was a car standing in the yard; it was a medium-sized car, neither very old nor very new, in fact just the sort of car one might expect to find in the possession of a retired Colonel.

"Hop in," said Colonel MacLean. "It's five miles to Seacliff, and I don't drive very fast; you've got to be careful on these narrow winding roads, so we can chat as go along. First of all why did you answer my advertisement?"

"For several reasons," Ken replied. "Principally because I

20

was fed-up with my job. Sitting on an office-stool all day long isn't much fun — and of course there was the money."

"You want money?"

Ken smiled and said, "Most people do. I'd like to go to Canada, or somewhere, and get a more interesting sort of job. A bit of money would be helpful."

"You have nobody dependent on you?"

"Nobody. As a matter of fact I was engaged to be married but — but we didn't see eye to eye so — so she broke it off. I have a sister who is married to a doctor near Bristol but she won't bother if she doesn't hear from me for a bit. The fellow who shares my flat has gone off to Greece on business and I don't know when he'll be back. We never interfere with each other's affairs. So you see there's nobody to bother."

"What about the office?"

Ken laughed a trifle bitterly. "I'll never go back there. They were as sick as mud when I said I was leaving."

"You've burnt your boats with a vengeance!"

"Yes, I know. Even if you decide I'm not the right person for the job I shall never go back. What's the use of toiling and moiling day after day for a mere pittance? That's not life."

"I think you're the right fellow for me, but you haven't heard what the job is," said Colonel MacLean soberly. "You may decide not to take it on; if so I shan't blame you."

"I suppose it's somewhere abroad?"

"No, it's in England."

"What is it, sir?" asked Ken.

For a few moments the Colonel was silent, and then he

said, "We'll leave it until after dinner. You'll be all the better of a bath and some food after your long journey."

Ken could not deny this. Although it was only April and London had been cold and cloudy it was very warm here. The sun was shining in a bright blue sky and the lanes were full of dust. "I suppose you couldn't give me some idea —" he began.

"No, it's a long story and you'll have to hear the whole thing, but I'll give you some idea of my household and then you'll know where you are when we arrive. I'm a widower with one son of eighteen. Four years ago he had a serious accident and he's been a cripple ever since. I've taken him to a dozen different doctors but none of them seem to be able to do much for him. You'll see Wallace, of course. He's very plucky —"

"How dreadful!" said Ken in a low voice.

"We live at Seacliff together," continued the Colonel. "I've got a man and his wife to look after us, a fellow called Shanks — he was my batman when I was in the Service. Seacliff is very isolated but fortunately they don't seem to mind. Then there's Ingram Whitehill; he's staying with us at the moment, collects pictures, you may have heard of him."

"No," said Ken.

"Do you know anything about pictures?"

"No," said Ken.

"About your engagement," said the Colonel after a short silence. "Is it really broken off for good and all?"

Ken hesitated.

"Of course I've no right to ask," said the Colonel hastily.

22

"I just wondered. Sometimes young people quarrel about something unimportant and —"

"We quarrelled about something very important indeed," declared Ken. Quite suddenly he felt that he wanted to talk about his affairs. "As a matter of fact we had quarrelled about it before, several times, but this last time was absolutely final. We were having supper together in a restaurant and she took off her ring and threw it onto my plate and walked out."

"Good lord!"

"Yes, it was final all right," said Ken bitterly. "I never felt such a fool in my life. Everybody in the place was staring at me — and laughing. A girl who can do that, I mean make a scene in a restaurant, isn't the sort of girl I want for my wife."

"She wouldn't make a very comfortable wife," the Colonel agreed.

They drove on in silence for a time. Ken was bursting with curiosity. He had answered the advertisement in the *Daily Clarion* because he was furious with Margaret and absolutely fed-up with the monotony of his life. The advertisement offered Adventure and Money — and those were what he needed.

> Retired Army Officer offers a large sum of money to a young man who wants Adventure. Must be of Good Appearance and free from dependants. Engagement for two months. Apply Daily Clarion Box 35672.

Ken had written off in haste and had received a telegram asking him to come to Cornwall for an interview so he had burnt his boats (as the Colonel had said) and come as directed. The spirit of defiance which had prompted him to this reckless course had lasted until he was in the train, actually on his way, and then he had begun to have doubts and to wonder if he had been crazy.

Of course it was crazy to throw up a settled job and plunge into the unknown — anybody would tell you that, thought Ken. He was somewhat reassured by Colonel MacLean's appearance, but he was still a bit anxious. What on earth could the job be?

Seacliff was well-named. It was a large house, built of grey stone, and it stood upon the very edge of a high cliff overlooking the sea. The place was extremely isolated, there was not another human habitation to be seen, and despite the warm afternoon sunshine it looked bleak and a trifle eerie.

"Parts of the house are very old," said Colonel MacLean as he led the way in. "There are huge cellars and a rough sort of stair-case down the cliff. Wallace used to have a great time playing at smugglers — "

Smugglers, thought Ken. Yes, this would be a grand place for smugglers. Perhaps the job was something to do with smuggling.

Inside the house was comfortable though a trifle old-fashioned and shabby. It was a man's house with deep leather chairs and heavy furniture; there were no cretonnes nor flowers and there were very few cushions. Ken's suitcase was carried upstairs by Shanks, the Colonel's manservant, and it was Shanks who showed Ken the bathroom and informed him that dinner would be ready in

24

half an hour.

Ken bathed and put on grey flannel slacks and a tennis-shirt (he had been told not to dress), and he went downstairs feeling a good deal better.

He found the rest of the party in a long low-ceilinged room with four windows facing the sea. At one end of the room was a table laid for dinner; the other end of the room was furnished as a lounge with comfortable chairs. Colonel MacLean greeted Ken in a friendly manner and made the introductions. Mr. Whitehill was short and stout and bald. His head had the appearance of being too big for his body and this peculiarity was stressed by the fact that he wore very large tortoiseshell-rimmed spectacles. Wallace MacLean was thin and delicate and his face was marked by lines of pain, but his smile was eager and friendly. As the boy limped across to the sideboard and got out the drinks for his father's guests Ken's heart went out to him in a flood of sympathy. Ken had been feeling depressed, he felt life had treated him badly, but now suddenly he was ashamed of himself. If one were strong and fit one had no right to complain.

"Who will have what?" asked Wallace looking round.

"You know my tipple, Wallie," said Mr. Whitehill. "If I can get Scotch I don't look for anything else."

"You'd better have the same, Leslie," said the Colonel. "There's nothing to beat it after a tiring day. I'll have gin and lime, but make it a long one, Wallace. My throat is full of dust."

They sat and chatted for a bit and then moved over to the table for dinner. It was an excellent meal and Ken was hungry so he did it full justice. He gathered that Mr. Whitehill and Wallace had been out in the boat and caught the fish themselves; certainly the fish had quite a different flavour from a London fish which has been packed in ice and sent by train. They talked about various things but there was an odd sort of feeling in the air and every now and then the conversation flagged and died away, and was started again by Mr. Whitehill. It was obvious that they were all abstracted, they were all thinking of something else.

When at last dinner was over Wallace went away and the other three stood up.

"Well, Colonel," said Mr. Whitehill. "I guess the time has come to tell this young man what you want him to do. Wallie has cleared out and I better follow his example."

"I would rather you stayed," said Colonel MacLean quickly.

"Well, if you say so —"

"Yes, you know the whole thing and you may be able to help."

They sat down at the other end of the room. Mr. Whitehill lighted a cigar and the Colonel took out his pipe. Ken noticed that his hands were trembling as he filled it.

CHAPTER 4
The Discovery of Saskia

"IT'S A LONG STORY," said Colonel MacLean. "You've got to know everything from the very beginning, but before we start I must ask you to swear most solemnly that whether or not you undertake the job you'll keep the whole matter a dead secret. You're at liberty to accept the job or turn it down but you must promise absolute secrecy."

"I understand," nodded Ken.

"You promise?"

"Yes, I promise."

There was a short silence.

"Well that's okay," said Mr. Whitehill. "You've got your promise, Colonel, so you can go right ahead. If this young man turns down your offer you can try one of the other applicants. You got over thirty replies to that little advertisement of yours if I remember rightly."

"Thirty-four," said the Colonel. He lighted his pipe, settled himself in the big shabby leather chair and began his story.

"I was an only child," said Colonel MacLean. "My father was in the Indian Army so I used to spend most of my holidays with my mother's brother, Sir Frederick Carr, who had a big property in the north of England. My uncle lost his wife many years ago in a railway accident; he had one son, Gregor Carr, who was some years older than myself. My uncle was good to me and I was very fond of him. As a matter of fact most people liked Uncle Frederick, he was a fine old man —"

"He was indeed," put in Mr. Whitehill. "I only saw him once but he made a big impression upon me."

"He died last year," said Colonel MacLean. "The property went to Gregor, of course. Gregor Carr is a very rich man, not only because he inherited the family money but because he was a successful man of business. He was a director of a very large oil company and, although he has now practically retired and lives at Grey Gill with his daughter, I believe he still has a good deal of influence in the business. That's the present state of affairs."

Ken nodded. He was wondering what all this family history had to do with him.

"Gregor always disliked me," continued the Colonel. "I think he was a bit jealous if the truth be told. Uncle Frederick made no secret of the fact that he liked having me at Grey Gill. When I was a boy I spent my holidays there and later, when I was in the Service, I went there when I got leave. Wallace used to come with me and we had good fun. Sometimes Gregor's daughter was there too. She's a bit older than Wallace but they got on well together. Gregor himself was too busy to spend much time at Grey Gill, and as a matter of fact country life never appealed to him. It appealed to me tremendously. There's plenty of rough shooting and there's fishing too; sometimes we had picnics on the moor. Yes, it was good fun," added the Colonel reminiscently. "Shooting and fishing and then, in the evening, a game of chess. Uncle Frederick was very good at chess and usually beat me, but we had some stiff battles."

"He travelled a lot, didn't he?" put in Mr. Whitehill. "His hobby was collecting pictures, and he knew a good deal about them, what's more."

Ken saw his two companions glance at one another significantly.

"Yes, he knew about pictures," agreed Colonel MacLean. "He used to pick them up at sales and in out-of-the-way places in Belgium and Holland. He liked talking about his finds and I was interested in his stories. As a matter of fact I'm fond of pictures myself."

"You've got a flair," declared Mr. Whitehill. "You know a good thing when you see it, Colonel."

"Well — perhaps," agreed Colonel MacLean smiling. "A fine picture gives me a great deal of pleasure, I admit. Unfortunately my cousin Gregor had no use for pictures. He thought it a waste of money to spend hundreds of pounds on canvas and paint and his father's stories bored him to death. He used to argue with his father and say it was ridiculous to have so much capital tied up in pictures; they produced no dividends. This annoyed the old man and he would fly into a rage. 'Dividends!' he would shout. 'You think of nothing but money. That picture gives me a dividend of pleasure every time I look at it.' Gregor would smile and say nothing. He has a very unpleasant smile.

"About five years ago Wallace and I went up to Grey Gill for a holiday. I hadn't been to see Uncle Frederick for some time and I found him depressed. He was suffering from rheumatism and had given up shooting and fishing. He was a bit bored with life, poor old fellow. While I was there he told me that he had decided to leave me all his pictures in his will. 'Gregor will get everything else,' he said 'but I'd like you to have my pictures.' 'Not all of them!' I exclaimed. 'Yes every one,' declared the old man smiling. 'Even the water-colour of the haunted mill in the spare bedroom. Gregor shall have Grey Gill without a single picture in it.'

"I was a bit worried. Gregor and I had never been friends but I didn't want a family quarrel, and I knew he would be furious. Grey Gill was full of pictures; good, bad and indifferent. Some of them were family portraits. It seemed to me that Gregor should have those at least and I said so. At first Uncle Frederick wouldn't listen; he pointed out that if he left me all the pictures I could take the ones I wanted and let Gregor have the others, but I didn't like the plan."

"Your cousin Gregor wouldn't have liked it either," said Mr. Whitehill.

"No, I knew that. I could see frightful trouble ahead. Uncle Frederick and I talked about it a lot and finally I managed to persuade him to change his mind. I suggested that he should leave me the pictures he had brought himself and that the others should be left to Gregor with the house. We were sitting in the library at the time; it's a fine big room and my uncle always used it to sit in so all his best pictures were there. He looked round the walls and nodded. 'Very well,' he said. I'll leave you all these. I daresay you're right. Gregor ought to have the others.'

"I was very pleased with this arrangement and thanked him as best I could. It's difficult to thank a man who tells you he's going to leave you something in his will, but my uncle was sensible and we understood each another. There were seven pictures in the library; my uncle had picked them up himself, every one of them, and they were all valuable. The gem of the collection was a Rembrandt."

"A Rembrandt!" exclaimed Ken in surprise.

Colonel MacLean nodded. "You said you didn't know much about pictures but you probably know that most of Rembrandt's work has been bought by public galleries or well-known collectors. This picture was a find; nobody knew it existed. Uncle Frederick discovered it himself in a junk-shop in Leyden."

"These things happen sometimes," Mr. Whitehill said. "Not often nowadays — nothing of the kind has ever come my way, worse luck. Your uncle found it in an attic, didn't he, Colonel?"

"Yes, it was stacked amongst a lot of rubbish and although it was dirty and in bad condition it caught his eye. He didn't actually know what it was but he had a feeling about it — I've heard him tell the story several times and that's what he always said."

Mr. Whitehill nodded. "I know the feeling — we call it a hunch — you can't explain it. Something inside you tells you to buy the thing."

"That's what happened to Uncle Frederick — he had a hunch — so he bought the picture for a few pounds and took it home with him and started to clean it. Fortunately there was no need to send it to an expert, he knew exactly how to do it himself. Gradually the dirt and grime of centuries melted away and the glowing colours appeared. The force and vigour of the brushwork were unmistakable and, to clinch the matter, it was a portrait of Saskia who was Rembrandt's wife. Rembrandt painted at least half a dozen portraits of Saskia.

"Uncle Frederick was wildly excited about his find, but he kept quiet about it; in fact he told no nobody about it except me. I persuaded him to let Mr. Whitehill see it so Mr. Whitehill came to Grey Gill and had a look at it."

"I did," said Mr. Whitehill. "It was a memorable occasion. I was able to confirm the fact that the picture was a Rembrandt and I offered Sir Frederick Carr fifty thousand dollars for it, but the old gentleman wasn't interested. All he wanted was my promise to keep it dark."

Ken was speechless.

"I expect you're wondering why he was so anxious to keep it a secret," said the Colonel after a pause. "The fact was Uncle Frederick hated publicity. He was aware that the discovery would create a stir; it would be News. His life would be upset; he would be plagued by picture-dealers from all over the world. Collectors would write to him offering to buy the picture; reporters from newspapers would descend on Grey Gill — all that sort of thing. He didn't want to be plagued; he just wanted to hang the portrait of Saskia on his wall and enjoy it, so that's what he did."

"Your uncle was a sensible man," declared Mr. Whitehill.

"Yes, I think he was," agreed Colonel MacLean. "The secret was well kept. He was very careful about it. Even when he was talking about it to me he called the picture 'Saskia' and never mentioned the magic name. He said it was safer, and I suppose it was, but as a matter of fact he enjoyed the secrecy and I'm sure the picture gave him even more pleasure because nobody knew about it except me.

"Well then," continued Colonel MacLean. "Saskia hung on the wall of the library where Uncle Frederick could see her from his chair, so when he said he intended to leave me the seven pictures in his library I turned and looked at her. I didn't want the old man to die — I was very fond of him — but I couldn't help being pleased and excited at the thought that someday Saskia would belong to me. Of course Uncle Frederick knew what I was thinking. 'Yes, my boy,' he said. 'You're to have my Saskia. Gregor doesn't even know who painted her portrait, and doesn't care.' He chuckled and added, 'I won't say Gregor wouldn't appreciate the money she'd fetch; he'd like that all right, but he's not going to get her.' "

"It was natural," said Ken nodding. "I mean of course Sir Frederick wanted to leave his treasure to somebody who really valued it. I suppose Mr. Gregor Carr was very angry when he found his father had left it to you."

Colonel MacLean did not answer.

"Tell Mr. Leslie about the copy of the picture," said Mr. Whitehill.

"Oh yes, the copy," nodded the Colonel. "My uncle managed to find a young painter and got him to come and stay at Grey Gill and make a copy of Saskia. He had it done for me and gave it to me for my birthday. As a matter of fact I was rather amused, it was so typical of Uncle Frederick. He adored Saskia and he knew I was fond of her so he thought I would like the copy. There was something very child-like about him; I suppose some people would say he was eccentric."

33

CHAPTER 5
Adventure for a Young Man

KEN WAS VERY MUCH INTERESTED in Colonel MacLean's story but he still had no glimmer of an idea where it was leading. He had answered an advertisement for a Young Man who wanted Adventure — what had this story of a newly discovered Rembrandt to do with him?

"I don't see —" he began.

"No, of course not," said Colonel MacLean hastily. "You'll see the point in a minute or two. I wanted to give you a clear idea of the position first."

"If I may so, Colonel," said Mr. Whitehill, "you've made it all very clear."

"I've been a bit long-winded, I'm afraid," Colonel MacLean replied. "But it was necessary to tell Leslie the whole thing." He turned to Ken and continued. "Last year my uncle had a serious heart attack and the doctor ordered him to bed and said he must remain there for some weeks. Gregor was abroad at the time (as a matter of fact he gone to Australia to see about some important oil concessions) so I offered to go to Grey Gill. But my uncle wrote me a cheery letter saying that he was improving daily; he had a good nurse and was very comfortable and he would rather I postponed my visit. I must come later on and bring Wallace and we would go for spins in the car and have some games of chess. It would be something to look forward to. He added that it would be a waste for me to go and stay with him when he was in bed and good for nothing. I wrote

34

back saying Wallace and I would come whenever he gave the word and I hoped it would be soon. A few days later I had a telegram telling me that he had had another heart attack and was critically ill. Of course I went north at once but it was too late; Mrs. Aldine the housekeeper, met me at the door and told me he was dead.

"Poor old fellow," added Colonel MacLean with a sigh. "I wished I had gone before, but there it was."

"There was no need to reproach yourself, Colonel," declared Mr. Whitehill.

"No, there wasn't, really, but I felt very sorry. I was fond of the old man and I know he liked me. Mrs. Aldine told me that he asked for me before he died. Mrs. Aldine was very upset of course, she had been at Grey Gill for years and was devoted to him. She took me upstairs to see him; he looked very peaceful. The nurse was there and I had a chat with her. She seemed a kindly creature. I asked her if he had been a difficult patient. I was afraid he might have been a bit restless, for he loved pottering about in the garden and going out for spins in his car, but the nurse said he been quite happy in bed. 'He had his books and his radio,' she said, 'and he had his picture. He would lie for hours looking at his picture.' She pointed to the wall and I saw that they had brought the Rembrandt upstairs and hung it where he could see if from his bed. 'It's a lovely picture,' said the nurse. 'I suppose it's a picture of Sir Frederick's wife when she was young, isn't it?'

"It amused me that she would think it was a portrait of my aunt but I didn't undeceive her. I told her it was a very good plan to bring it upstairs. 'Sir Frederick asked for it,' she said. 'He was very fond of that picture. Sarah and I got the steps and took it down off the wall and brought it to him — he was ever so pleased. It left a mark on the library wall and Mrs. Aldine was rather unhappy about it, so Sir Frederick told us to find another picture the same size and hang it over the mark, and that's what we did.'

"I nodded. I wasn't surprised to hear that Uncle Frederick had wanted his beloved Saskia to look at while he was laid up in bed, but I must admit I thought it odd of Mrs. Aldine to fuss about the mark on the wall, especially when my uncle was so ill."

"You don't know women, Colonel," remarked Mr. Whitehill. "Women are odd creatures. They like to see the place looking tidy no matter if the skies fall."

"Yes, and of course she's very house-proud," admitted Colonel MacLean. "She likes things to look spick and span — not like Sarah. In fact she and Sarah wage a constant war about tidiness at Grey Gill. Sarah is really the cook but she does a certain amount in the house as well; it's difficult to get girls to help in the house nowadays."

"About the picture," said Mr. Whitehill, bringing him back to the point.

"Yes, the picture was now mine and I intended to take it home with me and enjoy it — and keep quiet about it. For one thing I knew that by doing so I should be carrying out my uncle's wishes and for another I didn't want publicity any more than he did. This house is very isolated and if it was known that I possessed a valuable Rembrandt I should never have a moment's peace. You see that, don't you, Leslie?"

36

"Yes, of course," agreed Ken. "The picture was yours and you could do what you liked with it."

"That was exactly my view," said Colonel MacLean. He paused for a moment and then went on with his story. "Gregor arrived in time for the funeral. He had flown home, leaving his job half-finished, and he was in a very bad humour; he seemed to resent my presence at Grey Gill. But I felt I had a right to be there so I took no notice of his manner. After the funeral we went into the library with Mr. Sloane, my uncle's lawyer, and prepared ourselves to listen to the Will. It was exactly as I had expected; there was a list of bequests to various people, amongst them five thousand pounds to Gregor's daughter, Anne, and two thousand to my son Wallace. To me Uncle Frederick had left two thousand pounds and the seven pictures in the library. Everything else was left to Gregor.

"When Mr. Sloane had finished Gregor looked round the walls and said unpleasantly, 'Well, that's that. You can get all this junk of yours moved out of my house, and the sooner the better.'

"I told him I would get the pictures moved at once. Then a thought struck me and I added, 'But of course the picture in Uncle Frederick's bedroom belongs to me.'

" 'What do you mean?' asked Gregor.

"I explained that the picture which was now hanging in Uncle Frederick's bedroom really belonged *here*, and therefore was one of the seven which had been left to me. I explained exactly what had happened and why it had been moved. Gregor smiled unpleasantly and replied that he didn't care how or why it had been moved. The seven pictures in the library were mine, and I could have them."

"Good heavens!" exclaimed Ken.

"Yes, you can imagine my dismay! I tried to explain all over again but it was like beating against a wall. Then I turned to Mr. Sloane and appealed to him but he refused to give an opinion on the subject. There was a long argument. I told them that I knew for a certainty that my uncle wanted me to have that particular picture, that he had told me so over and over again. Gregor repeated that the seven pictures in the library had been left to me. 'There they are,' he said. 'Take them.' Mr. Sloane kept on saying it was pity that Sir Frederick had not described the pictures he intended me to have, then there would have been no doubt of his intentions. 'There's no doubt of his intentions,' declared Gregor. 'The Will is as plain as a pikestaff. Colonel MacLean is to have the seven pictures in the library. He can take them and go.' "

"But it wasn't right!" cried Ken. "The old man wanted you to have his Rembrandt. Why didn't you go to law about it?"

"I did," replied Colonel MacLean. "The case came off a couple of months ago and was given against me."

"But that's incredible!" Ken exclaimed.

"It seemed so to me," agreed the Colonel. "I felt certain of winning the case. I knew I was in the right and I believed that any unprejudiced person would see it from my point of view."

"Your cousin Gregor had a very good lawyer," said Mr. Whitehill.

"Yes," agreed the Colonel with a sigh. "He was very

plausible, I admit. He made a great point of the fact that the picture was extremely valuable and said that if my uncle had intended me to have it he would have mentioned it especially in his will. I knew why he hadn't of course. It was because he didn't want to give away the secret. Then there was Sarah — poor Sarah is muddle-headed at the best of times and Gregor's lawyer twisted her round his finger — but the case really was decided by the fact that the picture had been moved from the library by my uncle's orders and another picture hung in its place."

"But that was — that was an accident!" cried Ken. "I mean one can see exactly how it happened. Sir Frederick wanted it to look at while he was laid up in bed. It would never occur to him for a moment that — that —"

"I'm sure it didn't. I'm perfectly certain Uncle Frederick meant me to have the picture."

There was a moment's silence.

"Do you never read the daily newspapers, Mr. Leslie?" enquired Mr. Whitehill.

Ken looked at him in surprise.

"There was a great deal of publicity about the case," explained Mr. Whitehill waving his cigar. "There was a great fuss about the Rembrandt and there were pictures of Grey Gill — in fact just the sort of publicity that Sir Frederick Carr would have deprecated, just what he wanted to avoid. I'm surprised you didn't notice it in the daily newspapers."

"Oh, I believe I did," said Ken vaguely. Now that he thought of it he remembered seeing something about "a newly discovered Rembrandt" which had come to light in an old house and about a lawsuit for its possession. But Ken was not interested in pictures and it had all happened soon after he and Margaret were engaged, so the "Romantic Story" splashed over the front pages of the daily picture papers had made very little impression upon his mind.

"Leslie isn't interested in pictures," said Colonel MacLean with a smile.

Mr. Whitehill nodded but he still looked doubtful. It was difficult for him to believe the discovery should not have excited Ken's interest.

"Well, that's the whole story," said Colonel MacLean. "The law says the picture belongs to Gregor, but I still think it belongs to me. There's your job, Leslie. What about it?"

"My job?" asked Ken in surprise.

"Yes, are you willing to take it on?"

Ken gazed at him. "You mean — you mean you want me to — to steal it for you?" he asked incredulously.

"I want my own picture," declared the Colonel, setting his lips in a stubborn line. "If you call it stealing to take what's your own property then I suppose you'd call it stealing."

"But — but I had no idea —"

"I'd do it myself like a shot. I'd go and get my picture. In fact that's what I meant to do but Mr. Whitehill said —"

"I said it was crazy — and so it would be," declared Mr. Whitehill. "You'd be spotted straight off. Every soul in the district knows you. That's why I said it would be crazy. I offered to go myself but—"

"But they know you," Colonel MacLean pointed out.

"You stayed at Grey Gill."

"Six years ago," agreed Mr. Whitehill. "Six years is a long time."

"People wouldn't forget you," declared the Colonel. "I mean — "

"All right, Colonel," said Mr. Whitehill smiling. "I know what you mean. They wouldn't be likely to forget a fat guy with spectacles and no hair. Anyhow we've discussed all that before; the point is will this young man take on the job?"

They both looked at Ken.

"But how!" he exclaimed. "It seems mad. Even if I could get hold of the picture — I mean the moment they discovered it had been stolen there would be a hue and cry all over the country."

"They wouldn't miss it," said the Colonel. "You see I have the copy which was given me five years ago by my uncle. All you need to do is substitute one for the other." He rose as he spoke and opening a cupboard he took out a picture and propped it up on a side table. It was the portrait of a young woman sitting in front of a small mirror combing her hair. The canvas was about two feet by one and a half and was unframed. "There," he said. "That's Saskia".

"It's beautiful!" Ken said. "It really is — beautiful." There was a sort of magic about it. The girl was graciously posed, her arms raised, her head slightly bent. Her profile was reflected in the mirror.

"It's quite a good copy," agreed Mr. Whitehill. "But if you were to see the real thing you would soon realise the difference. You would realise this was a milk and water affair."

"Gregor would never notice," said Colonel MacLean quickly. "He doesn't *look* at pictures. They mean nothing to him."

"But other people —" began Ken.

"How many people really look at the pictures on their walls?"

"That's true," Mr. Whitehill said. "The answer is one in twenty. It might be months, or even years, before anyone discovered this was not the real thing. Of course your cousin might take it into his head to show the picture to an expert, but we've got to risk that."

Ken's thoughts were in a turmoil. He had never imagined in his wildest flights of fancy that the "adventure" would be so crazy.

"If you succeed I'll give you five hundred pounds," said Colonel MacLean. "I'd make it more if I could, but I'm not a rich man and —"

"Five hundred pounds!" exclaimed Ken. It seemed a fortune to him.

"It's not enough, Dad," said another voice.

They all looked up and saw Wallace standing at the door.

"It's not enough," Wallace repeated. "Mr. Leslie will be taking a big risk. He might be caught and if so he would be sent to prison, so —"

"He mustn't get caught," interrupted the Colonel. "Anyhow, Wallace, it's nothing to do with you."

"Oh yes it is," replied Wallace gravely. "If I were any use I'd be doing the job myself — so you see it has a lot to do with me. I'll add two hundred pounds to the money. I can use some of the money Uncle Frederick left me, can't I, Dad? I mean it's my own money to do what I like with and I believe Uncle Frederick would approve of the plan. I'd like Mr. Leslie to have the two hundred pounds whether he succeeds in getting the picture or not."

"Well done, Wallie!" exclaimed Mr. Whitehill. "I'll add a hundred to the score, just for the fun of it, just because I want to see that picture hanging here, in it's proper place."

There was a feeling of excitement in the room and Ken was swept away.

"Gosh!" he cried. "Yes, I'll have a crack at it! There ought to be some way —" He rose to his feet and began to pace up and down.

There was a chorus of delight from the others.

"Good man!" exclaimed Colonel MacLean.

"Fine!" cried Mr. Whitehill. "I knew you were the right stuff!"

"You'll let me help, won't you?" said Wallace eagerly. "I mean I wouldn't be any use physically, but I've been thinking about it a lot and I've got some ideas."

"I'm full of ideas, too," declared Mr. Whitehill. "Now just you listen to me, young man. To begin with —"

"Tomorrow will be time enough for plans," said Colonel MacLean rising from his chair. "Look at that clock — it's nearly midnight! Leslie has had a long tiring day and I'm tired, myself. We'll go into ways and means tomorrow morning."

CHAPTER 6
Planning the Job

KEN HAD NOT EXPECTED to sleep a wink, but he was very tired and the bed was comfortable so he went off to sleep almost immediately and did not awaken until seven o'clock. This was his usual time for waking and it was habit that woke him now; usually he awoke to the irritating summons of an alarm clock.

At first Ken could not think where he was. Then he heard the sea roaring at the bottom of the cliff, and smelt the tang of seaweed, and the events of yesterday came flooding into his mind. It was like a bad dream, but unlike a dream it became clearer as he thought about it. In the sane light of day the whole affair seemed crazy — Colonel MacLean must be mad — somehow or other he must back out of the adventure — he must pack his bag and go.

These were his first thoughts, but after a bit he began to swither. The adventure beckoned him for there was a streak of knight errantry in Ken. His life had been drab and monotonous but he had found an outlet for his adventurous spirit in books — stories by Stanley Weyman and Buchan and Dumas. *The Three Musketeers* appealed to Ken tremendously, it always had. When life depressed him more than usual Ken went to his bookcase and took out the shabby volume and went adventuring with D'Artagnan and his friends. D'Artagnan would have gloried in this adventure.

It would be a crime in the eyes of the law to break into a man's house and steal a valuable picture, but this did not worry Ken unduly. The law had made a wrong decision. Colonel MacLean had a moral right to the Rembrandt. He had been cruelly swindled by that cousin of his.

Then there was the money. With eight hundred pounds in his pocket Ken could go to Canada in comfort and he would have time to look about for the sort of job he wanted instead of going steerage and taking the first job he could get. Eight hundred pounds! thought Ken. It was a staggering sum of money, absolutely staggering.

The money tempted Ken, but it was really the thought of Wallace that was the deciding factor. How could he back out now and let Wallace down? He remembered the look on the boy's face when he had said, "If I were any use I'd be doing this job myself." Ken valued his own health and vigour and he had enough imagination to realise how ghastly it must be to be crippled, to hobble about leaning upon a stick! Yet there was no self-pity in the lad; he was brave; he was even cheerful. Ken's heart had been stirred to sympathy and admiration.

He was still thinking about Wallace and marvelling at his courage when the door opened very quietly and Wallace himself looked in.

"Oh, you're awake!" he said. "I just wondered. May I come in, Mr. Leslie?"

"Yes, come in and talk to me — and you can call me Ken."

Wallace smiled in a friendly manner and sat down on the edge of the bed. "You aren't regretting it, are you — Ken?"

he asked.

"I was, a little," replied Ken honestly.

Wallace nodded. "I don't wonder. It will be risky. If you get caught they'll send you to prison. You know that, don't you? It seems rotten to ask you to take risks for us. Why should you?"

"But you want me to take on the job."

"With your eyes open," said Wallace gravely. He hesitated for a few moments and then went on, "I'd do the job if I could, I'd do it like a shot, but that's different because I'd be doing it for Dad. I'd do anything for Dad. You've no idea how good he is, so frightfully kind and understanding. It must be pretty rotten for him to have a son like me; I mean I can't go into the Army or play cricket or anything. He must be disappointed, but he never shows it. And in a way I'd be doing it for poor old Uncle Frederick. I suppose it's ridiculous to think Uncle Frederick minds what happens to Saskia *now*, but I can't help feeling he does."

"Did you ever hear him talking about the picture?"

"Yes, often. I wasn't in the secret of course and I used to wonder who Saskia was, and why Uncle Frederick was so fond of her." Wallace smiled and added, "I knew jolly well it wasn't a portrait of my great-aunt."

Ken smiled too. "So you thought the worst? But I really meant, did you know that your father was to have the picture?"

"We all knew Dad was to have the seven pictures in the library and of course Saskia was one of them."

"What about your Cousin Gregor? Did he know?"

"I'm sure he did — that's what makes it so beastly. He didn't know it was a Rembrandt, but he knew Uncle Frederick valued it very highly. Everybody knew that. I think Cousin Gregor had his suspicions and when he saw the chance to get the picture himself he took it, and of course the more fuss Dad made the more determined he became."

"He seems a very unpleasant character."

"Yes," agreed Wallace. "As a matter of fact I haven't seen him for years. Dad never took me to Grey Gill if he knew Cousin Gregor would be there, because — well — because he used to look at me in an odd sort of way," added Wallace in a low voice.

Ken was silent. He felt certain that he would dislike Mr. Gregor Carr profoundly.

"But Anne is a dear," continued Wallace. "She's Cousin Gregor's daughter. She used to go to Grey Gill in the holidays, when her father was abroad, and we had great fun together — but I really came to talk to you about plans and to show you this." He took a large sheet of oiled paper out of his pocket and unrolled it.

"A map!" exclaimed Ken. "That's just what I want."

"I enjoyed making it," said Wallace. "I've always loved maps and I know Grey Gill and the country round about so well that it was easy." He paused and then added, "I often dream about Grey Gill — but Uncle Frederick is always there. Somehow I can't imagine Grey Gill without the old man."

Ken felt more hopeful about his task when he saw the map. It showed Grey Gill standing upon the side of a hill; it showed the village and the woods and the river. The house looked isolated; it was about half a mile from the village. Wallace had made a detailed plan of the house as well.

"It's a rambling sort of place," he explained. "At one time it must have been quite small and then somebody built on a wing. The library is on the right as you go in at the front door; it's the new part of the house. There are three big windows which look out onto a terrace with a stone balustrade. At the far end of the library there's a door and two steps which lead down to the terrace, and then two more steps from the terrace to the rose-garden. Uncle Frederick loved his roses, he used to potter round the rose-garden all day. Sometimes he used to sit on the terrace in the sun. Now look, Ken, I think your best plan will be to get into the house by the window of the bathroom. It's round at the back, quite near the back door. You can climb up the ivy onto a low roof — it's the roof of the coal-cellar — and the bathroom window is on the left."

They looked at the plan together and Wallace explained his idea; he told Ken that when he used to stay at Grey Gill in the summer holidays he had found this entrance very convenient indeed.

"Sometimes I wanted to get in or out without being seen," said Wallace reminiscently. "And sometimes I used my secret entrance just for fun. It was more amusing to climb onto the roof and crawl in through the bathroom window than to walk in by a door. Unfortunately the bathroom is in the old part of the house at the end of a long passage. You'll have to get the plan of the house clear in your head. There's another passage here," said Wallace, pointing with a pencil. "And there are two steps down — the new part of the house is on a different level — then you come through an archway onto the landing and the front staircase which leads down to the hall."

"Yes, I see," said Ken nodding. The plan was very clear.

"Have you decided to take it on, really and truly?" asked Wallace anxiously.

"Yes," replied Ken.

"It won't be difficult," Wallace assured him. "I don't see how it can go wrong. You get in at the bathroom window and come down to the library; then when you've got the picture you can go out by the side-door. I wish I could come with you and be some help —"

"The map will be a tremendous help," said Ken. "In fact you've made it seem possible. If it hadn't been for you and all you've told me, I wouldn't be taking on the job. I wonder where I should stay," he added thoughtfully.

"You must take a tent with you. Hire a small car — you could get one in London — and camp on the moors. Gosh, I wish I could come with you! But it's no use wishing that. I would just be a nuisance."

"You think I should camp?"

"People are so inquisitive, aren't they? If you stay in a hotel everybody will wonder who you are."

The conference took place after breakfast and Ken found that the two older men had quite different suggestions as to how he should tackle the job.

"You want to lose yourself in a crowd," declared Mr. Whitehill. "There's a big hotel about five miles from Grey

Gill with a swimming pool and tennis courts and all the rest of it. You know the place, Colonel, we went there to lunch one day while I was staying with you. Well, that's the place for Mr. Leslie to stay."

"A tent would be better —" Wallace began.

"No, no, Wallie. If you want to be inconspicuous you must mix in with a crowd and establish your identity as a good sort of guy, then you've got something to fall back on. If I were going to take on the job I'd study the personalities of the household. For instance there's the cook, Sarah, we know the woman is a fool —"

"That would take too long," interrupted Colonel MacLean. My idea is that Leslie should hire a small van and take some samples with him. He could tour the district as a commercial traveller."

He'd soon get found out," said Mr. Whitehill with conviction. "Drummers all know each other and they've got a jargon of their own."

Ken sat back and listened to the argument. It seemed to him that all these schemes were far too elaborate. There was no need for secrecy; there was no need to hide, either in a crowd or on a moor. If he managed to exchange the pictures there would be no hue and cry, no trouble of any kind would ensue. If he bungled the job he would be caught, and that would be that. The idea of having a car appealed to Ken, but it would be better to buy a small second-hand car rather than to hire one as Wallace had suggested. Ken had saved up a little money, enough for that. If the car were his own property he could do what he liked with it and it might be possible to make a secret hiding-place below the floor, or perhaps behind the back seat.

"You haven't said much, young man," said Mr. Whitehill at last.

"I've been thinking, but I haven't got a cut and dried plan. I think I had better go and have look round before I decide what to do."

"Any questions?" asked Colonel MacLean.

"Yes, are you sure the pictures are exactly the same size? Will it be quite easy for me to take the real Saskia out of the frame and put in the false one?"

"So you've arrived there already!" exclaimed Mr. Whitehill smiling.

The Colonel nodded approvingly. "It's a good point," he said. "Fortunately I can set your mind at rest about that. The pictures are exactly the same size."

"I'll show you how to do the job," declared Mr. Whitehill. "That won't be difficult. It seems to me your chief difficulty will be to get into the house."

"By the side door in the library," said Colonel MacLean. "There's a bolt on the door but it's a flimsy affair. You could insert a screw driver in the jam and burst it open."

"That's all very well, Colonel," objected Mr. Whitehill. "But if the door is tampered with it will arouse suspicion and the fat will be in the fire. The whole idea is that the pictures are to be exchanged without arousing suspicion. I can't see why he need go at night. It might be easier to do it in the day-time."

"In the day-time!" exclaimed the Colonel in amazement.

"Leave it to Ken," said Wallace with a little smile. "He'll

51

find some way of getting in."

"It seems we'll have to leave it to him," agreed Mr. Whitehill.

Ken saw no object in revealing the plan. "What is the village like?" he asked. "I see from Wallace's map that it's called Hillfoot."

"It's quite a small village, just one street with shops and a post office," said Wallace. "At one end of the street there's the church and at the other end there's the Black Bull Inn. It's always full of men talking about fishing."

"About fishing?" asked Ken with interest. "I wonder —"

"Perhaps you'd like the loan of my rod," suggested the Colonel smiling.

"Yes," said Ken thoughtfully. "Yes, I think I would."

CHAPTER 7
The Black Bull Inn

THE BLACK BULL was an old-fashioned hostelry. The door of the bar opened onto the village street and beside it there was a wide stone arch leading into the yard. When Ken pulled up at the door he saw that the bar was brightly lighted and he heard a buzz of talk. The buzz grew louder when he opened the door and then died away. Everybody stopped talking and turned to stare. The inn-keeper was standing behind the counter serving beer; he was fat and cheerful with a round red face and greying hair. Ken walked across the room feeling somewhat self-conscious and leant upon the counter.

"Good evening," he said politely. "Can you give me a meal and a bed? I've been having trouble with my car."

"Why — yes, I think so," replied the inn-keeper. "You'll not be wanting a grand dinner? We can give you eggs and some cold ham —"

"That will do splendidly," nodded Ken. "I'm on my way north and I got delayed. This looks very pleasant country — is there any fishing?"

"Why — yes, there is," said the inn-keeper. "I'll just see about a meal for you, and a room. Jim can tell you about fishing, can't you Jim?"

"What Jim doesn't know about fishing isn't worth knowing," said a tall lanky individual with a hatchet face.

But it was not only Jim who knew about fishing. There

53

were eleven men in the bar and they were all anglers, or so it appeared. The buzz of conversation broke out afresh as they put forward their views on the subject, advising Ken to hire a boat and have a day on the lake or to take his rod and try a particular pool on the river. Ken had hoped for a friendly reaction to his question and he had got it in full measure. By the time the inn-keeper returned to say that the meal was ready, Ken had allowed himself to be persuaded to stay at Hillfoot for a few days before proceeding north. He had arranged to go out with Jim and be introduced to the best pools in the river Fleece.

Mr. Winter, the inn-keeper, was quite pleased to hear that his unexpected guest had decided to stay on but he raised the point of a permit.

"A permit!" exclaimed Jim in surprise. "But the river's free. We never bother about no permit, Mr. Winter."

"You didn't in Sir Frederick's day," Mr. Winter agreed. "But Mr. Gregor's a different pair of shoes. If you take the gentleman fishing without a permit you'll be in for trouble, mark my words."

"I don't want trouble," said Ken quickly.

Jim's face was a study in disappointment and frustration.

"You could telephone to the big house," suggested the hatchet-faced man.

The others voiced their opinions for and against this course of action and they were still arguing when Ken went into the parlour to have his supper.

Mr. Winter served the supper himself and chatted the while. "I'm sorry about that permit," he said. "It's like this, you see, Sir Frederick was a very kindly old gentleman and he never bothered, but he died last year and his son isn't so easy-going. The chaps from the village go out with a rod in the evenings and so far they've got off with it, but it's different for a stranger like you."

"I don't want trouble, either for myself or anybody else," Ken told him.

"Why no, of course not," agreed Mr. Winter. "My advice would be to go up to the big house and ask for a permit. Mr. Gregor doesn't fish himself and I expect he'd say yes. Then it would be plain sailing. He isn't a very agreeable gentleman but I daresay he'd like a few trout from his own river, if you see what I mean."

Ken had made up his mind that he would not ask a favour from "Cousin Gregor" but the inn-keeper's suggestion put the matter on a different footing. Obviously it would not be a favour if he were to provide the big house with a basket of fish.

"Why not go up tonight?" continued Mr. Winter. "It's a fine evening and barely half a mile to the big house. If you was to go up there yourself and ask to see Mr. Gregor it would be better than telephoning — more polite to my way of thinking."

"You think I should?" asked Ken doubtfully.

"Why yes, I do," replied Mr. Winter. "Then you could have a nice day's fishing tomorrow with Jim."

The affair seemed simple to Mr. Winter, but not so simple to Ken. He shrank from the idea of an interview with "Cousin Gregor". He shrank even more from the idea of asking him for a fishing permit — yet, on the other hand, it was such an excellent excuse to go up to the house and have a look round. Ken had not expected to plunge into his adventure so quickly; his idea had been to hang about the village for a few days and try to form a plan. He thought about it seriously and then decided that his reluctance to go up to Grey Gill this evening was cowardice, no more and no less, so he had better go.

It was dark by this time but the moon was bright and the sky was cloudless. Jim offered to accompany Ken to the gates of Grey Gill and show him the way, so they set forth together, chatting as they went.

"I wonder what he'll say," said Jim anxiously. "I think it would have been better to risk it, really. If he says no we're done, if you see what I mean."

"Why shouldn't he say yes?"

"He's a funny sort of gentleman. He was born and brought up at the big house but for all that he seems like a stranger. A funny sort of smile he has, as if he was laughing at you in a nasty sort of way."

Ken had heard about "Cousin Gregor's" smile before.

"I daresay you'll have heard tell about the picture," continued Jim. "A very valuable picture it is. Old Sir Frederick bought it in foreign parts."

"I saw something about it in the papers," said Ken cautiously.

"You would! There was a lot about it in the papers. The village was full of reporters; they drank up all the beer in the Black Bull. Some of them brought their cameras and took photos of everything they could see. Why, one of them took a photo of old Mrs. Brown and it came out in the papers — the oldest inhabitant in Hillfoot — that was what

56

it said. Mrs. Brown was as pleased as punch. Yes, there was a fine old stir, there hasn't been nothing like it in Hillfoot in the memory of man." He chuckled and added, "Why, you could get a pint off any of them by saying as how you'd seen the picture hanging on the wall."

"You've seen it, I suppose?"

"Well, I have — and I haven't," replied Jim. "I've been in the liberry half a dozen times or more, and I've got my eyesight, but between you and me I couldn't say what the pictures on the wall was like. If I'd known it was a Rembrandt and worth all those thousands of pounds I'd have had a good look at it. Thousands and thousands of pounds for a picture — it's a funny life, isn't it?"

Ken agreed that it was.

"Colonel MacLean ought to have got that picture," continued Jim. "He's a nice gentleman — I've known him for years — very keen on fishing, he is. It's my belief old Sir Frederick liked him a lot better than his own son. It's my belief old Sir Frederick meant him to have that Rembrandt picture whatever the judge might say."

"Why do you think that?" asked Ken, showing a little interest but not too much.

Jim could not explain why he thought so, except that the Colonel was "much nicer than Mr. Gregor", but he rambled on happily and vouchsafed a good deal of useful information. Ken was rather startled to discover that everybody in the village knew all about the picture and the lawsuit, but then he realised it was natural. It is not every day that a small out-of-the-way village wakes up to find itself News, and to see itself depicted on the front pages of

57

the picture papers.

"You ought to have a look at that Rembrandt picture, Mr. Leslie," said Jim as they parted at the gates of the big house. "It's hanging in the liberry in the same place as it used to in Sir Frederick's day. I know that because Nancy Cole goes and helps Mrs. Aldine three times a week. Nancy says it's a picture of a young woman in a petticoat combing her hair — very pretty, Nancy says. All the same you wouldn't think a picture of a young woman in a petticoat would be worth all that amount of money."

"I don't know much about pictures," said Ken quite truthfully.

"Nor me, neither;" agreed Jim. "But it's funny what a lot of interest people take in pictures — I mean, people you wouldn't think would take any interest in them. There was two chaps in the Black Bull last night asking about it."

Ken had turned to go in at the gates, but he hesitated. "Who were they?" he asked.

"They were rough sort of chaps," replied Jim. "I didn't like the looks of them. One was a little chap with a monkey face. They were foreigners, both of them."

To an English villager everybody who does not live within a radius of twenty miles from his home is a "foreigner" and Ken was aware of this, so he realised that the two men were not necessarily visitors from foreign lands. They might easily be Londoners — or Aberdonians for that matter. He was about to ask Jim for more information on the subject but Jim was walking away and Ken did not like to call after him.

The drive was not very long and a turn in it brought the

house to view, flooded with silver moonlight. Ken stood and looked at it. He had memorised the plan which Wallace had given him and now he was able to apply his knowledge to the actual building. It was an ugly house, for it had been added to without regard for its outward appearance and the two styles did not blend very happily. On his left was the old part of the house with small windows and a gabled roof and tall chimneys; in the middle was the front door with a short flight of broad steps and a pillared portico; on the right was the library with its three tall windows and beyond those the side door. He noted the terrace with its stone balustrade and the steps of which Wallace had spoken. It was all exactly as he had imagined it — so much so that he almost felt he had seen the house before.

He crossed the broad gravel sweep and rang the bell.

CHAPTER 8
Interview with Cousin Gregor

THE DOOR WAS OPENED by a plump young woman with black frizzy hair. She looked doubtful when Ken asked if he could speak to Mr. Carr.

"I don't know," she said, hesitating. "P'raps I better ask Mrs. Aldine if you can see 'im. You can wait in the 'all."

Ken went in and waited. It was a square hall with several heavy pieces of furniture in it and several large pictures on the walls. The staircase was broad, with a carved bannister, and went curving up to the floor above. Ken had plenty of time to look about him. He looked at the hall table; it was of polished mahogany with carved legs; he looked at the enormous cupboard — it also was of mahogany and there was heavy carving on the doors. It was raised a few inches from the ground upon four carved feet. In one corner of the hall there was a grandfather clock with a large white face; it was ticking away industriously. On the walls were pictures in heavy gilt frames: portraits of old-fashioned gentlemen, some in pink hunting-coats and others in broad-cloth with carefully arranged cravats (probably these were the family portraits of which Colonel MacLean had spoken).

Ken looked at the door on his right which led into the library and wondered whether he would have time to open it and peep into the room. It would be interesting to have a look, just to make sure that the picture was still there. Jim

60

had said it was there, but perhaps it would be a good thing to make sure.

Ken was gazing at the door and trying to make up his mind when the door opened and a man came out. The man was tall and heavily built; he was clean shaven and his hair was iron grey and slightly wavy.

"What are you doing here?" he asked, looking at Ken in surprise.

"I wanted to speak to Mr. Carr," replied Ken.

"I suppose you're a reporter. If so you can clear out."

"No, I'm not a reporter. I came about the fishing. I'm staying at the Black Bull for a few days and Mr. Winter suggested I should ask Mr. Carr to allow me to fish."

"Why should he?"

"Well, I don't know, really," replied Ken smiling. "I like fishing so I thought it was worth while asking for a permit. Mr. Carr could say yes — or no."

The man smiled (it was not a pleasant smile and it confirmed Ken's guess that this was Mr. Gregor Carr himself). "You'd better come in for a minute," he said. "But I warn you if you're from some blasted newspaper and this is just a ruse to get into my house you'll be thrown out."

Ken did not reply. He followed Mr. Carr into the library and waited to see what would happen next. It was difficult not to look round the walls but he kept his eyes glued to Mr. Carr's face — rather a pale face with a curious full-lipped mouth and a jutting nose.

"Well, what about it?" asked Mr. Carr. "Why should I give you permission to fish my river? Let's hear your reasons."

"There are no reasons," Ken replied. "If you don't want me to fish your river you have only to say no."

For a few moments Mr. Carr hesitated. Then he said, "All right. You can have a permit for two days fishing. If you like to spend two days flogging the water you can get on with it. But the fish are mine, not yours. You can bring them up to the house when you've caught them."

It was so rudely said that Ken had some difficulty in controlling his anger.

"You don't seem pleased," said Mr. Carr with his famous smile.

"Of course I meant to offer you the fish."

"But you didn't expect me to accept them?"

"Some of them. I mean usually —"

"Well, now we know where we are, don't we? You may have the pleasure of catching my fish for me. If you catch too many for me to eat I shall sell them. Is that clear?"

It was perfectly clear. Ken did not really mind about the fish but the rudeness was almost beyond bearing. He felt inclined to turn and walk out, but there was too much at stake for him to indulge his natural inclinations.

"Do you want the permit or not?" asked Mr. Carr.

"Yes please," said Ken meekly.

Mr. Carr crossed the room to his writing-desk and sat down. "What's your name?" he asked. "You had better have a written permit because I've told my keeper to turn people off the river. The villagers seem to be under the impression that the river belongs to them, but they'll soon be undeceived. If we can catch one of them red-handed I'll have him up before the magistrates for poaching and make

62

an example of him. That's the best way to tackle the matter. What did you say your name was?"

"Kenneth Leslie."

Ken had not been asked to sit down so he stood and waited patiently while the permit was being written, but now that Mr. Carr's back was turned he was at liberty to use his eyes. He glanced round the library walls and saw the portrait of Saskia hanging in the far corner just above the desk. Ken gazed at it, trying to make up his mind whether the real Saskia looked different from the copy (which at that moment was wrapped in a cloth bag and stowed away in neatly contrived hiding-place behind the back seat of his little car). Did it look different? Mr. Whitehill had said that when he saw the real Saskia he would realise that the copy was "a milk and water affair", but to Ken it looked exactly the same. It was not hanging in a very good light, of course, and he realised that if he could see the two pictures together he might be able to see the difference, but here and now there seemed no difference at all. It was very odd that whereas one picture was worth a small fortune the other was worth a few pounds.

"I see you're looking at the famous Rembrandt," said Mr. Carr.

Ken started. He had been so intent upon Saskia that he had forgotten to watch her owner.

"I suppose you saw all the fuss in the papers," suggested Mr. Carr. "Perhaps you think it's worth all the fuss?"

"Not really," replied Ken quite truthfully. "But I suppose it might be to somebody who could appreciate it."

"No picture on earth is worth thousands of pounds,"

declared Mr. Carr. Anybody who thinks so is a fool. It's absolute lunacy to tie up capital in a picture when you could get good interest on an investment. I shall sell it, of course. I've had offers from Art Galleries and collectors all over the country."

"Yes," said Ken. "Yes, I suppose — are you going to sell it soon?"

"Oh, I shall bide my time. I expect eventually it will go to America, but I'm in no hurry. The picture can hang on my wall until I find the fool with the biggest bank-roll. It's a nuisance, of course," he added, glancing at the picture in a casual sort of way. "I shall be glad to get rid of it. I've had to have burglar-alarms put on the windows and a solid bolt on the side-door. The insurance company insisted upon it."

"Yes, I suppose they would," said Ken.

"It was all that damned publicity," continued Mr. Carr. "Every thief in the Kingdom knows that the thing is here, in my house. Yes, I shall be glad to get rid of it." He folded up the permit and handed it to Ken as he spoke.

"Thank you, Mr. Carr," said Ken.

"You can bring the fish tomorrow night — if you catch any. And please ring the bell. I dislike strangers walking into my house without permission."

"But I didn't!" exclaimed Ken.

"You didn't? What d'you mean? You were wandering round the hall when I found you."

"I rang the bell and a girl answered the door and said she would find out whether you could see me."

"That's Ida," said Mr. Carr. He hesitated and then added, "We've only had her for a week and she knows nothing.

I'm sorry about it."

Ken was surprised to receive the apology. "I ought to have explained —" he began.

"The girl is hopeless," declared Mr. Carr. "It seems impossible to get an intelligent servant nowadays, especially in an out-of-the-way place like this. My daughter advertised in the local paper for a housemaid and this one applied for the post. She's an absolute fool and lazy into the bargain. I'm not surprised she left you standing in the hall — she probably forgot all about you. Well, I hope you'll have a good day's fishing."

"Thank you," said Ken. It was obvious that Mr. Carr was regretting his rudeness (in fact he had become quite genial) but Ken did not like him any better and was very glad to get away.

CHAPTER 9
Six Fine Trout

JIM SLATER CALLED FOR KEN at the Black Bull early next morning and they set off together for the river. The best pools were higher up than the village, beyond the bridge. Jim was disgusted when he heard the terms of the permit and said so in plain language. To his practical mind part of the pleasure of fishing was the pleasure of eating a nice fat trout, split and fried to a golden brown. His description of this dainty morsel, as prepared by his mother, made Ken's mouth water.

"She won't half be disappointed," declared Jim. "I told her I might be bringing in a few trout for supper. My idea was you would have two and I would have two and we'd take the rest to the big house."

"We haven't caught them yet," said Ken smiling.

"But we will — it's a grand day for fishing."

"Well anyhow that wasn't Mr. Carr's idea."

"He's a curmudgeon, that's what he is. He's a mean stingy old curmudgeon. Why should you and me fish for a whole day to get him his breakfast! Rolling in money, he is. What does he do with it? Hoards it like a miser. He wouldn't even give a subscription to the cricket-pavilion — what d'you think of that? If I'd gone to Sir Frederick and asked him for a subscription he'd have headed the list with a fine big cheque, but not that old curmudgeon. Not a penny!"

The topic of Mr. Carr's stinginess lasted until they

arrived at the river and then was abandoned for pleasanter things. Jim was a keen angler and when he saw his favourite pool, its surface ruffled by a gentle breeze, his eyes glistened with delight.

The rod was taken out of its case and put together carefully.

"That's funny," said Jim, looking at it with interest.

"What's funny?" asked Ken.

"Why it's the dead spit of Colonel MacLean's rod. I used to go out fishing with him when he stayed with old Sir Frederick. If I didn't know it couldn't be I'd say this was his rod. Feels like it, too," added Jim, waving it gently from side to side.

"What should I put on the tail?" asked Ken diplomatically.

The diplomacy succeeded. Jim put down the rod and threw himself eagerly into a discussion about the rival merits of a Butcher and a Greenwells Glory. The fly-hook also belonged to the Colonel but Jim did not seem to notice this. He made up a cast with skilled fingers while Ken arrayed himself in the waders.

It was a perfect day for fishing. There was a breeze from the west and though it was bright there was not too much sun. The river was in perfect condition, neither too high nor too low. In fact the only trouble was that the trout were not hungry. Ken liked fishing but he was not crazy about the sport and when he had fished for half an hour without a single rise he handed the rod to Jim.

"You can have a go," he said.

"I'll just have a few casts," said Jim who was torn

67

between his desire to handle the rod and his idea of what was the right thing. "I'll just try that pool — "

"Go ahead," said Ken, sitting down on the bank.

Jim went ahead. He was the type of angler who can fish happily all day and half the night without seeing the glitter of a fin. He crawled along the bank and cast across the pool; he waded into the shallows; he climbed onto the rocks and balancing precariously dropped the flies with exquisite precision into each little snug backwater. No fish rose. There might not have been a single trout in the river.

Ken watched with interest. It is always interesting to see an expert at work, and he was learning a good deal from watching Jim, and when Jim moved slowly up the river from pool to pool Ken followed him. Apparently Jim had forgotten that he was just going to have a few casts, but Ken did not mind.

Soon after twelve Ken began to feel hungry so he called to Jim to come and share his lunch. Mr. Winter had provided plenty of sandwiches and plum cake and coffee in a thermos flask and Jim waded out of the river reluctantly and sat down.

"Are there any fish in the Fleece?" asked Ken teasingly.

"It must be thunder," replied Jim. "Fish don't rise when there's thunder about. Maybe it will have cleared in the afternoon. I've known days like this before, when there wasn't a rise for hours and then all of a sudden they'd start taking and you couldn't pull them in quick enough. There was one special day I'm thinking about when me and the Colonel — Colonel MacLean that is — were fishing below the bridge and we didn't have a rise all morning —"

Jim went on to tell Ken all about this occasion, and other occasions, for he was a great talker and enjoyed the sound of his own voice. Ken had a feeling that his stories were slightly exaggerated to say the least of it.

"Look, Mr. Leslie!" exclaimed Jim suddenly. "Look there! Across the river!"

Ken looked and saw a man standing upon the hill. He was a long way off but Ken's eyes were good and he could see that the man had a pair of field-glasses.

"That's Mr. Curmudgeon Carr," declared Jim. "See what he's doing? He's having a look at us. He's counting how many fish we're catching. Funny, isn't it?"

Ken did not think it funny. The feeling that you are being observed through a pair of field-glasses is unpleasant.

After lunch Ken took the rod and fished for a while. He had one rise but he had ceased to expect a fish so he failed to strike at the right moment. This annoyed him a good deal, and mortified him, for he was aware that if Jim had been in his boots the fish would have been well and truly hooked.

"It was a big one, too," declared Jim who had been watching eagerly. "It was all of two pounds. I could see it was big by the splash it made."

Ken's impression was that the fish had been quite small but he did not say so. He surrendered the rod to Jim and sat down with his back against a rock.

The air was warm and pleasant and Ken was almost asleep when a sound disturbed him. It was a queer metallic sound like the clank of an empty bucket against a stone — and that was exactly what it was. A man appeared from among the trees with a bucket in his hand. He was a small man with long arms and a queer little wizened face. He paused at the edge of the river and looked about him with a curiously furtive air — then he dipped the bucket in the pool and hurried away.

The incident was not particularly interesting. Probably there was a camp somewhere near and the man had come down to the river for water. Ken would have thought nothing of it if it had not been for the way he looked about him, as if he did not want to be seen. Why that furtive air? There was nothing wrong in taking a bucket of water from the river; even Mr. Gregor Carr would not grudge him that.

The puzzle intrigued Ken so he went along the bank of the river to the place where the man had filled his bucket, and looked about. There was a track leading up the hill through the trees. It was not a path, it was merely that the grass had been crushed by the passage of feet. Ken followed the track, smiling at himself for being so inquisitive. The track wound up the hill for a couple of hundred yards and ended in a little hollow where the trees had been cleared. In the clearing there was a small brown tent and, beyond the tent, there was a car half hidden among the bushes. The small man had put down the bucket and was standing beside it. Another man, a big tough looking individual with a bull neck and a red face, was shaking out some blankets. They were campers — just as Ken had thought.

He stood in the shelter of the trees and watched them. They *were* camper, but there was something a bit odd about them. Campers were usually cheery. These two looked glum. They certainly did not look as if they were enjoying themselves — and what a strange place they had chosen to pitch their tent! Why hadn't they chosen a sunny hill-side instead of a small damp clearing in the woods? However it was no business of Ken's, so after watching them for a few minutes he turned and went back to the river.

While he was away Jim had caught a trout; it was a nice fish, about a pound in weight, with beautifully mottled markings. Jim described the fight it had given him with a wealth of detail and bewailed the fact that Ken would not be able to have it for breakfast. When at last Jim paused for breath Ken described his own small adventure.

"It's those chaps!" exclaimed Jim excitedly. "I told you about them, Mr. Leslie, you remember? They was in the bar night before last — a little monkey-faced man and a big enormous chap with a red face. You're quite right when you say they're up to no good."

Ken had not said they were up to no good but by this time he knew Jim's talent for exaggeration. Jim amused him considerably and he began to tease him.

"What can they be up to?" asked Ken, pretending to be very serious.

"That's just it," declared Jim. "There's no knowing what chaps like that might do. They ought to be watched. The police ought to keep an eye on them."

"We might report them for stealing water out of the river."

"That's a joke," said Jim nodding.

"It was intended to be a joke," admitted Ken.

"Yes, but it wouldn't be a joke if they was to take it into

71

their heads to steal that Rembrandt picture or break into the Black Bull and make off with all the money in the till."

"So you think they ought to be watched," said Ken hiding a smile.

"That's right. You never know what chaps like that will do. My brother is in the police — he's at Leeds now — and he was telling me about some chaps that stole some lead off the roof of a church. That's a funny thing, isn't it?"

"Very funny," agreed Ken.

Jim plunged into the story but Ken did not listen very carefully for he was busy making up a new cast. When it was ready he waded into the river and began to fish in earnest. The fish had begun to rise, for some reason best known to themselves, and Ken caught two nice trout in a few minutes.

At seven o'clock they knocked off and went back to the inn for supper. By this time they had six very nice fish in the basket . . . but according to Jim the two they had lost were much bigger and better.

"It's a shame you've got to take them to that old curmudgeon," said Jim. "He can't eat six trout. Why not keep one for your breakfast? Mrs. Winter would cook it a treat. He'd never know. He wasn't watching us all the time, and there's parts of the river you can't see from the hill. Keep one, Mr. Leslie. Keep that nice big one you caught yourself."

Ken did not want the fish — he felt it would choke him — but he wished he could offer one to Jim. However it was no use wishing that because they were not his to offer. They were Mr. Carr's fish and he should have the lot.

Directly after supper Ken put the fish in a bag and walked up to Grey Gill. It was still quite light, for the sun had just set behind the hills and the skies were clear. This time Ken went round the house to the back door and had a good look at the coal-cellar and the ivy which was growing on the wall. He was relieved when he saw it for he had been wondering if perhaps it had been removed. People sometimes tore down ivy if it became too strong and tough — but there it was, providing a very satisfactory ladder to the coal-cellar roof.

The cook answered Ken's knock. She was a little wisp of a woman with greying hair and a surprised look in her pale blue eyes. Ken handed her the fish and said they were for Mr. Carr.

"Six of them!" she exclaimed. "Did you catch them all yourself? You want to keep some, don't you?"

"Mr. Carr wants them all," replied Ken, showing her the permit.

She took the paper and held it a long way from her eyes and then handed it back. "I haven't got my glasses," she explained. "And anyhow it's writing, isn't it? I can't read writing."

"You can't read writing?" asked Ken in bewilderment.

"I can read reading but not writing — but never mind. You can tell me what it says."

Ken read it out to her. The permit stated clearly that Mr. Kenneth Leslie had permission from Mr. Gregor Carr to fish his reach in the river Fleece but that all fish caught were to be delivered to Mr. Gregor Carr at Grey Gill.

The old woman listened intently and then she took two

of the fish and handed the remainder to Ken. "You better keep them," she said. "Mr. Gregor won't be wanting them all. One for him and one for Miss Anne for breakfast. That's enough."

"But he wants them all," said Ken.

"Sir Frederick always let people keep the fish if they caught any. Sometimes he'd have one for his own breakfast, but —"

"But Mr. Carr is different —"

"Yes, indeed," she agreed nodding her head seriously. "Quite different, he is. Why nobody wouldn't never think they was father and son. I was just saying that very thing to Mrs. Aldine this morning: 'nobody wouldn't never think they was father and son' I said, and Mrs. Aldine said, 'Sarah,' she said, 'you've never said a truer word'."

"Yes, well —" began Ken.

"I could ask Mrs. Aldine," suggested Sarah, looking at the fish. "I'm pretty sure Mrs. Aldine would say you was to have them."

"You had better keep them all. It might cause trouble if I —"

"There's lots of trouble in this house nowadays," declared the old woman. "There used to be no trouble when Sir Frederick was alive — well, I mean he used to shout at you sometimes but nobody minded that. Mr. Gregor is different, he's interfering, and interference is a thing I can't stand. Why, only this morning when I came downstairs — I get up at six every day of the week except Sundays. You can get on with your work if you get up early, that's what I say. These girls nowadays they lie in their beds till goodness knows when and then wonder why they're all behind like a cow's tail. That Ida! She's a lazy good-for-nothing! Calls herself a housemaid! She hasn't got no idea of polishing brasses no more than a babe in arms — " Old Sarah paused for breath.

"When you came downstairs this morning — " suggested Ken, who was interested for private reasons to know what Sarah had discovered at dawn.

"Yes, when I came downstairs I saw at once somebody had been tidying up my larder so I said to Mrs. Aldine, 'Were you poking about in my larder last night?' I said. But it wasn't her, it was him. He doesn't go to bed till all hours. He wanders round the house with a pistol in his pocket and looks for burglars. It was him that was in my larder last night because he said so. 'Sarah,' he said. 'What are you going to do with that mutton bone? You better make some soup' — telling me to make soup out of an old bit of bone that was only fit for the pig's pail! Very mean, he is. You wouldn't hardly believe it if I was to tell you — "

Sarah told him a good deal, including the fact that she "wouldn't stay on here a day if it wasn't for Miss Anne."

It was difficult to escape from the garrulous old woman without being rude but he managed it somehow, reminding her as he said goodbye that the fish were to be taken straight to Mr. Carr. As he walked back to the Black Bull he remembered what Colonel MacLean had said about Sarah, that she was muddle-headed at the best of times, and he could not help smiling. All the same there was something rather nice about her, and she had told him one or two very interesting things.

CHAPTER 10
The Adventure Begins

KEN SPENT THE REST of the evening in the bar, chatting to the habitués. Jim Slater was there, talking enthusiastically about the day they had had on the river. Everybody that came in had the whole story described to him and each time Jim told his tale there were fresh embroideries. Ken saw some of the other men glance at one another and smile, but the smiles were kindly and it was obvious that they were used to Jim's exaggerations and he was popular. The local police-sergeant dropped in for a pint and he, too, heard the tale, including the fact that two tough-looking characters were camping in the woods, but he did not pay much attention and merely said he supposed they must have got permission to camp from Mr. Carr. Probably Sergeant Merton knew Jim's propensity for making a good story out of nothing.

Presently the door opened and an elderly man with a thin weather-beaten face appeared.

"Good evening, Doctor Stott," said Mr. Winter. "This is Mr. Leslie, he's staying here for a day or two on his way north. He's been fishing."

Ken was not surprised to hear he was the doctor, for there was something about his keen face and confident bearing that proclaimed his profession.

"Fishing, were you?" he asked, smiling at Ken. "Did you have any luck?"

Ken was about to reply but he did not have a chance for everybody began to talk at once, telling the doctor what had happened.

Presently the buzz of talk died down and Doctor Stott moved along the counter to have a few words with the newcomer.

"Have you been in this part of the world before?" asked the doctor in a friendly manner.

"No," replied Ken. "It's very beautiful country."

"I think so," admitted the doctor. "But I was born here, so probably I'm a bit prejudiced. I've never been tempted to leave the place — I've got my work and my garden and that's all I need. Are you keen on roses?"

"Yes, but I don't know much about growing them."

"This is a good place for roses," declared the doctor. "I've got the best roses in the whole district. At one time my roses were the second best." He sighed and added, "Sir Frederick Carr had the best."

"He died last year, didn't he?" said Ken.

"Yes, and I lost a good friend. We had a great deal in common, not only roses but other things as well. I miss the old man even more than I expected, which is saying a good deal. Are you staying here long, Mr. Leslie?"

"I'm not sure," replied Ken. "It depends on — on the fishing and —"

"You must come and see my garden," said Doctor Stott. "Just drop in any time you feel inclined. If I'm there I'll be delighted to see you and if I'm out you can have a look round yourself. I'm a bachelor and my housekeeper won't bother you, so be sure to come along."

Ken accepted the invitation; he liked the doctor and he had a feeling that the doctor liked him.

"That's right," said the doctor. "You just drop in. It's no use fixing a time because my movements are so uncertain."

At closing time Mr. Winter cleared the bar as usual and Ken went up to his room. He felt sleepy after his long day in the open air and was tempted to get into bed, but he resisted the temptation for he had made up his mind that the great adventure was to take place tonight. He was not looking forward to it; he did not feel very brave, nor very confident of success, but it was no use putting it off on that account.

All his arrangements had been carefully thought out beforehand. He had intended to take Wallace's plan of the house with him, and then he decided not to, for if by any chance he were caught it would give him away completely. There was no need to take it; he had memorised every turn in the passages, he knew every step and every door. Ken had a last look at it and then burnt it and reduced the ashes to powder. When this was done he put on a dark brown suit and brown suede shoes with rubber soles; he put his electric torch in his pocket and a small screwdriver. There were all the "tools" he would need and the less he had to carry the better. The grey cloth bag which contained the copy of Saskia was an awkward sort of burden but he had made a sling for it so that he could strap it onto his back and have his hands free for climbing.

It was just after midnight when Ken set forth from the Black Bull. Everything was very quiet. Everybody was asleep; there was not a light to be seen in the village. Last night the moon had been clear and bright, but tonight it was hidden by heavy clouds and there was a thin mist lying in the hollows and amongst the trees. Ken found the gates of Grey Gill open (they had been shut last night) and this puzzled him and added to his uneasiness. He made his way up the drive, peering about him in the gloom, starting nervously when a bush loomed out of the darkness. An owl flew past with an eerie screech and made his heart pound like a steam hammer.

When he approached the house he saw that there was a light in the window just above the front door so he sat down and waited. It was Mr. Carr's bedroom window — one of the interesting things that Sarah had told him was that Mr. Gregor had moved into Sir Frederick's room. She had also told him that Mr. Gregor prowled about at night "with a pistol in his pocket" but Ken hoped that by this time he had finished prowling and was undressing and going to bed.

After a few minutes the light went out but Ken did not move. He had decided to give Mr. Carr half an hour to go to sleep.

The half hour went past very slowly. Every now and then Ken switched on his torch, shading it carefully, and looked at his watch and each time he did so he was astonished. When at last his watch informed him that he had been waiting for half an hour he felt as if he had been sitting there for at least two hours — it was most extraordinary. He rose and stretched himself and went all round the house just to make sure that there were no lights anywhere. There was not a chink to be seen. Grey Gill was dark and silent. Having made sure of this Ken wasted no more time but made his way to the coal-cellar.

The roof of the out-house was about ten feet from the ground and the gnarled stem of the ivy made an easy ladder. Ken thought of Wallace as he climbed up. He wished Wallace could know that the adventure was taking place tonight and could be thinking about it. Ken was doing this for Wallace; for other reasons too of course but principally for the lame boy who could not take on the job himself.

There was no difficulty in the climb. In a few moments Ken had found the gutter and pulled himself up onto the flat roof. If the rest of the job were as easy as this he would have nothing to worry about. There were two windows facing Ken, he moved quietly to the one on the left and looked in, using his torch. Yes, it was a bathroom. Somebody had been having a bath quite recently for the window was slightly steamy and it had been left open at the top to air the room. Slowly Ken eased up the window from the bottom. Then he put one leg over the sill and climbed in.

For a few moments he stood there hesitating. Should he shut the window or not? He felt rather unwilling to shut it, and so cut off his escape, but his intention was to go out by the side-door in the library, and if this window were found open from the bottom it might cause some surprise. He shut it very carefully. Then he tiptoed from the bathroom and opened the door into the passage. The passage was pitch dark.

Ken had switched off his torch and put it in his pocket

while he was fiddling with the window but now he took it out and switched it on. The passage was narrow; it ran straight for a few yards and then curved to the right. Ken moved along silently, he remembered that there were two steps down just beyond the turn — yes, here they were! One of the steps creaked as he trod upon it!

The noise seemed so loud and so alarming that he felt sure somebody must have heard it — the creak had been loud enough to waken the dead! Why hadn't Wallace warned him about the creaking step! Wallace must have known. He switched off his torch and stood still, listening intently, but he could hear nothing. Then he saw something in the darkness; it was a faint light reflected upon the wall where the passage divided. He was so petrified with fright that he could not move. The light grew brighter rapidly and a figure appeared round the corner, the figure of a woman in a dark coat with a torch in her hand. She was coming towards him, hurrying, almost running, and if she had raised the torch she would have seen him; but she was not looking for burglars, she was not looking for anything. When she reached the back stairs, about three yards from where Ken stood, she turned swiftly and ran up them and vanished.

If was the girl with the frizzy black hair who had opened the door to Ken on his first visit to Grey Gill — it was Ida. She had come and gone so quickly and silently that she had seemed like a ghost, scarcely real.

Ken's heart was beating violently; he could hear it pounding. He had had a narrow escape. But now that the girl had gone he realised that he had nothing to fear from her. She had been attending to some business of her own and now obviously was on her way back to bed. What could she have been doing wandering about the house at this hour? Perhaps she had been out at a dance, or perhaps to meet somebody — yes, that must be the explanation.

After a few moments Ken's heart stopped pounding; and switching on his torch he went on. He passed the back stairs and turned left down another wider passage — it was all exactly as he had expected — and a few more steps brought him through an archway and onto the main landing.

The landing was wide and was carpeted with rugs. Ken crossed it and looked over the banisters into the hall. A faint glimmer of light was coming through the fanlight above the front door. All was quiet except for the ticking of the grandfather-clock. Softly and silently Ken went down the broad staircase.

He had been in the hall before of course but it looked different tonight. He had seen it brightly lighted but now it was dark except for the light of his torch and the shadows moved about in an alarming way. The huge cupboard with the carved doors looked bigger than ever . . .

Now that Ken was here, within a few yards of his objective, he began to feel more confident of success. The most difficult part of his adventure had been accomplished and, except for his fright when he had so nearly been discovered by Ida, everything had gone well. Ken crossed the hall with assurance and, seeing that the door of the library was slightly ajar, he pushed it open and looked in. The room was empty but it had not been empty for very long for there was a strong smell of cigar-smoke in the air. The remains of the cigar was on an ash tray on the table; also upon the table was a decanter of whisky about a third full, a siphon of soda-water and a glass. There was a dying glimmer of a fire in the big old-fashioned grate. The armchair which stood at one side of the fireplace was disarranged, as if somebody had been sitting there a few moments ago and had got up and gone away. On the floor, beside the chair was a tousled heap of newspapers.

Ken wondered how long it was since the room had been occupied by its owner. Obviously Mr. Carr had been sitting up late, drinking and smoking and reading the papers. He wondered how late. He wondered how much whisky Mr. Carr had drunk. He would have given a good deal to know the answers to these questions. Of course he had seen the light in Mr. Carr's bedroom window and watched it go out, but did that really mean he had gone to bed?

It was no good worrying. The best thing to do was to carry on with the job as quickly as possible and get it over. Ken flashed his torch round the walls and saw the picture hanging above the desk. There it was, waiting for him. But before starting on the job Ken felt he would like to make sure of his retreat. He went over to the side-door intending to draw the bolt, and discovered to his amazement that the door was unbolted. He turned the handle and the door opened. It was easy as that. What on earth was the meaning of it?

Ken closed the door and stood there, wondering. Perhaps Mr. Carr had forgotten to bolt the door. What other explanation could there be? Yes, thought Ken, it must be that, but how annoying it was! How absolutely ridiculous! The door was unbolted and he could have walked into the library without the slightest trouble. Instead of climbing in at the bathroom window and wandering about in the dark passages he could have walked straight in at the door. He had never thought of trying the door — the idea had never crossed his mind. Mr. Carr had told him that he had been obliged to put "a solid bolt" on the side-door, so naturally he had supposed it would be used.

But it was foolish to waste time in idle speculation. Ken set his torch upon the table, fetched a chair, mounted upon it and unhooked the picture. He laid the frame face-downwards upon the table and taking out his screwdriver set to work. Mr. Whitehill had showed him how to do the job, and it was not difficult, but Ken's hands were shaky with excitement and the light was bad. He could not risk putting on the table-lamp; he had to prop up his torch with a book so that the beam was pointed in the right direction. It seemed to Ken that the simple task was taking a very long time. Once or twice he thought he heard a sound and paused and listened, but it was only his imagination.

At last he had finished. The real Saskia was removed from the frame and the false Saskia fitted into place. Ken climbed upon the chair and hung the picture on the wall. He straightened it carefully. Then he put the real Saskia into the grey cloth bag. The deed was done. Ken heaved a sigh of relief; he took out his handkerchief and wiped his forehead which was wet with perspiration.

CHAPTER 11
Thieves Break In

IT WAS AT THIS MOMENT, when Ken had completed his job of changing the pictures and the tension had slackened, that he heard a sound. He had thought so often that he heard a sound, but this time it was real, not imaginary. At first he thought it had come from the fireplace, perhaps a piece of coal had fallen from the grate. He strained his ears to listen and heard the scrape of a boot on the steps outside the side-door. Somebody was coming in!

Ken seized the picture, switched off his torch and, running across the room to the other door, slipped into the hall. He left the door slightly ajar and stood there waiting to see what was going to happen.

The side-door opened with a slight squeak. "It's okay," said a man's voice in a hoarse whisper. "She's left it open like I told 'er."

"There was a light in the room — I saw it," declared a second voice.

"It's the fire, that's all. There's a bit of fire left."

"Looked more like a torch to me."

"Got cold feet, ain't you?"

"There's something queer about this job. I don't like it."

The hoarse voice gave an unpleasant sort of chuckle. "There's nothing queer about the dough. Two 'undred shiners ain't to be sneezed at!"

The two men were speaking quickly and in such very

85

low tones that Ken had to strain his ears to hear what they were saying. He was peering through the partially open door and after a few moments one of them moved into his line of vision; it was the little man with the wizened face who had filled his bucket in the river. Presumably the other, the one with the hoarse voice, was his camping companion.

"Wot are we waitin' for?" asked the monkey-faced man in a whining voice.

"There ain't no 'urry," declared the other. "We got plenty of time. Look 'ere! The old geezer's left some booze for us — nice of 'im, ain't it?"

"Stop it, Rough. You don't want no booze, not now!"

Ken heard the chink of a glass. Evidently Rough was not taking his friend's advice.

"Stop it, Rough," repeated the whining voice. "We'll be 'ere all night if you start boozin'. Where's the pickcher? Old Lee said it was a pickcher of a dame brushin' 'er 'air."

The beam of a torch flickered round the walls.

Ken was wondering what to do. The absurdity of the affair struck him suddenly and he wanted to laugh. The two burglars would make off with the copy and would be quite happy until they discovered their mistake. He wanted to laugh, but that would be fatal, so he ground his teeth and controlled the rising hysteria. What was he to do, that was the question. He tried to think out a sensible plan but he was too excited and strung up. His throat was dry and his nerves were jumping. Should he allow them to get away with the picture? But no, that would never do. If they got away with the copy it would spoil everything; there would be a hue and cry all over the country! He must do something before it was too late.

The real Saskia was clutched tightly under his arm and he realised that if he intended to tackle these men he had better get rid of it. He had better hide it somewhere. He remembered the big carved cupboard — it was here, beside him — should he put the picture inside? No, underneath, thought Ken. Quick as thought he bent down and slipped the picture underneath the cupboard — there was just room for it to slide in and no more. It was a perfect hiding-place.

Ken felt safer now and his brain began to work. His first idea had been to rush into the library and scare the men away, but now he realised that this would be foolish; they could escape by the side-door, taking the picture with them. The better plan would be to go round and wait for them on the terrace and leap upon them in the dark. The unexpected attack would terrify them and it would be easy to seize the picture and slip into the library and bolt the door. They would be so surprised that they would scarcely know what had happened. Then, thought Ken, he would hang up the picture on the wall, get the real Saskia from her hiding-place and run.

The plan had several drawbacks, but he could think of no other, and he must not waste any more time. He let himself out of the front door and closed it behind him. It shut with a slight noise but he was in too great a hurry to mind. He ran round to the terrace on winged feet.

All this had happened in a few moments and when Ken reached the side-door of the library the men were still in

87

the room. The door was slightly open and the light of their torches was moving about inside. He could hear the scrape of a chair on the wooden floor and the murmur of voices. As he waited there in the darkness he began to lose confidence in his plan and to think he had been a fool. The men were desperate characters and they were two to one. Why was he interfering? He had had the precious picture in his hands and should have made off with it then and there — it would have been easy. By this time he could have been half-way down the drive with his task accomplished. Yes, he had been mad.

Ken had just arrived at this uncomfortable conclusion when suddenly there was a blaze of light in the library and a voice shouted, "Hands up, both of you! Drop that picture and put up your hands!"

Immediately there was confusion and shouting and the crashing of furniture; two shots rang out with ear-splitting bangs followed by a scream of pain. Somebody wrenched open the side-door and blundered out almost knocking Ken over in his haste. It was the monkey-faced man and he had the picture in his arms.

Ken leapt at him and hit him on the side of the head; the man yelled with fright and, dropping the picture on the steps, ran for his life.

Having accounted for Monkey-face Ken decided to see what was happening inside the library. He pushed open the door and looked in. He had expected to find Mr. Carr in charge of the situation, for it was he who had switched on the lights and shouted, "Hands up!" But Mr. Carr was not in charge of the situation and the sight that met Ken's eyes was so puzzling that for a moment or two he could not understand it at all. Just in front of Ken with his back to the door stood the big man with the bull-neck. He had a revolver in his hand. At the other end of the room stood Mr. Carr with his back to the fireplace. Mr. Carr was in his pyjamas and a blue silk dressing-gown, his right arm was hanging down helplessly and his sleeve was stained with blood.

"It's funny, ain't it?" the bull-necked man was saying in his hoarse sneering voice. "It's you that's got shot, not me. People shouldn't never say, ' 'ands up' unless they means it serious. P'rhaps you meant it serious, but you wasn't quite quick enough, see? An' it takes a bit of doin' to 'old up two chaps wif one gun, see?"

"All right, you've won," said Mr. Carr faintly. He swayed as he spoke and held onto the table with his left hand. "You've got what you — wanted. Why don't you — go away?"

The man chuckled. "I'm going," he said. "I just got one little job to see to before I clear out. I've got to be on the safe side, see? I can't risk you blabbing. It's a pity, but there it is. You better say a prayer, Mr. Gregor Carr. It's curtains for you."

He raised his revolver as he spoke but before he could take aim Ken sprang upon his back, jerking his arm sideways. The revolver flew out of his hand and clattered across the room knocking over a vase of flowers which stood on the side-table. Ken locked his arms round the man's neck and pushed him in the back with his knee. For a brief moment he thought he had the better of the man

89

but it was only the surprise of the unexpected attack which had taken him a disadvantage and when he had recovered from it he twisted himself free.

Ken rushed at him and aimed a blow at his chin but the man caught his arm in a vice-like grip and pushed him over backwards. Ken held on and they both fell on the floor. They rolled over twisting this way and that, fighting desperately. The table was upset and fell with a crash. The man was tremendously strong; his muscles were like iron. Ken knew it was hopeless. He felt the man's hands tightening round his throat and hit out with all his might. The choking grip slackened.

"Help!" cried Ken struggling to free himself. "Help! Help!"

The next moment something hit him on the head and he knew no more.

When the monkey-faced man escaped from Ken's clutches he ran like a hare, stumbling over steps in the rose garden and clawing his way through shrubberies and hedges. He had been scared before and now he was nearly mad with terror. The mist and darkness bewildered him; he wandered hither and thither, breathing hard, his heart thumping. At last, after what seemed like hours, he came to a wall and climbing over it found himself in the road just outside the village. He knew now where he was and turned to his right ran on down the road and across the bridge and up the path through the woods. When he reached the encampment in the clearing he was gasping for breath and he could do nothing but fling himself upon the ground. It was some time before he recovered enough to be able to think, and thinking was unpleasant. What should he do? Wait here for Roughie? but he did not know what had happened to Roughie in that room. For all he knew Roughie might be dead, or wounded. He hoped with all his heart that Roughie was dead, then he couldn't squeal. If Roughie were wounded and captured he would squeal all right, Monkey knew that, he had no illusions about his partner. If he could be sure that Roughie was dead the best thing to do would be to pack up and go as quickly as possible — but how could he be sure? If Roughie escaped he would come up to the camp and if he found the camp dismantled and his partner gone there would be trouble. Monkey writhed with terror. He was terrified of the big ugly man with the broken nose. He was so terribly strong, as strong as an ox, and his sudden rages were devastating. But it was no use lying here on the damp ground waiting. Monkey got up and began to pack. He had taken down the tent and was rolling it into a bundle when suddenly he had an uncomfortable feeling, the feeling that he was being watched. He swung round quickly and saw Roughie standing near the car, staring at him.

"Hullo — Roughie — " he said with a little gasp.

Roughie said nothing.

"You — got away — all right," said Monkey.

"No thanks to you," declared Roughie. "You wretched miserable rat. What d'you mean — doing a bunk with the picture. Never thought of me did you? Left me to sink or swim, thought you'd got rid of me, thought you'd make off with the goods. I daresay you hoped I'd get copped. Well I didn't see? I'm 'ere. Where's the picture?"

91

"The picture?" exclaimed Monkey in amazement.

"That's wot I sed. Where's the — picture? You got it didn't you? You made off with it an' left me to stand the racket. Wot 'ave you done with the blasted thing?"

"I dropped it. That feller bashed me on the 'ead an' I dropped it —"

"Wot's that!" shouted Roughie. "You dropped it. I bet you did! It's 'ere somewhere. You're trying to double-cross me you pop-eyed rabbit. You got it 'idden somewhere, that's wot." He advanced threateningly and Monkey backed away, his eyes fastened upon other man like a frightened rabbit.

"Honest Roughie," he said. "Honest I didn't — the feller biffed me an' I dropped it — honest Roughie — I dropped it on the steps outside the door — an' I didn't rat on you — I thought you 'ad the show taped — I thought it was all buttoned up — that's why I took the goods and ran for it. 'Ow was I to know that feller was waitin' ouside the door? Socked me, 'e did. Give me a proper old bash — near as not knocked me out."

"You dropped it — eh?"

"That's right — I dropped it —"

"You fool! You 'ad the thing in your 'ands — and you dropped it! You've messed the 'ole bloomin' show. Five 'undred smackers gone west because you're such a rotten little — I'd have done better myself. Gee I wish I'd never set eyes on you — five 'undred smackers we was to get for this job and you go an' muck it up —"

"I thought you 'ad it taped —" declared Monkey backing away.

"An' so I 'ad. If you 'adn't let that buster come in behind my back I'd 'ave finished off the old chap as easy as pie."

"Finished 'im off!"

"That's wot I sed — finished 'im off."

"But — you didn't?"

"I couldn't," declared Roughie bitterly. "That feller knocked the gun out of my 'and. We was 'aving a bit of a rough an' tumble when the 'ole place woke up an' the nex' minute the room was full of people. It was as much as I could do to get away wiv a 'ole skin. A feller came after me with a gun an' we played 'ide an' seek in the garden but I jinked 'im an' got away."

"We'd better get away," said Monkey. "We better pack the car an' clear out."

They began to pack hastily pitching their belongings into the car.

CHAPTER 12
Dreams and Visions

KEN BEGAN TO HAVE the most horrible dreams: he was walking down a long dark passage but his feet were weighted with lead so that he could hardly drag himself along. He knew he must hurry because Wallace was waiting — he had to get the picture for Wallace, the Saskia picture —if he did not hurry the monkey-faced man would get to the library before him. There were two steps in the passage and they creaked as he went down. Wallace was watching him and he tried to call out, "You should have warned me!" but he could not make a sound. Then suddenly, he found himself in the library struggling madly with a great tough fellow with a bull neck — they were rolling over and over on the floor — the fellow was kneeling on his chest. "Help!" shouted Ken. "Help, help!"

"It's all right," said a gentle voice. "It's all right. You're quite safe."

Ken opened his eyes and saw an angel. The angel was bending over him; her eyes were large and very blue and she had long golden hair in two plaits which hung down on either side of her face. She was wearing a blue gown which was exactly the same colour as her eyes. Ken gazed at her in astonishment. He had never seen an angel before.

"It's all right — you were dreaming," said the angel stroking his head. "You were having a bad dream, weren't you?"

Ken tried to speak but the effort was agonising. Pains shot through his head like knives and he was engulfed in black clouds.

Years passed, or so it seemed, and then Ken struggled out of the black clouds and found a cup being held to his lips.

"Just a little sip," said a voice. "It will do you good."

Ken thought for a moment that it was the angel, but it was not. The face looking down at him was a plain kindly middle-aged face, framed in smoothly brushed grey hair.

"Where is the angel?" whispered Ken.

"The angel? Never you mind about angels. You drink this up and go off to sleep."

"Pain — in my head," Ken murmured.

"Yes, I know. You got a bad knock on the head, but you'll be better soon."

He drank a little milk and drifted off to sleep.

The next time Ken woke he felt a good deal better. The pain was still there but it was dull and heavy, not sharp and agonising like knives. Where on earth am I? He wondered. He raised his head slightly and looked round. He was in a comfortably furnished bedroom; a room that he had never seen before. The blind at the window was lowered but bright sunshine streamed in below its fringe making an oblong patch of golden light upon the green carpet. The angel had come back. She was sitting in a small armchair at the window reading a book. Her graceful neck was bent forward as she held the book to the light, and the golden plaits were coiled round her head like a crown. Ken lay and watched her. He watched her turn the pages of her book. After a little while she looked up and came over to the bed.

"You're awake!" she said smiling at him.

Ken gazed at her. "I don't remember — anything."

"It's all right," she replied. "The doctor said you'd feel a bit bewildered. He said you mustn't try to remember —"

"But where am I?"

She hesitated for a moment and then she said, "The doctor told us not to bother you, but I expect it would bother you more not to know. You're at Grey Gill. The house belongs to my father, Mr. Gregor Carr."

Ken began to remember vaguely. "The picture — " he said.

"Yes, the picture is quite safe."

"There was a little man with a wizened face — like a monkey."

At that moment the door opened and the older woman came in. "Oh, Miss Anne!" she exclaimed. "You know the doctor said he wasn't to talk."

"Yes, I know, but —"

"Your father is asking for you, Miss Anne."

Anne hurried away without another word.

Ken was given some beef tea and toast and went to sleep again. When he woke up his brain had cleared and he began to remember what had happened. Bit by bit the pieces fell into place. He remembered the day on the river with Jim Slater and the camp in the woods; he remembered coming to Grey Gill in the mist and climbing up the ivy. He had got in at the bath-room window and made his way through the dark passages to the library, but what happened next? His head was beginning to throb with the effort he was making but he struggled on. It was like trying to remember a dream — you managed to grasp a bit of it and the rest slipped away.

"He's looking better this morning, Mrs. Aldine," said a deep voice.

Ken knew the voice. He had heard it before — somewhere. He opened his eyes and saw Doctor Stott.

"Hullo, doctor!" he said.

"Hullo, young man!" replied the doctor cheerfully. "You're a lot better, aren't you? It's lucky you've got a thick skull and a good thatch of hair. I wish my other patient was making such satisfactory progress."

"Mr. Carr?" asked Ken.

"That's right. He was shot in the arm — but you mustn't worry. You must just lie there and pretend to be a cabbage for the next few days. Mrs. Aldine will look after you. I'm going to take off that bandage and have a look at the wound. Can you raise his head a little, Mrs. Aldine?"

"Mrs. Aldine?" asked Ken, looking at her.

"I'm Mr. Carr's housekeeper," she explained, smiling at him.

Ken remembered now. Colonel MacLean had mentioned Mrs. Aldine.

When the wound had been dressed and the bandage replaced the doctor began to repack his bag.

"I wish you'd tell me," said Ken fretfully. "You say I'm not to worry, but it's much more worrying not to know what happened. I've been trying to remember, but it makes my head ache."

"Wait until tomorrow," said the doctor.

"But I want to know. I remember bits of it. Did those

men get away?

"Yes, they escaped."

"They haven't been caught?"

"Not yet. The police are looking for them but they seem to have vanished into thin air."

"They were camping in the woods. I saw them —" began Ken.

"We know all that," declared Doctor Stott. "Jim Slater told Sergeant Merton the whole story. Now look here, you mustn't worry about it. You've had a very nasty crack on the head and you really must take it easy."

"But, Doctor —"

"Tomorrow," said the doctor firmly. "I'll ask Anne to come and talk to you tomorrow morning. Will that do?"

Ken agreed. The idea of seeing Anne tomorrow morning was very pleasant. It was his last thought as he drifted off to sleep.

Mrs. Aldine brought his breakfast and tidied his room. "Miss Anne will be coming up presently," she said. "Mr. Carr took a bad turn in the night and Miss Anne didn't get much sleep, so she's having a little rest."

"Is Mr. Carr very ill?"

Mrs. Aldine nodded. "There's another doctor coming to see him today and we're getting a nurse from Manchester. It's far too much for Miss Anne looking after him all the time."

"Do you think I could shave?"

"Shave!" exclaimed Mrs. Aldine in horrified tones.

"Well, I feel such a — such a tramp," explained Ken. "I must look awful. I just thought — "

"Certainly not," said Mrs. Aldine firmly, and she went away.

Ken lay and waited patiently until Anne appeared. She looked strained and anxious but she smiled at him in a friendly manner and sat down beside his bed.

"I'm so glad you're better," she said. "I'm to tell you all you want to know, but I'm not to tire you. Those are my orders."

"I want to know everything," declared Ken eagerly.

"That's rather difficult — it was all such a muddle. In fact we haven't got it properly sorted out even now."

"What wakened Mr. Carr?" asked Ken.

"Oh, that was a funny thing," replied Anne. "Daddy was late in going up to bed and just as he was dropping off to sleep he thought he heard somebody shut the front door. You see his bedroom is just above the front door." She hesitated and then added, "But he must have been mistaken. How could the burglars have come in by the front door?"

Ken was silent. He thought it quite likely that Mr. Carr had heard somebody shut the front door.

"He got up at once," continued Anne. "He took his revolver and went downstairs to see what was happening and he heard the two men moving about in the library; so he switched on the lights and shouted to them to put up their hands. Daddy never thought they would have a revolver, but one of them had. He whipped it out as quick as lightening and shot Daddy in the arm. The other one seized the picture and rushed out at the side-door. You were there waiting for him, weren't you?"

"Yes," nodded Ken. "I gave him a biff and he dropped the picture and made off."

"Daddy was helpless," continued Anne. "The pain was so agonising that he almost fainted. The man taunted him and said he was going to kill him so that he couldn't 'blab'. Daddy thought he was done for when suddenly you appeared from the side-door and leapt at the man and knocked the revolver out of his hand. Daddy said you pulled the man down and you were both rolling on the floor fighting like tigers — but he couldn't do anything to help. He just managed to stagger to the bell and ring it before he collapsed." Anne looked at Ken and added, "It was terribly brave of you!"

"I never thought about it," declared Ken, half pleased and half embarrassed. "I mean I was sort of het up — it was just a natural reaction. I remember now. I remember rolling over and over on the floor and the table falling down. I suppose I must have hit my head against something."

"Doctor Stott says the burglar must have hit you with something sharp and heavy," said Anne with a little shudder. "The police looked for it, whatever it was — but they couldn't find it."

"The police came?"

"Not then. They came later. Fortunately I had been wakened by the shots. I went to Daddy's room and found him gone, so I knocked up Barr, the chauffeur, who sleeps in a room on the first landing. We ran downstairs and dashed into the library just in time. The man had got up off the floor and was looking for his revolver but when he saw us he turned and ran. Barr picked up Daddy's revolver and went after him but he had disappeared in the mist. That's all, really."

"But it isn't *nearly* all! What happened to the picture?"

"Oh the picture! It was lying on the terrace. Barr found it there when he came back after trying to catch the burglar. As a matter of fact he fell over it in the mist and darkness and he couldn't think what it was, so he picked it up and brought it into the library, but we were far too worried to bother about the wretched picture. You were unconscious and Daddy was fainting — his arm was bleeding terribly. Fortunately Mrs. Aldine knows a little about First Aid, so she helped me. The telephone wire had been cut so Barr had to get out the car and go for the doctor. How thankful I was when he arrived!"

"The telephone wire had been cut?"

Anne nodded. "It's a mystery," she said. "We don't know who did it, of course. Another mystery is how the burglars got in." She hesitated and then added, "I wondered if you knew."

"They came in at the side-door."

"But it was bolted! Daddy is certain he bolted it, and he looked at it again to make sure before he went up to bed."

"Somebody must have opened it for them — " began Ken. "Yes!" he cried excitedly. "Yes, of course! I remember now. The big chap said, 'It's O.K., she's left it open like I told her' — or something like that. So it must have been somebody in the house! Yes, and I know who it was — that girl with the frizzy black hair!"

Anne gazed at him in amazement. "You mean, Ida?"

"Yes, I'm positively certain it was Ida." He *was* positively

101

certain. That was what she had been doing when he met her in the passage. She had been down to the library to unbolt the door and cut the telephone wire.

"But I can't believe it!" exclaimed Anne in dismay. "Of course we only had her for a fortnight, and she wasn't a very good housemaid, but I liked her and —"

"Don't you see?" said Ken earnestly. "She must have come here under false pretences on purpose to do the job."

"Oh no —"

"Yes, really. She's an accomplice."

Anne's faith in Ida began to waver. "Well, perhaps you're right," she said. "As a matter of fact I suppose it must have been Ida; it couldn't have been anyone else."

"You must tell the police at once."

"Yes, I'll tell them," said Anne in rather a sad little voice. "But it won't be much use. She's gone home."

"Gone home!"

"She had a telegram to say her mother was dying and she must come home at once, so of course I let her go. I was so sorry for her that I gave her five pounds and sent her in the car to the station."

"It was a ruse to get away," declared Ken with conviction.

"But she was crying," objected Anne. "She was in floods of tears!"

"That's easy — with onions."

Anne sighed. She said, "Oh dear, I'm afraid I've been an awful fool, but I was so sorry for the girl."

"You weren't a fool," said Ken comfortingly. "How were you to know it was all put on? You thought the girl was in trouble so you were kind to her."

"You don't think it was awfully silly?"

"Not a bit silly. It's just that you have a beautiful nature, that's all."

Anne blushed — and then she smiled. "It really is rather funny, isn't it? Mrs. Aldine and I were so upset about poor Ida. Mrs. Aldine helped her to pack and I gave her the money for her fare to London and sent her to the station. I wonder what Sergeant Merton will say when I tell him. I know what he'll think. He'll think I'm the world's biggest idiot."

"You must have had a dreadful time," said Ken, changing the subject tactfully.

"Yes, it was dreadful! At first we didn't know what had happened. You and Daddy were both unconscious so there was nobody to explain. Mrs. Aldine thought you must be one of the burglars, but that was silly because you didn't look in the least like a burglar, then Sarah came downstairs and she said you had been fishing and had brought some fish to the back-door. Doctor Stott knew you, of course. He said you were staying at the Black Bull. Then Daddy recovered a little and was able to tell us his part of the story which cleared things up a bit, and Doctor Stott heard your part of the story from Jim Slater."

"My part of the story?"

"They were all talking about you at the Black Bull. Jim said you tracked the two men to their camp and you were certain that they were bad characters — that's why you followed them, wasn't it?"

"It wasn't quite like that —" began Ken uncomfortably.

103

"Well, you caught them," said Anne. "It was very lucky that you were here at the right moment and tackled them so pluckily." She shivered and added, "Daddy thought his last hour had come."

"The chap was probably bluffing."

"Daddy doesn't think so — nobody thinks so. Jim told Doctor Stott that the two men were horrible creatures, scarcely human. The smaller one was a like a gorilla with a wizened face and long sinewy arms and the big one was enormous, well over six feet tall and broad in proportion, like a huge grizzly bear."

Ken began to laugh. "That's Jim all over! He can make a good story out of nothing."

"Oh, I know that," agreed Anne smiling. "I've known Jim Slater for years. My cousin and I used to go out fishing with him when we were children. Of course in those days we believed everything Jim told us — it was thrilling to listen to his stories. But in this case Jim's story is true, isn't it?"

"No, not really," said Ken with a sigh. "There's a grain of truth in it, but not much more."

"You're tired," declared Anne, looking at him anxiously. "Yes, I can see you're tired. The doctor will be very angry with me."

"Never mind the doctor," said Ken.

"Never mind the doctor!" echoed Anne. "Goodness, you don't know Doctor Stott! Everybody has to do what he says. Even old Mrs. Brown who's the oldest person in the village and as stubborn as a mule does exactly what Doctor Stott tells her!"

Ken laughed.

"You can laugh if you like," said Anne seriously, "but you'll soon find out it's true — and now I'm going to leave you to have a sleep."

Ken was a little tired; he was also rather unhappy. He wished he could tell Anne everything.

CHAPTER 13
Visitors to the Sick-Room

FOR THE NEXT FEW DAYS Ken saw very little of his angel. Mrs. Aldine brought his meals and did what was necessary for him but by this time he was so much better that he needed very little attention; he was able to get up and have a bath and shave. Mr. Carr's condition was much more serious, his arm had been severely injured and he had lost a great deal of blood, but it was his heart that was causing most anxiety. Doctor Stott was worried and had sent for a heart specialist; he had also engaged a nurse but until the nurse arrived Anne was busy looking after her father.

Occasionally old Sarah came up to see Ken and have a chat. Sarah thought Mr. Leslie was a beautiful young man. She had liked him the first time she saw him, when he had brought the fish to the back door. The next time she saw him, lying unconscious on the floor with his head covered with blood, her heart had gone out to him in a wave of sympathy. Later it had been discovered that he was a hero — everybody in the village said so — and Sarah, who was a romantic old woman, adored heroes. So whenever she had time and could escape Mrs. Aldine's eagle eye Sarah trotted upstairs to worship at his shrine.

Ken welcomed her visits; he was a little bored and he could not read for long without making his head ache. Besides, he found Sarah a very interesting study; he had never met anybody like her before. She was so kind, and so

106

silly; she was so scatterbrained — and yet there was a shrewdness in her which showed itself at unexpected moments. She was always in a muddle — and yet she was an exceedingly good cook.

One morning he asked her if there had been anything in the papers about the attempted burglary,

"Not worth bothering about," replied Sarah scornfully. "Not nearly so good as last time. There wasn't no pictures nor nothing. Last time it was really good — quite exciting it was — with lovely pictures of Grey Gill and people in the village and all —"

"Yes," said Ken. He knew about that, of course. What he really wanted to know was whether a highly coloured report of the affair had found its way into the London papers, whether Colonel MacLean had seen it and if so what he was thinking about it. Ken could not write and explain matters to the Colonel because he had no means of getting the letter posted — even old Sarah would have been surprised if she had been asked to post a letter addressed to Colonel MacLean.

Doctor Stott at last gave permission to the police for a short interview with Ken. As a matter of fact Ken was not looking forward to this at all; he had a feeling that Sergeant Merton might ask some awkward questions — Sarah had told Ken that the Sergeant was "nosy" — but it was not Sergeant Merton who was ushered into his room; it was a tall good-looking man of about forty, in a lounge suit.

"Here's Detective Inspector Halliwell to see you," said Mrs. Aldine.

"Good morning, Mr. Leslie," said the Inspector

cheerfully. "The doctor said I could come and chat to you for a few minutes. You see I'm taking over the case and I think perhaps you could help me."

"Yes," said Ken. "I'll do what I can. I suppose you want me to — to make a statement or whatever you call it."

"That won't be necessary. I've got all the information from Sergeant Merton. Miss Carr has told me her story and I've spoken to Mrs. Aldine. I've seen Jim Slater and several other people in the village and I've had an interview with Mr. Carr. The doctor wasn't very pleased about *that,* but Mr. Carr is so keen to get the case cleared up that he insisted on seeing me. Well, one way and another, I've got the picture fairly clear so there's no need for you to give me a detailed statement. I just want to ask you a few questions, that's all." He smiled and added, "I don't want to get into trouble with Doctor Stott."

"What do you want to know?" asked Ken rather anxiously.

The inspector took out his notebook. "Miss Carr says the men got in at the side-door. You're sure of that, I suppose?"

"Yes, they walked straight in. It wasn't bolted."

"You heard one of them say, 'She's left it open like I told her'."

"Yes."

"The girl was an accomplice of course. That's obvious. She opened the door, cut the telephone wire and cleaned up the room."

"Cleaned up the room?"

"We'll come to that presently. The next question is, can you describe the two men?"

108

Ken did his best. It was easy enough to describe the smaller man, for Ken had seen him clearly and he was an unusual-looking creature, but the bigger man was a more ordinary type.

"It's the big chap that interests me most," said Inspector Halliwell. "He was armed — it was he who shot Mr. Carr and laid you out."

"I didn't see him properly," Ken explained. "Of course I saw him for a few moments at the camp, but that night in the library I was much too excited to see what he was like. In fact I'm doubtful if I would know him if I saw him. He was just a big hulking sort of chap with a thick neck and a red face. He had a hoarse voice — I remember that. The other chap called him 'Rough'."

"Rough!" exclaimed the Inspector, looking up from his notebook with a startled expression.

"It sounded like that. I'm still a bit muddled you know. Bits of it keep coming back to me in a funny sort of way. But yes, I'm almost sure he said, 'Stop it, Rough'."

"What did he want 'Rough' to stop doing?"

"Drinking Mr. Carr's whisky."

The Inspector nodded. "That sounds like Rough Bates. He used to be a boxer at one time; he was pretty good until he took to drink and fell on evil days."

"He was very strong," said Ken ruefully. "I'm no weakling but I felt like a baby when he got me in his clutches."

"It could be Rough Bates," said Inspector Halliwell in thoughtful tones. "I wish it had occurred to Sergeant Merton to take finger prints. Sergeant Merton is a good chap but he's a bit slow and of course he isn't used to this kind of thing. It occurred to him next morning to take prints off the door handles but by that time somebody had been round the room with a duster."

"That girl!" exclaimed Ken.

"Yes, obviously. You see everything was in such a turmoil that night and everybody was so worried that it was quite easy for her to clean up the room. And even if she had been discovered polishing up the door-handles — well, that was her job, wasn't it? Then, when she'd finished her job the telegram arrived and off she went, in floods of tears. It was all very neat — very carefully planned."

"Have you traced the girl?"

The Inspector shook his head. "No, the address she gave Miss Carr was false. Of course Sergeant Merton should have held her for questioning but by the time he got round to it she had gone. I don't really blame him; he was searching the woods for the place where the men had been camping and he couldn't be in two places at once."

"They seem to have covered up their tracks pretty thoroughly."

"Yes, they're old hands at the job, that's quite certain. Now Mr. Leslie, is there anything else you can remember? Anything they said?"

Ken tried to think. "They mentioned somebody called Old Lee. Yes, that was the name! The monkey-faced man said, 'Old Lee said it was a picture of a girl brushing her hair' or something like that."

"It couldn't have been Old Levy, could it?"

Ken thought it might have been. "Do you know

somebody called Old Levy?" he enquired.

"Yes, we do," replied the Inspector smiling rather grimly. "We have a feeling that the gentleman has been a prime mover in quite a lot of trouble, but he's a slippery customer and we haven't been able to get any definite evidence against him. I don't suppose this will help much, it's all too vague, but it's just as well to know."

Inspector Halliwell stood up and shut his notebook.

"Is that all?" asked Ken in surprise.

"That's all," replied the Inspector smiling. "I promised Doctor Stott I wouldn't tire you. Of course if you remember anything else that you think might help — "

"No — " said Ken doubtfully. "At least — I suppose you found that chap's revolver, didn't you? It went flying across the room when I knocked it out of his hand."

"Sergeant Merton found it next morning. It had been thoroughly polished," replied the Inspector significantly.

"I'm sorry I haven't been any help."

"You've given me a ray of light. I was absolutely in the dark before. I shall set the wheels turning and get hold of Rough Bates, if I can, and find out what he was doing on the night of the burglary and if he happens to have a girlfriend with frizzy black hair. That's how it's done," added Inspector Halliwell with his pleasant smile. He said goodbye and went away.

Ken heaved a sigh of relief. He had been sure that the Inspector would want to know what he had been doing at Grey Gill on the night of the burglary. That would have been difficult to answer. It would have been equally difficult to explain how he knew that the side-door had

111

been unbolted. Apparently the Inspector had taken it for granted that he had been following the two men and watched, from outside, when they walked into the library. Somebody must have told the Inspector that this was what had happened. Somebody had cleared Ken's path of all the awkward obstacles — he felt certain it was Anne.

CHAPTER 14
Child's Play

THE FIRST THING KEN DID when he was able to go downstairs was to make sure that the real Saskia was safe. He knelt down and groped underneath the cupboard in the hall — yes, she was still there. As a matter of fact he had not been worrying for the cupboard was so enormous that it would have taken two strong men to move it — he could not have found a better hiding-place if he had searched all day. When he went into the library he expected to see the false Saskia hanging upon the wall, but the space above the desk was empty. He looked about somewhat puzzled, and then he saw the picture leaning against the wall beside the desk, with its face to the wall. He went over and had a look at it. The picture seemed none the worse of its adventure but the frame had come adrift; it would have to be mended before it could be hung up again. The damage was not serious, if Ken had had some glue he could have mended it himself, but he had no glue — and it was none of his business.

Now that he was on his feet again, clothed and in his right mind, he decided he must make some plans. Half his task was done and the other half should not be difficult. All he had to do was to walk down to the Black Bull and get his car and bring it to the front-door; he must await an opportunity when nobody was about, remove Saskia from beneath the cupboard and stow her away in the specially constructed hiding-place behind the back-seat. She could remain there with perfect safety until he was able to leave Grey Gill and drive away. It would be the easiest thing in the world; it would be child's play compared with what he done already, but somehow Ken did not feel very happy about it. He felt disinclined to complete his job — in fact he felt disgusted with the whole affair.

He sat down in the one of the big armchairs beside the fire and argued with himself about it. What was the matter with him? He was still convinced that Colonel MacLean had a moral right to the picture; he was still perfectly certain that old Sir Frederick had intended to leave the Rembrandt to his nephew and not to his son. Well then, thought Ken, that's all clear, isn't it? I had better get on with the job.

Ken was still arguing with himself when Anne came in.

"Oh, there you are!" she exclaimed, smiling at him. "Mrs. Aldine said you were getting up. How are you feeling?"

"Very lazy. Otherwise not too bad."

"I'm afraid I've been neglecting you. Daddy has been so ill, but we're getting the nurse today, so it will be easier."

"I think I ought to go —"

"Oh, not yet! You aren't nearly well enough — besides, I like having you in the house." She hesitated and then added in a low voice, "You see, I'm rather — frightened."

Ken understood her feelings. She had nobody to help her, nobody to lean on. He felt so sorry for Anne that he could not speak.

"Mrs. Aldine is very kind," continued Anne. "But — but — it's the responsibility that's so — frightening. Doctor

Stott suggested I should get somebody to come and stay; but Daddy doesn't like any of our relations, so you see —"

Ken saw.

"Of course I know it must be very dull for you here — "

"It isn't a bit dull. I'll stay as long as you want me," declared Ken.

Their eyes met for a moment and then they both looked away.

Ken knew now why he felt disinclined to complete his job. He knew he could not possibly go through with it. Somehow or other he would have to change the pictures again and put the real Saskia back in the frame. There was no hurry of course. The real Saskia was perfectly safe in her hiding place. He could wait until he was better and more able to tackle the job — any time would do — but the mere fact of having made the decision lifted a cloud from his spirits and he felt free and happy.

Of course it would not be plain sailing — there were snags. It was hard on Colonel MacLean. Ken realised that he would have to explain the whole matter to Colonel MacLean and that would not be easy. Ken's own future would not be very pleasant for he would have no money to go to Canada and look for a job as he had intended. He could not accept Wallace's money — he was not entitled to a farthing of it. All Ken possessed in the world was the little car and about ten pounds in the Savings Bank. But it was no good worrying.

"What are you thinking about?" asked Anne.

Ken started. His thoughts were not very suitable to put into words.

"You look worried," Anne explained.

"I was just wondering what I could do when I leave Grey Gill. I gave up my job in a dull dreary London office because I couldn't bear it any longer. I shall have to find another job."

"Daddy will find you a job. He says you saved his life, and it's true."

Ken was silent. It was true of course, but all the same he did not like the idea of accepting favours from Mr. Gregor Carr.

"Just wait till Daddy is better," continued Anne, "then we can talk it over and decide what you want to do. Daddy can easily find you a job in his oil-company. He's a little — a little difficult at times but he isn't ungrateful. He often talks about you. He keeps on asking how you are and whether we're looking after you properly."

"Does he? That's very nice of him," said Ken uncomfortably.

"He wants to see you," declared Anne. "He wants to thank you for tackling that great enormous burglar and saving his life, but the doctor wants him to be kept as quiet as possible so we'd better wait until he's a little stronger."

Ken was not anxious to see Mr. Carr and be thanked for saving his life. "Oh yes, we'd better wait," agreed Ken fervently.

"Meanwhile you must just take things easy and not worry about anything. Daddy will get you a good job, I know he will."

"Well, we'll see," said Ken.

Ken had promised to stay at Grey Gill as long as Anne

wanted him and that meant until her father was well on the road to recovery. He was in no hurry to go, for his convalescence was pleasant. Everybody in the house was kind to him and he was pampered and cosseted like an invalid child. Ken had never been pampered before so it was no wonder he enjoyed it. Once the nurse had been installed to look after Mr. Carr, Anne had more leisure and she and Ken went for walks together or sat on the terrace; they talked about all sorts of things but they avoided the subject of the picture. Ken had no wish to discuss that subject and apparently Anne did not care to talk about it either.

Anne told Ken about her childhood and her schooldays but she did not say much about the last few years when she had lived with her father in London and run his house. They had not been happy years and there were incidents in her father's life which had distressed her. Ken had his reticences too; he could not speak of his visit to Seacliff, he could not mention the MacLeans. But in spite of these hidden reefs Anne and Ken sailed along together very happily.

Sometimes Ken felt tempted to tell Anne the whole story, but he could not tell her because it was not his secret. He had given his solemn promise to Colonel MacLean that he would tell nobody — his lips were sealed. Perhaps it was just as well Ken's lips were sealed, for of course if he told Anne the real story of what had happened on the night of the burglary he would have to go. Anne would never forgive him. The friendliness in her blue eyes would change to coldness and reproach. Yes, it was just as well he

117

could not tell her.

Ken could not tell Anne about Saskia, but one day when they had walked up the hill together and were resting in the shelter of some rocks he told her about Margaret Coke.

Anne listened to the story and sympathised.

"Oh, you needn't be sorry," said Ken cheerfully. "It was all a frightful mistake. You see Margaret and I had quite different ideas about things — about important things — so we wouldn't have been happy together. I feel as if it had happened long, long ago. In fact I had almost forgotten about her."

"I wonder if she has forgotten about you?" said Anne thoughtfully.

"Goodness, yes," declared Ken. "She didn't really love me. If she had loved me she would have understood what I felt about that horrible job — and that horrible man. She wouldn't have minded living in a small flat and not having much money. You see, Anne, when two people love each other it doesn't matter about money."

"Money doesn't matter, one way or the other, when two people love each other," said Anne in a very thoughtful voice.

This was exactly what Ken had said, or at least he thought it was, and he reflected, not for the first time, that it was wonderful to have found somebody whose ideas on every important matter harmonised with his own. He looked at Anne. Fortunately he was able to look at her quite comfortably for she was lost in thought, gazing across the valley. It was delightful to look at Anne. She was so beautiful to look at. His first impression of Anne had been that she was an angel, straight from Heaven — it was an illusion of course but it was not so very far from the truth. Anne looked like an angel and her nature was angelic; there was an air of goodness and innocence about her which was not of this world. She believed ill of nobody — anybody could take her in with a hard-luck story — but this innocence was part of her charm and Ken adored her all the more because of it.

He adored her. He had never thought of marrying her of course. Ken had known from the beginning that Anne was not for him. Anne was an angel, she was as far above him as the stars. It was enough happiness to look at her and talk to her and to serve her in any way he could. When he went away he would never see her again, but he would always remember her. As long as he lived he would remember her.

Ken realised that it was lucky he felt like this about Anne because obviously he could never ask her to marry him. There were insurmountable barriers between them. For one thing there was the secret, which could never be told, and for another thing Ken had no money and Anne had a great deal. Their ways lay apart. This was just a short interlude in their lives; it was a very happy interlude but nothing more.

CHAPTER 15
The Difficult Letter

THERE WAS NOW NO EXCUSE for not writing to Colonel MacLean — Ken could walk to the village and post the letter himself — so he decided he had better get on with it. His first intention was to explain the whole thing in detail, but this was so difficult that he abandoned the attempt. What was the use of telling Colonel MacLean that he had changed the pictures when he was going to change them back? It sounded crazy. So he started the letter all over again and just said that he had come to Grey Gill to take the picture and had become involved with a couple of tough characters who had broken into the house with the same intent. A mêlée had ensued in which Mr. Carr had been wounded and he himself had been laid out with a crack on the head.

"Since then," wrote Ken. "I have been lying here in bed and everybody has been so kind to me that I feel I cannot carry out my job. I am very sorry about it, and I am afraid you will think it very silly. I still feel that the picture belongs to you by right, in fact I am more than ever convinced that Sir Frederick intended you to have it, but after staying here in the house as a guest and being so well looked after I feel I cannot take the picture away. Naturally I shall keep my promise to tell nobody about our arrangements, so you need have no fears on that score. When I am better I intend to go to Canada and start life

120

afresh. I hope you and Wallace will forgive me and understand."

Ken read the letter over and thought it would do. That afternoon he walked down to the village and posted it. The matter was now settled and he felt greatly relieved. He need not worry about it any more.

When he got back to Grey Gill he met Doctor Stott in the hall. The doctor had been to see Mr. Carr and was just going away.

"May I speak to you for a minute, sir?" asked Ken.

"Of course," replied the doctor cheerfully.

They went into the library.

"I'm wondering what I ought to do," said Ken. "I really ought to go and look for a job, but Anne has asked me to stay on until her father is better."

Doctor Stott did not reply at once. He walked over to the window and stood there looking out.

"You see my difficulty, don't you?" continued Ken. "I'm all right now and I feel I ought to go, but I can't leave Anne all by herself when her father is so ill. Could you give me any idea when Mr. Carr is likely to get better?"

"He isn't likely to get better," said Doctor Stott.

"Not — get better?"

"He's losing ground. We've done all we can but he hasn't responded to the treatment — his heart is in a very bad condition. Between you and me Gregor Carr has been drinking pretty heavily for years. I don't mean he was a drunkard, in the usually accepted sense of the word, but he certainly took far more than was good for him. If you do that for long it's liable to undermine the strongest

121

constitution."

Ken was silent. For some reason it had never entered his head that Mr. Carr might not recover. The news upset all his plans. He felt bewildered.

"I haven't told Anne," continued Doctor Stott. "She'll be upset, of course, but I don't think it can be a great grief to her. Gregor Carr hasn't been a good father; in fact he's given Anne a very bad time. I don't know how much she's told you but it can't have been pleasant for her to live with him these last few years."

"She hasn't told me much, but I had a feeling —" began Ken.

"Yes, well — there it is," said the doctor with a sigh. "Anne has borne a lot, and very bravely." He paused for a few moments and then went on, "I wish she had some relative who could come and stay with her, but Gregor Carr has quarrelled with all his relations. For instance there's Alec MacLean; he's a cousin of Gregor's and a very good fellow, but it's no use asking him to come because there was that row about the Rembrandt."

"Yes, of course."

"I feel responsible for Anne. You see I've known her since she was a small child; she used to come to Grey Gill and stay with her grandfather. Sir Frederick was a fine old man. I was very fond of Sir Frederick — "

The doctor went on talking about Sir Frederick but Ken was thinking of his own affairs.

"Perhaps I really ought to go away —" he began in a doubtful voice.

"Don't do that," said the doctor quickly. "It's good for

Anne to have somebody to talk to. The only thing is —" he paused.

"The only thing is you don't know anything about me," said Ken. "Well, the fact is I've got no money and no job and no prospects. There's not much more to tell you except that I've promised Anne to stay as long as she wants me."

"And after that?"

"I shall try to get to Canada and find a job."

"Mr. Carr intends to help you. He told me so."

"I don't want that," declared Ken.

"I see," said the doctor. He was still standing near the window, looking out and jingling the money in his pocket as if he could not make up his mind about something.

"You needn't worry," said Ken, breaking a long silence. "I'm not a fortune-hunter."

"That isn't what's worrying me," replied Doctor Stott. He sighed and added, "I don't know what to do. Perhaps Mr. Sloane will be able to advise something."

"Mr. Sloane?"

"Yes, he's Gregor Carr's lawyer. Gregor wants to see him so he's coming down for a night.

Afterwards when Ken thought about this conversation he was puzzled. What was the doctor worrying about? On the face of it one might presume he was worrying about the condition of his patient's heart, but somehow Ken did not think it was that.

123

CHAPTER 16
The Unexpected Visitor

ON THE MORNING following his conversation with Doctor Stott, Ken was sitting on the terrace reading the papers and enjoying the sunshine. He was waiting for Anne to go for a walk. Suddenly he looked up and saw a young man approaching the house. The young man had no hat and the sun was shining upon his bright red hair so that it looked like flames. Ken gazed at the blazing head; surely there could not be two heads like that in the world! It must be — it was — Copper!

"Hullo!" said Copper, leaning upon the balustrade and smiling his wide friendly smile.

"Great Scott!" exclaimed Ken.

"Surprised to see me?" asked Copper cheerfully. "Pleased, I hope? I must say you seem to have found very comfortable lodgings — and you don't look much the worse for your adventures. I suppose you're wondering how I found you? That's how." He took a newspaper out of his pocket and dropped it onto Ken's knees; it was a copy of a sensational London newspaper about ten days old.

"I don't usually buy this rag," explained Copper. "I just happened to see somebody reading it in a bus. Most of the London papers gave a very tame account of the affair, but this is quite exciting. You read it and you'll see."

Ken read it.

124

DARING ATTEMPT TO STEAL WORLD-FAMOUS PORTRAIT
YOUNG MAN THWARTS THE THUGS

The famous Rembrandt which was discovered last year was the object of a daring raid on Thursday night when two heavily armed men broke into the North Country Mansion of Mr. Gregor Carr the well-known Oil King. Under cover of a thick fog the burglars scaled a fifteen foot wall and attempted to remove the valuable picture from the library. Mr. Carr who had been sitting up late dealing with his correspondence was disturbed by a noise and discovered the thieves at work. He endeavoured to hold them up at the point of a revolver but without success. Fortunately Mr. K. Leslie, a young medical student who was on his way north in his car happened to be on the spot at the psychological moment and with consummate bravery came to Mr. Carr's aid. Having disposed of one of the thugs and rescued the picture he proceeded to tackle the other with his bare hands. A fight ensued in which Mr. Carr was seriously wounded and Mr. Leslie was hit on the head with a sharp instrument and rendered unconscious. Aroused from sleep by the crack of revolvers Miss Carr ran downstairs in her night attire and found the library a shambles. She immediately summoned the police who arrived in force shortly afterwards. The priceless picture was discovered in the garden where it had been thrown by the burglars in their headlong flight. The gilt frame was scratched and damaged but the picture was intact. The police took charge of the situation and are searching for the criminals high and low; they have discovered several important clues and an arrest is imminent. The abortive burglary calls to mind the romantic story of the discovery of the Rembrandt by the late Sir Frederick Carr and the lawsuit for its possession which followed his death . . .

"It's not true," said Ken. "At least some of it is, but —"

"But it is frightfully exciting, isn't it?" said Copper. "Absolutely lurid! For instance I like that bit about Miss Carr running downstairs in her night attire and finding the library a shambles — it must have given the poor girl a nasty shock — and I like that bit about your consummate bravery. But look here, Ken, it's a frightful mistake to thwart thugs with your bare hands. Always wear gloves, my boy. It's dirty work thwarting thugs — and how difficult it is to say!" exclaimed Copper. "Even when completely sober, as I am at present, it's almost impossible to get your tongue round the words."

"But I'm not a medical student! How did you know it was me?"

"Oh the medical student is just poetic licence," said Copper airily. "I mean if you're sent to report an incident and you can't find out much about it you have to use your imagination — and I didn't actually know K. Leslie was you; I just thought he might be. I'd have come up last week but I was billed to give a talk on the Radio and I couldn't get away. It's nice to see you, old cock."

"But Copper — "

"Then of course I thought this little imbroglio was probably part of the Adventure. It sounded as if it might be. Mr. Seton and I put two and two together and decided that it was worth looking into. So I jumped onto the old bike and zoomed north. I stayed last night at an inn called the Black Bull and had a chin-wag with some of the local inhabitants. You seem to be a sort of hero in this place."

"But look here, Copper — "

"It's just a flying visit. As a matter of fact I've got to be back in London tonight because I'm doing another broadcast tomorrow morning. Mr. Seton stood me the petrol for the trip."

"But I don't understand," declared Ken.

Copper sighed. "I thought I had explained it all so clearly."

"To begin with who on earth is Mr. Seton?"

Copper swung himself onto the balustrade and sat there dangling his legs. "Mr. Seton is an old codger who

127

interferes in a benignant sort of way with other people's affairs. Of course that Margaret girl has been urging him on and badgering him about you — "

"Margaret!" cried Ken in dismay.

"Not to worry," said Copper soothingly. "The Margaret girl has no idea where you are. We didn't tell her. We had a feeling you would rather not."

"But the papers — "

"She didn't recognise you as K. Leslie, the medical student — at least I suppose not or she would have mentioned it. It takes great minds like Mr. Seton and me to penetrate the disguise. Besides she didn't know about the Big Adventure for the Young Man of Good Appearance free from Dependants."

"Good heavens!" exclaimed Ken. "Then you've been to Seacliff — "

"No, definitely not. What happened at Seacliff?"

Ken was silent.

"Ah, a secret," said Copper nodding. "I suppose that's where the retired Army officer hangs out."

"How do you know? I mean — "

"You seem a bit wandered," said Copper kindly. "I expect that's the result of being hit on the head with a blunt instrument — no, it was a sharp instrument, wasn't it? Fact is I'm calling this "The Case of the Missing Advertisement! Quite good, don't you think?"

"I don't know what to think," said Ken. "I wish you'd explain."

"I wondered where you'd gone," explained Copper. "I thought you might be tilting at a windmill, or something, so when I found the *Daily Clarion* in the waste paper basket with a bit cut out I put Mr. Seton on the trail. He waddled along to the *Clarion* office and found the missing advertisement. It was the work of a moment. Unfortunately neither he nor I could induce the young woman behind the counter to divulge the identity of the advertiser. I'm getting old or something," declared Copper sadly. "I'm losing my sex-appeal — or perhaps she has an allergy to auburn hair. Anyhow she wouldn't play and we were stumped."

"How could you be stumped if she wouldn't play?" asked Ken who was beginning to recover from his bewilderment.

Copper waved aside the interruption. "Only temporarily stumped," he said. "When we saw the account of the 'abortive burglary' we put two and two together, as I said before, and here I am."

"But why?" asked Ken. "I mean I'm very pleased to see you, but why all this fuss?"

"Several reasons," replied Copper. "For one thing you went off with the key of the store-cupboard —"

"I didn't —"

"You did."

"I didn't," declared Ken indignantly. "I left it in the tobacco jar on the mantelpiece. I knew you'd find it."

"I've knocked off smoking," Copper said.

They looked at one another and laughed uproariously.

"But it wasn't really that," objected Ken. "Surely you wouldn't have — "

"Well, what could I do?" asked Copper. "Of course I brought a bottle, but that cupboard is the only safe place in the flat — you know as well as I do that our Mrs. Mop snoops into every other place. That wasn't the only reason. I wanted to know what silly-ass trick you were up to and the old bike wanted a bit of exercise. Then there was the Margaret girl. She's been a confounded nuisance — "

"That's all off," declared Ken earnestly. "She gave me back the ring. It's absolutely off."

"All right, all right! Keep your hair on. I'll tell her you're going to Timbuctoo."

"Canada," said Ken. "When I've — when I've finished what I'm doing here I'm off to Canada to find a job."

"What are you doing here?" asked Copper with interest.

"Oh, just — just hanging about. I've been ill, you know."

"Why not go to Brazil? It's a marvellous place. Brazil is News these days. People have just discovered it's bigger than Australia. As a matter of fact I've been thinking of pushing off to Brazil myself — what about you and me going together? There's an idea!"

"Brazil?"

"You like nuts, don't you?" said Copper persuasively. "We'll sail up the Amazon and take photographs of crocodiles basking in the sun. It will be terrific sport. Yes, Ken, that's what we'll do. I'll write a series of articles and make pots of money."

"But what about me?"

"You'll snoop round and get a first class job. I tell you, Ken, it's the thing to do. Honest it is. Now listen to me — "

They were still talking about Brazil when Anne came out of the side-door, ready for a walk. She was surprised to find Ken and a strange young man in earnest conversation.

"Oh, this is Copper," said Ken. "He's a friend of mine.

Copper, this is Miss Carr."

"How do you do," said Anne politely.

Copper said nothing. He was gazing at Anne, wide-eyed.

"Copper saw an account of the burglary in a paper," explained Ken. "So he just dropped in to see me."

"How nice of you!" said Anne smiling at Copper in a friendly manner. "I expect you were worried about Ken. He was very ill for a day or two but he's getting on splendidly."

"That's good," said Copper in a dazed sort of voice.

"I'm perfectly fit now," declared Ken.

"Not really," said Anne. "You must still take things easy. Doctor Stott says you mustn't get overtired."

"He looks — all right," said Copper.

Anne nodded. "Oh, he's ever so much better of course, and it will do him a lot of good to have a chat with you. You'll stay to lunch won't you, Mr. Copper?"

"Yes, rather," said Copper. "I mean no, I can't. I mean it's most awfully kind of you but I'm on my way back to London."

"But surely you could stay to lunch!"

"I'd stay if I could," declared Copper earnestly. "Wild horses wouldn't drag me away — but I've got to get back tonight. I've got to be on the air tomorrow morning."

"Broadcasting," Ken explained proudly. "Copper does a lot of talking on the air."

Anne looked at Copper admiringly. "How clever of you!" she said. "We must listen tomorrow morning. What are you going to talk about?"

"Greece," said Copper.

"He's just come back from Greece," explained Ken.

"How wonderful!" Anne said. "I've always wanted to go to Greece. It must be perfectly lovely — do tell us about it."

Copper had recovered by this time and he was able to talk about some of his experiences. He found he could talk better if he did not look at Anne. When he looked at her it took his breath away and he could only gasp like a fish removed from its native element.

When they had chatted for a little Copper said he must go. He had left his motor-bike at the gate and Ken walked down the avenue with him to speed him on his way.

"It's been grand to see you, old boy," said Ken. "I'm awfully glad you came; I just wish you could stay a bit longer."

"So do I," said Copper fervently.

"You'll tell Margaret, won't you? I mean it's absolutely off. She gave me back the ring. In fact she took it off and threw it onto my plate — in a restaurant — so you see —"

Copper saw. "How foul!" he exclaimed. "I'll choke her all right. Trust your Uncle Copper to make up a first class yarn."

"But there's no need to make up a yarn. Just tell her the truth. Say that you and I are off to Brazil together, that's all. Of course I'm not sure when I shall be free, but I'll let you know."

"I wouldn't go to Brazil if I were you," said Copper, wheeling his bike into the road and preparing to mount.

"You wouldn't! But Copper, you said — "

"If I were you," said Copper earnestly, "if I were you I'd stay here as long as I could — and then head off to Greece for my honeymoon."

"But you don't understand!" cried Ken.

His words were drowned by a series of deafening explosions which was the normal manner of starting for Copper's bike. Copper kissed his hand gracefully towards the house and vanished in a cloud of evil-smelling smoke.

CHAPTER 17
Weighty Matters of Business

Two DAYS LATER Mr. Sloane arrived. He arrived just before dinner and it had been arranged that he was to see Mr. Carr the next morning. Anne and Ken and Mr. Sloane had dinner together; it was not a very comfortable meal.

Of course Mr. Sloane had heard about the attempted burglary but he wanted to know details of the affair, he wanted to get to the bottom of the matter. Anne answered his questions; she described how Ken had saved the situation and praised his courage in glowing terms, but Mr. Sloane was not impressed. It was obvious that Mr. Sloane regarded the young man with suspicion, which under the circumstances was not unnatural, and he wanted to know how the young man happened to be on the spot at exactly the right moment.

"It was clever, wasn't it?" said Anne. "He knew those horrible men were after the picture, so he followed them."

"How did you know they intended to steal the Rembrandt, Mr. Leslie?" asked Mr. Sloane.

This was the question that Ken had been dreading. He had thought of so many different answers to it that he could not make up his mind which one to offer. He hesitated.

"Oh, Ken just put two and two together," said Anne. "You see Jim Slater had heard them asking questions about it in the Black Bull, and then Ken saw the camp in the woods and he realised there was something very queer

134

about the men."

Ken felt miserable. He longed to escape, to sink through the floor and disappear from view.

"Very clever," commented Mr. Sloane in disbelieving tones. "Mr. Leslie has missed his vocation. He ought to be in the C.I.D. By the way what is your profession, Mr. Leslie?"

"I haven't got — " began Ken.

"He was in an office in London," said Anne, "but he didn't like it. Daddy is going to find him a post, something really worth-while and interesting. There's no hurry about it, of course. He must stay here until he's better."

"Well, we'll see," said Mr. Sloane.

These were the very words Ken had used but on Mr. Sloane's lips they sounded somewhat sinister.

Dinner was over now, and Anne got up. She always sat with her father when the nurse was off duty.

"You must ask Daddy about it," she said. "You'll be seeing Daddy in the morning; he'll tell you what he means to do for Ken."

"Yes, I shall look forward to seeing Mr. Carr," declared Mr. Sloane. "There are several very important business matters to discuss."

But Mr. Sloane did not have the promised interview with his client. Gregor Carr had a serious heart attack during the night and he was much too ill to see anybody. In the afternoon he rallied a little, but the improvement in his condition was only temporary and by the following morning he was dead.

Anne had been with her father all day long and she was

135

so worn out that Doctor Stott ordered her straight to bed and told Mrs. Aldine to keep her there for two days and to allow nobody to see her.

"There's no need for her to bother about anything," declared Doctor Stott. "She must have a complete rest. Mr. Sloane is here and can make all the necessary arrangements. You understand, Mrs. Aldine?"

Mrs. Aldine understood and bowed to the doctor's decree.

Mr. Sloane was very busy indeed. He took over a small room at the back of the house and settled down to go through his client's papers. This room had been used by Gregor Carr as an office and was equipped with a filing cabinet and a large roll-top desk. All day long Mr. Sloane laboured with stacks of papers and documents and endeavoured to bring order out of chaos.

With Anne in bed, and Mr. Sloane shut up in the office, Ken was left to his own devices and to tell the truth he felt extremely miserable. He felt he had no right to be living here, doing nothing, now that he was perfectly well, and Mr. Sloane, whom he met at meals, was obviously of the same opinion. Yet how could he go away now, before Mr. Carr's funeral, and without seeing Anne to say goodbye?

It was fortunate for Ken that Mr. Sloane had so many weighty matters on his mind — even at meal-times he was abstracted — and although he showed by his manner that he did not approve of Ken he seemed to have lost all desire to examine him about his movements on the night of the burglary.

"It's a great pity I didn't see Mr. Carr before his death,"

136

said Mr. Sloane after a long silence.

"Yes," said Ken in a non-committal tone.

"I blame Doctor Stott," said Mr. Sloane. "If I had had any idea Mr. Carr was so seriously ill I would have come before. There were several very important matters connected with his estate — but it can't be helped."

"No," said Ken.

"I suppose you will be leaving Grey Gill immediately after the funeral?"

"Yes," said Ken.

"Miss Carr must shut up the house and go away. It is must unsuitable for her to live here alone. I must engage a trustworthy companion to look after her; she will be a very rich young woman and must be protected from adventurers."

Ken said nothing.

"Miss Carr is not wise in the ways of the world," continued Mr. Sloane. "She is — er — very childlike — er — easily taken in. It is essential that she should have a trustworthy person to look after her. I shall see to it myself."

Ken still remained silent. There was nothing to say.

After tea Ken decided to go for a walk. Mrs. Aldine was out so he called to Sarah that he was going up the hill for a breath of fresh air.

"Yes, you should," said Sarah. "It'll be nice up there — but don't you go too far and get too tired."

Sarah watching him striding off across the garden. As has been said before she was devoted to Mr. Leslie — he was simply beautiful, and so pleasant and kind. It would be nice if he and Miss Anne got married, thought Sarah. Miss Anne couldn't find anybody nicer, and a wedding at Grey Gill would be lovely.

Sarah was thinking about the wedding and how lovely it would be, when the door-bell rang. She remembered that Mrs. Aldine was out so she trotted across the hall and opened the front door. There was a short, stout gentleman standing on the steps. He had thick curly grey hair and was very well dressed in a brown lounge suit and nicely polished shoes. At the bottom of the steps there was a small van.

"Good afternoon," said the gentleman smiling pleasantly. "I'm from Messrs. Shuttleworth and Brown. I've called for the picture."

"What picture?" asked Sarah, gazing at him vaguely. "Mrs. Aldine is and out and I don't know nothing about it."

"When will Mrs. Aldine be back?" enquired the gentleman.

"About six," replied Sarah.

"That's a pity," said the gentleman frowning. "I particularly wanted to see Mrs. Aldine but I'm afraid I can't wait. You see I must be back in Manchester before six. Mrs. Aldine knows all about it of course. I was told to call for a picture that needs repairing. The frame is damaged." He produced a card from his pocket-book and handed it to Sarah.

Sarah took the card and looked at it. She had not her spectacles, but the printing was very large and clear so she had no difficulty in reading it: MESSRS SHUTTLEWORTH AND BROWN, PICTURE DEALERS AND REPAIRERS,

MANCHESTER.

"Are you Mr. Shuttleworth, then?" asked Sarah.

"No, just a representative of the firm," replied the gentleman.

"Well, I don't know," said Sarah. "Perhaps I'd better ask Miss Carr —"

"Oh, we mustn't trouble Miss Carr," said the gentleman hastily. "I wouldn't think of disturbing her — at a time like this."

"No, p'raps not," agreed Sarah. "She's resting. The doctor said she was to."

"Well, that is a pity," said the gentleman with a sigh. "If only Mrs. Aldine were here. I suppose you don't know which picture it is? The frame has been damaged."

"Why yes, of course!" exclaimed Sarah. "It'll be the Saskia picture, that's what. The picture nearly got stolen by the burglars and the frame got a bit knocked about. Mrs. Aldine was only saying this morning that it would need to be mended before it could be hung up again."

By this time the gentleman had come into the hall. "That's right," he declared. "Yes, that's the one. Mrs. Aldine wants the frame mended."

Sarah hesitated. She had a sort of feeling that she knew the gentleman — she had met him before — somewhere — but when she looked at him again the feeling disappeared and she felt sure she had not seen him before. He was not the sort of gentleman you would be likely to forget, with his nice curly grey hair and his funny screwed up eyes.

"I'll take it today," said the gentleman with easy assurance. "If I take it today we can put it in hand at once

139

and I can bring it back on Friday."

"On Friday," said Sarah nodding. "That's the day the laundry comes." She led the way into the library and lifted the picture which was leaning against the wall.

"Allow me," said the gentleman politely. "You really mustn't bother —"

"I can carry it for you."

"No, no. I'm used to dealing with pictures."

"You'll get it mended at once?" asked Sarah anxiously.

"Oh yes. At once," he replied. He glanced at it and added, "It just needs a little glue — and perhaps we should touch up the gilding — but that won't take long."

"I'll tell Mrs. Aldine you called for it."

"Yes, be sure to tell her," said the gentleman as he walked across the library with the picture tucked under his arm. "Tell her that I'll bring it back on Friday. I'm sorry not to have seen Mrs. Aldine, but you've been most helpful. Thank you very much indeed."

"That's all right," said Sarah as she opened the front door.

The gentleman went down the steps and put the picture into the van. "Goodbye — and thank you again!" he said, waving cheerfully. Then he got into the driving-seat and drove off very slowly.

The card was still in Sarah's hand; she put it into the pocket of her apron. What a nice gentleman! she thought. So polite and pleasant spoken! Mrs. Aldine would be glad that the picture had gone to be mended.

Sarah glanced at the clock and saw that it was high time the joint for dinner was in the oven; she hurried away into the kitchen.

140

CHAPTER 18
The Pleasant-Spoken Gentleman

AFTER DINNER Ken sat in the library by himself and looked at the papers, but he had so much on his mind that his attention wandered. Tomorrow was the day of Mr. Carr's funeral and after that was over he must see Anne and say goodbye. Tonight was his last night at Grey Gill — and he still had to change the pictures. He glanced across the room to the corner where the picture usually stood, leaning against the wall, but it was not there. That was funny! Ken got up and looked for it; he looked behind the desk and all round the room but it had gone. Obviously Mrs. Aldine must have put it away somewhere; she was a very tidy woman and she had a mania for putting things away. Where could she have put it?

Ken was worried for it upset his plans considerably. He had intended to come down tonight when everybody was in bed and asleep and return the real Saskia to her frame. He simply must do the job tonight. Ken was annoyed with himself for not doing it before. Why on earth had he left it till the last moment? He did not want to make a fuss and ask Mrs. Aldine where she had put the picture, but he would have to. He decided to wait until Mrs. Aldine came in with his milk. (Ken still was treated as an invalid and was regaled with a glass of hot milk at bedtime) and then he could ask her in a casual sort of way where she had put the picture.

141

He was about to sit down again in the big chair when the door opened and Anne came in. She was in a blue dressing-gown, the same blue dressing-gown that she had worn the first time Ken had seen her and mistaken her for an angel, but her hair was neatly coiled round her head, not hanging down in plaits. Ken had not seen Anne since her father's death, so he took her hands and said in a stumbling way that he was sorry.

"Yes, poor Daddy," said Anne. "Thank you, Ken."

She was pale, but quite composed and he was glad to see she looked more rested.

"I had to see you," she continued. "I wanted to talk to you, Ken. It's about Mr. Sloane. He wanted to see me on business, so he came up to my room. Mr. Sloane says you're going away tomorrow."

"Yes — I think I had better."

"But why? And where are you going? You haven't got a job!"

"I'll find one all right," declared Ken.

They sat down in the two big chairs at either side of the fire.

"Oh dear," said Anne miserably. "I don't know what to do. Mr. Sloane seems to think he can arrange my life for me. He says I ought to shut up Grey Gill and go away and he says he's going to find a companion for me — but he hasn't really got any right to arrange my life. I can do what I like."

"Perhaps he's your trustee," suggested Ken.

"No, he isn't," replied Anne. "That's what he wanted to see Daddy about. He wanted to arrange for me to have

142

trustees. You see I'm twenty-one now and I can do exactly as I like. Daddy didn't make a Will."

"Didn't make a Will?" echoed Ken.

She shook her head. "He didn't like the idea. Mr. Sloane wanted him to make one but he kept on putting it off, so I shall get everything belonging to him."

Ken gazed at her. She looked so young, sitting there in her blue dressing-gown with her little blue shoes. She would get everything belonging to Gregor Carr without let or hindrance!

"It's a great responsibility," said Anne with a sigh. "But I shall do what I think is right. I'm not going to let Mr. Sloane dictate to me. The first thing I want to do — Mr. Sloane doesn't approve at all, but I don't care — the first thing I want to do is to give the Rembrandt to Cousin Alec."

"What!" exclaimed Ken.

"It's his, really," said Anne. "Grandfather meant him to have it." She gave a little shudder and added, "I shall be glad to get rid of it. Everything has gone wrong since we got that horrible picture — everything has gone wrong, and now it has killed Daddy."

Ken's thoughts were in such a turmoil that he could not speak.

"Of course it isn't really the picture," continued Anne after a short silence. "I mean the picture is only a picture, it can't be unlucky in itself, but I think if a person does something very wrong it brings misfortune. Don't you agree?"

"Yes, perhaps, but — "

143

"Oh, I know it seems dreadfully disloyal to talk like this, but I've been so miserable about it and I do want you to understand. I think the picture brought Daddy all these terrible troubles because it was wrong for him to have it."

Ken felt they were getting into deep waters. "But perhaps your father thought it really was his — " he began.

"No, he didn't," said Anne in a low voice. "At least — it's rather difficult to explain. Daddy won the case, so of course the picture was his by law but law isn't always right — you know that, Ken." She paused and looked at him and then continued. "Grandfather wanted Cousin Alec to have the picture. We all knew that. Even Mr. Sloane knows it in his heart of hearts. Mr. Sloane keeps on saying the Rembrandt is mine by law and I mustn't give it to Cousin Alec — but he can't stop me."

"You really mean to give it to him?"

"Yes," said Anne firmly. She looked across the room and frowned. "Where is it?" she asked.

"That's what I was wondering," admitted Ken.

"I'll ask Mrs. Aldine," said Anne. She rose and went away.

While she was gone Ken managed to sort out his thoughts. He was very glad indeed that Colonel MacLean was to get the Rembrandt and even more delighted that he was to get it in this way, as a gift from Anne. Nothing could be better. It finished up the whole affair in a most satisfactory manner. Colonel MacLean would be pleased, and so would Wallace, and they would both be very glad that the Adventure had not come off. All the same Ken realised, when he thought about it, that he had played a useful part in the affair; for if he had not been on the spot, Rough and his confederate would have got away with the real Saskia and Anne would not have been able to give it to her cousin and make the wrong thing right. This was a comforting thought. All his trouble had not gone for nothing. He could leave Grey Gill and go to Brazil with Copper knowing that he had not made a complete fool of himself.

Another good thing would come of it, thought Ken. Anne's generous gift would heal the breach between the two sides of the family and bring them closer together than ever before. Anne would not be so lost and lonely; she would have the MacLeans to look after her and see she was all right.

Yes, everything had turned out splendidly.

Anne was away a long time. She was away so long that Ken began to wonder what had happened. He had just risen from his chair to go and see what she was doing when she returned, followed by Sarah.

"Ken!" exclaimed Anne. "Something frightful has happened! The picture has been stolen!"

"What!" cried Ken.

"The picture has been stolen! Tell Mr. Leslie about it, Sarah."

Sarah was never very good at telling people anything and now she was upset which did not help matters. "He was a very nice gentleman," said Sarah in a shaky voice. "Such nice curly grey hair he had, and so pleasant spoken! He said Mrs. Aldine knew all about it so I never thought nothing wrong."

"But Mrs. Aldine knows nothing about it!" cried Anne.

"I forgot to tell her," admitted Sarah. "It was time the joint was in, so I never thought no more about it till this minute — and I had the card in my pocket and all — " She produced the card, slightly crumpled, and handed it to Ken.

He took it and looked at it in a bewildered manner.

"That's what he gave me," explained Sarah. "He was ever so nice. He said I wasn't to bother, he would carry it himself — so pleasant-spoken he was."

"It happened after tea," said Anne who realised that Sarah was incapable of explaining the matter. "A man drove up to the door in a van. When Sarah went to the door he said he'd come from a firm of picture dealers in Manchester to fetch a picture and have the frame repaired— "

"It's dreadful!" mourned Sarah. "I see now I didn't ought to have given it to him, but he said it was all right. He said Mrs. Aldine knew all about it and we wasn't to disturb Miss Carr — so gentlemanly he was, talking so pleasant and saying he could carry it himself and I wasn't to bother and all! Saying he'd have it mended right away and bring it back on Friday! I'll have something to say to him on Friday," added Sarah in significant tones.

"But he won't come back on Friday!" cried Anne.

"He said he would, for sure," declared Sarah with conviction.

Ken began to laugh. He could not help it.

"I know it sounds — funny," said Anne in a miserable voice. "It's absurd to think — to think anybody could walk into the house in broad daylight and — and steal it so easily. But what are we to do? We'll have to ring up the police — they won't think it funny. They'll think we're mad. They'll come here again and ask questions and upset everybody like they did before — I can't bear it!"

"Anne, listen! We needn't tell the police — "

"But we must. We must get it back! Somehow or other we must get it back. I want to give it to Cousin Alec — " She broke off with a little sob and sat down in the chair by the fire. "Oh dear!" she said in a trembling voice. "Oh dear, I'm so — so tired of that horrible picture!"

"Don't cry!" exclaimed Ken. "Anne darling, it's all right! Don't worry, *please* — it's all right —" He ran out into the hall and returned a moment later with the grey cloth bag.

Anne was sobbing helplessly, her face hidden in her hands, and Ken had to give her a gentle shake to make her look up. When she raised her eyes she saw the picture in front of her, propped up in the other armchair.

"But how — " she breathed, gazing at it incredulously.

Sarah was gazing at it too; she was speechless with amazement.

"That's the real Saskia," said Ken soberly. "The other was a copy."

"A copy!" exclaimed Anne. "You mean — "

"That's the real Rembrandt — so you see everything is all right. You can give it to Colonel MacLean as you intended."

"The other one was — a copy?"

"Yes," said Ken. He smiled and added. "I think we should just let the polite, pleasant-spoken gentleman get away with it, don't you? He'll be *so* pleased when he takes it out of the van and has a look at it — and he really deserves some reward for his cheek."

"But Ken, I don't understand — "

"I know you don't. I'm going to tell you the whole story. I'm going to explain everything. I couldn't tell you before because I promised faithfully not to tell anybody, but it doesn't matter now." He hesitated and then added, "When I've told you about it you'll never want to speak to me again."

CHAPTER 19
The Doctor's Orders

ANNE AND KEN had been so absorbed in their own affairs that they had quite forgotten Sarah. She was still standing near the door twisting the corner of her apron and gazing at the picture. How could it be here when she had given it to the gentleman and seen him put it in the van and drive away?

"When I've told you the story you'll never speak to me again," repeated Ken wretchedly. "But all the same I must tell you — I *want* to tell you. I've been wanting to tell you from the very beginning."

Anne wiped her eyes with her handkerchief and looked up at him; he saw she was smiling through her tears. "But I know," she said.

"You know!"

She nodded. "I've known all the time."

"You mean — "

"I knew you came here to get the Rembrandt for Cousin Alec."

Ken gazed at her in bewilderment. "You knew — all the time! But how? And don't you mind? I mean, I thought — I thought you would hate me."

"Oh Ken, how silly you are!" cried Anne. "Of course I don't hate you. The picture belongs to Cousin Alex. You came here to get it for him, didn't you?"

"I came to steal it."

149

Anne shook her head. "That isn't stealing — at least I don't think so. You were just taking Cousin Alec's picture and giving it to him. You were just putting a wrong thing right."

"Trying to," said Ken. "I didn't succeed. After a bit I decided I couldn't through with it. I wrote and told him so."

"Did he bring it back?" asked Sarah, who had been debating her own particular problem in her own muddled way and had just arrived at this possible explanation of the mystery.

"Bring what back?" asked Anne, looking up in surprise.

"He said Friday," explained Sarah with a worried frown. "I know he said Friday because it's the day the laundry comes."

"It's all right, Sarah, you can go to bed now," Anne told her.

"But, Miss Anne, I thought you wanted me to tell Sergeant Merton. That's what you said. You said I'd have to tell him all about the gentleman — "

"Not now," said Anne, waving her away. "You can go to bed."

Sarah was not sorry to go to bed. She turned to go and then hesitated. "Did he bring it back?" she asked.

Anne looked at Ken and he nodded.

"Well, there it is!" said Anne pointing to the picture and smiling.

Sarah was satisfied. "Yes, he brought it back," she said and trotted away happily to bed.

"Poor Sarah," said Anne. "I don't really blame her for

being taken in."

"You never blame anybody," Ken told her. "You don't even blame me for breaking into Grey Gill! I can't get over it — and I can't think how you knew."

"It wasn't difficult really," said Anne in a thoughtful voice. "You talked a lot when you were dreaming. Most of it was rubbish — Mrs. Aldine couldn't make head or tail of it — but sometimes you called for Wallace. It isn't a very common name. Then you called out, 'The step creaked! It'll waken everybody in the house! Wallace, you should have warned me!' You talked a lot about Saskia, of course, and once you said, 'I'll get her for you, Wallace!' Then there was another thing that helped me. When I went into the bathroom there was mud on the floor so I knew somebody had come in that way and Wallace and I were the only two people who knew about it. We used to call it our secret entrance — and of course your story didn't hang together properly. Obviously there was some mystery about it. You never said you had followed the burglars to Grey Gill and you always looked uncomfortable when you thought anybody was going to ask you about it. I don't understand it all," admitted Anne with a little frown of perplexity. "I've thought about it a lot and put all the pieces together but somehow it doesn't make a complete picture. Of course you got in by the bathroom window and came downstairs and you found the burglars in the library and heard them talking. Then I expect you decided it was no good dashing into the room and trying to frighten them away because they would have escaped by the side-door and taken the picture with them. So, instead of that, you went out of the

151

front-door — Daddy was right when he said he heard somebody shut it — and you waited for the burglars on the terrace. That's what happened, isn't it? What puzzles me is how you can have heard them say she had left the side-door open." She hesitated and then added, "And now it's more difficult than ever. I mean why were there two pictures?"

Ken was full of admiration. He was also full of amazement; somehow he had never credited his angel with so much shrewdness and perception. "It's very clever," he declared. "You've got it all right except one little bit. The burglars weren't in the library when I got downstairs. I was there before them. I'll you exactly what happened — "

He told her. The story took a long time to tell but at last it was all quite clear.

"Well, that's that," said Ken. "Now you know everything." He sighed with relief at having got it all off his chest and added, "It's terribly late. You ought to be in bed."

They rose and stood for a moment or two looking down at the fire.

"You won't go away, will you?" asked Anne in a low voice.

Ken hesitated.

"You promised to stay as long as I wanted you. Don't you remember?"

"Yes, but —"

"There are all sorts of things to do. If you go away I shall be left to do everything myself — to fight against Mr. Sloane — about the picture and — and everything. Please stay and help me."

"Yes, of course," said Ken quickly. "Of course I will — if you want me. How long do you think — "

"Always," said Anne.

"Always?"

She nodded. "I want you to marry me. That's what I want."

"Anne!"

"We love each other, don't we?" she asked, looking up at him confidingly.

Ken put his arms round her and kissed her. The kiss began with a gentle pressure on her cheek but it ended much more satisfactorily.

"Darling angel," whispered Ken. "Beautiful, darling angel."

"You do really love me?" asked Anne. There was no real necessity for the question because she knew that he loved her, but she felt it would be nice to have him say the words.

"Love you!" he cried. "Of course I love you! I loved you from the very first moment when I opened my eyes and saw your lovely face — and, after that, more every minute!"

"So did I," breathed Anne. "From the very first moment — and more every minute. Dearest Ken!"

It was quite a long time before they came back to earth. Anne arrived first.

"We must make plans," she said, disengaging herself gently.

"Plans?" said Ken vaguely.

"I'll tell Mr. Sloane tomorrow, and then — "

"Oh goodness!" exclaimed Ken in dismay

"He can't prevent us."

"He'll think — "

"It doesn't matter what he thinks."

Ken took a few steps away from Anne and gazed across the room with unseeing eyes. He had come down to earth with a very unpleasant bump. It was not only what Mr. Sloane would think — everybody would think the same. Ken had assured Doctor Stott that he was not a fortune hunter!

"It doesn't matter what he thinks," repeated Anne. "We can bear it, can't we? Nobody can come between us."

Ken was silent.

"I know what you're worrying about," declared Anne. "Doctor Stott told me — "

"Doctor Stott told you?"

"Yes, he's a very understanding sort of person. He said, 'If you want to marry that young man you'll have to ask him yourself'."

"Doctor Stott said that?"

She nodded. "So I did. It wasn't very — easy."

"But Anne, don't you see — "

"No, I don't!" cried Anne. "Oh Ken, do be sensible. You said money didn't matter if two people loved each other."

He remembered saying something of the kind — it was when they had been talking about Margaret. "But I didn't mean *that*," he told her. "What I meant was — "

"You meant it didn't matter being poor. If I had no money at all you wouldn't mind, would you?"

"Mind!" cried Ken, "Of course not. I'd get a job somehow

154

or other and — "

"But I can't help it!" exclaimed Anne with a little sob. "I can't help having lots of money. Oh Ken, you're being silly. You don't really love me at all. If you really loved me you wouldn't mind anything. You wouldn't mind whether I was rich or poor — it just wouldn't matter."

"But listen — "

"You're being selfish," she declared. "You're not thinking of me at all. You're just thinking of yourself, and what people will say."

It was true, of course. He *was* thinking of himself and of what people would say.

"It's the same sort of thing as the picture," said Anne, laying her hand on his arm. "When you said you would get the picture for Cousin Alec you saw the whole thing clearly; you saw what really mattered. Lots of people would think it was very wrong, but you knew it was right. I can't explain properly but I know what I mean."

Ken knew vaguely what she was trying to say. It was so like Anne's other-worldly innocence to see it in this light. Anne was trying to say that it did not matter what the World thought if your own conscience was clear.

"I need you so badly," said Anne in a hesitating voice. "And you promised, didn't you? You promised to stay as long as I wanted you. Of course if you don't love me — "

"I love you frightfully!" he exclaimed, and he put his arm round her and drew her close.

CHAPTER 20
Alan Seton Ties up the Loose Ends

THE STORY OF KENNETH LESLIE'S ADVENTURE ought to end here, but there are several loose ends which must be tied up neatly before I lay down my pen. Those who have followed the tale with interest may want to know whether Anne managed to get her own way with Mr. Sloane and marry her penniless young man; they may want to know what happened to the pleasant-spoken gentleman and whether Copper went to Brazil; they may be interested to hear a little more about Colonel MacLean and Wallace. There is Margaret, too, of course. Some people may feel a little sorry for Margaret, but they need not waste their tears. Margaret is one of those ruthless creatures who always know exactly what they want and usually get it. She did not get Ken, and for a time she was very upset, but she is now engaged to Mr. Ballintray and intends to marry him shortly. His books are selling better than ever so she is looking forward to moving into a large and commodious flat and having plenty of money for pretty clothes and fun and holidays on the Riviera. She can keep on her job if she likes, and intends to do so. Margaret does not think it would be a good plan for her husband to engage another young woman as his secretary.

Margaret got what she wanted; the pleasant-spoken gentleman was not so fortunate. When he had waved goodbye to Sarah he drove off slowly down the drive but before he reached the main road he stopped the van and taking a large pair of tortoise-shell spectacles out of his pocket he settled them firmly upon his nose. He did this because it was necessary; without his spectacles the world was foggy and driving would have been extremely dangerous. The pleasant-spoken gentleman then removed his hair — the beautiful grey curly hair which Sarah had admired so much — and folding it up carefully stowed it away in a square white box. If Sarah had happened to see the gentleman now she might have remembered him . . .

The gentleman took out a large yellow silk handkerchief and rubbed it over his hairless head — that darned wig had been uncomfortably hot — and then he let in his gear and drove on, feeling more comfortable. He drove quickly for he had a long way to go and was anxious to get to his destination. He just couldn't wait to see their faces when he walked into the house with the Rembrandt. They had no idea he was going to have a try for the picture; it would be a tremendous surprise. He imagined the Colonel's face of amazement and Wallace's delight! What would they say? What would they say when he told them he had driven up to Grey Gill in broad daylight and rung the bell and asked for the picture — and got it! When he told them he had picked it up and put it under his arm and walked away! They wouldn't believe it. As a matter of fact he could scarcely believe it himself, it had been almost too easy.

He chuckled with delight. "Ingram Whitehill," he exclaimed aloud. "You're a great guy! You're fifty years old and you've lost your hair and you're myopic as a bat — but

157

you're a great guy all the same!"

Yes, the pleasant-spoken gentleman was no other than our old friend Mr. Whitehill. He had been staying at Seacliff when young Leslie's letter arrived with the unwelcome news that he had decided not to go through with his job. The Colonel had been very angry with young Leslie, but Wallie had stood up for him manfully and Mr. Whitehill had started by being on the Colonel's side but had been converted by Wallie's arguments — it certainly would be a little difficult to rob a house in which one was being nursed back to health and treated as an honoured guest. But Mr. Whitehill was in quite a different position and owed nothing to the Carrs so there was no reason why he should not have a try for the Rembrandt himself.

He had thought about the matter seriously for several days. Having seen the account of the burglary in the newspapers Mr. Whitehill was aware that the frame of the picture had been damaged and from that small seed his plan had grown. Mr. Carr's death had been a lucky break; when there is a misfortune of this nature in a household there is usually a certain amount of disorganisation. Yes, he had been lucky but it was not all luck. He had planned his daring raid with a good deal of care. For one thing he had made it his business to discover when Mrs. Aldine would be out and he had waited until he saw young Leslie striding up the hill.

Now was the time. Sarah was easy game. Mr. Whitehill remembered Sarah. As a matter of fact there had been one rather uncomfortable moment when he had seen a vague look in Sarah's pale blue eyes, as if she sort of half remembered him, but it had lasted only for a moment and then had disappeared. It was the voice, of course. He had tried to talk with an English drawl but he must have slipped up. The old woman remembered the voice, but not the appearance. You could hardly blame her, thought Mr. Whitehill smiling to himself. Six years ago she had seen a stout man with no hair and a pair of thick glasses with tortoise-shell rims; today she had seen a stout man with no glasses and a thick crop of curls. There it was. The disguise was complete. Why, he had not known himself when he looked in the mirror! Some people were obliged to assume beards and dark spectacles when they wished to alter their appearance. He didn't need to! The fact was, thought Mr. Whitehill a trifle sadly, the fact was people didn't really see the man. When they looked at Ingram Whitehill they saw the spectacles and the lack of hair.

It had been a good idea to get that card, and quite easy. He had just walked into the store and taken the card from a pile on the counter. The assistant had been only too delighted for him to take it. Mr. Whitehill wondered whether the Carrs would call up Messrs Shuttleworth and Brown and make enquiries about their "representative" or whether they would get in touch with the police straight away. He just wondered — he didn't really care — it didn't matter one way or the other. The police could search the whole country for a stout individual with curly grey hair. There was the van, of course, but it was needless to worry about the van. There were thousands of small blue vans in England and he had been so certain that Sarah would not notice the number that he had not bothered to change it.

159

Mr. Whitehill was excited at the thought of that beautiful thing in the van behind him. Pictures excited him tremendously. Pictures were his passion. He had never had much use for women — all his love and romanticism had been centred upon pictures. The Rembrandt tugged at his heart and he was tempted to pull up at the side of the road and have a look at it, but it was too risky. Somebody might come along and see him. It was foolish to take an unnecessary risk. He would wait until he got to Seacliff and then he and the Colonel would look at it together — and gloat.

It was seven o'clock in the morning when he turned in at the gates of Seacliff and swept up to the front door. He ought to have reached here hours ago, of course, but he had got lost in the queer wandering English roads and then he had got sleepy and had pulled up for a nap. But it was just as well that he had been delayed and had not arrived in the middle of the night. The MacLeans would be up by this time; they were early birds.

Mr. Whitehill stopped at the front door and hooted madly and shouted at the top of his voice. "Hie, you guys! Come and see what I've got! Something pretty! Hie, there!"

Then he unlocked the doors of the van and took out the picture. This was to be his moment of triumph, one of the big moments of his life — "Holy Smoke!" exclaimed Mr. Whitehill gazing at the picture in dismay.

Colonel MacLean was shaving when he heard the hooting and the shouts. He put down his razor and ran downstairs, half his face was white with lather. Wallace had also heard the noise and hastened to the scene as fast as

160

he was able. Father and son came out of the front door in time to see their American friend executing a war dance of rage and fury, in time to see their American friend hurl a picture across the drive and shake his fist at it as it crashed onto the rockery.

"Hullo, Whitehill, what's up?" asked the Colonel in his quiet voice.

Mr. Whitehill's answer was unprintable.

Sarah had decided that a wedding at Grey Gill would be lovely; she had seen visions of Miss Anne in white satin with a veil and orange blossoms — there would be bridesmaids and a huge cake and the big drawing-room would be taken out of dust-sheets and would be filled with guests drinking champagne and chattering madly — so she was a little disappointed when the wedding day approached and she realised that there were to be no jollifications.

As a matter of face the wedding took place so soon after Mr. Carr's death that any jollifications were out of the question. Colonel MacLean and Wallace came north by car and stayed at Grey Gill; Copper and Ken took rooms at the Black Bull; Mr. Sloane came over for the day — these, and of course Doctor Stott, were the only guests. Ken's sister and her husband had been invited but were unable to come; Ken had also invited Mr. Whitehill (he had liked the old boy) but Mr. Whitehill had refused regretfully.

It was a beautiful day, the sun was shining brightly and the skies were blue. Copper was a very efficient best man; he got Ken dressed in plenty of time and the two of them walked up the village street to the parish church. Wallace and Doctor Stott and Mr. Sloane were there already, seated in the front pew; Mrs. Aldine and Sarah arrived shortly afterwards; the rest of the church was filled with villagers who had come to see the wedding. Ken, waiting at the altar steps, took a hasty glance round and saw quite a number of familiar faces; he saw Jim Slater with an elderly woman — obviously his mother who was such an excellent cook — and he saw Mr. and Mrs. Winter from the Black Bull. The faces were familiar but the bodies presented an unfamiliar appearance attired in Sunday garments instead of the usual week-day clothes.

After a few moments the organ began to play and Anne came in with Colonel MacLean. She was wearing a dove-coloured coat and skirt and a little hat of the same colour trimmed with blue forget-me-nots. She was carrying a large bouquet of roses which had been picked early that morning in Doctor Stott's garden. Ken's heart turned over when he saw her — she was so beautiful, more like an angel than ever — he felt quite dizzy, everything went round and round and he was obliged to clutch Copper's arm.

"It's all right," muttered Copper under his breath.

All right! Of course it was all right. Anne was really here. All night long Ken had lain awake envisaging all sorts of mishaps, serious and otherwise, which might prevent Anne from appearing here in church at the appointed moment. Now that she had arrived nothing short of an earthquake could prevent them from being married.

Fortunately no earthquake occurred. Anne and Ken stood side by side at the altar steps and promised to love one another for better for worse, for richer for poorer, in sickness and in health until death parted them, and having signed the register and received the congratulations of their friends they walked down the aisle to the strains of the Wedding March and out into the bright sunshine.

"We're married," said Ken in a dazed voice.

Anne smiled at him and agreed. She was just as happy as her bridegroom but much more composed.

Several press photographers were waiting outside the church and the bridegroom's dazed look and the bride's delightful smile were recorded faithfully to appear in the daily papers the next morning, wedged in between the picture of a wide boy who had murdered an old woman in an isolated cottage and a railway smash. The bride and bridegroom were quite oblivious of this; they got into the car and drove back to Grey Gill followed by their guests.

Sarah had put her best foot foremost to provide a suitable luncheon; there was no wedding-cake but there was plenty of champagne. Healths were proposed and drunk in the usual manner and everybody was happy.

Colonel MacLean was happy; he had liked young Leslie from the first and he was very fond of Anne. He thought they were well matched. In addition to the pleasure of the wedding he had the pleasure of knowing that he was to get his beloved Saskia after all. Anne had insisted that it was his by right and had told him that she did not want it — in fact she would be glad to get rid of a picture which had caused her father's death — so the Colonel was to take it home with him and hang it upon his wall.

Wallace was happy. He had always been devoted to Cousin Anne, and Ken was his hero. Ken could do no

163

wrong. They were a marvellous couple. They seemed to Wallace to be surrounded by an aura of golden light. He too was pleased about the Saskia picture, not so much for his own sake as for his father's — and the best part of it was that his father had forgiven Ken and everybody was friendly.

Doctor Stott was very happy indeed. He looked round the table with a beaming smile and decided that he had done well. If it had not been for him there would have been no wedding today — and that would have been a pity. These two young people were made for each other, they were healthy and beautiful and very much in love. He wished his old friend Sir Frederick could be here; that fine old man would have been in his element. He did not wish Gregor Carr could be here, it was just as well he could not. Doctor Stott looked forward to the future when possibly he might be called upon to attend in a professional capacity at interesting occasions. The eldest boy must be named Frederick, thought Doctor Stott. He decided to suggest this later on, at a suitable moment; there was no hurry, of course.

Copper was happy because he always enjoyed parties and good food — the fizz was absolutely super — and Ken had done jolly well for himself and deserved his good fortune. It was a pity Ken could not come to Brazil, thought Copper. It would have been fun to have Ken, but Copper was of a philosophical temperament and never worried over things that couldn't be helped. He was sailing for Brazil next week and was looking forward to the trip immensely

Even Mr. Sloane seemed happy. Of course he had been

thunderstruck when he learned from Anne's own lips that she intended not only to give away the valuable Rembrandt but also to bestow her hand and her riches upon a young man of whom he disapproved, but after a few moments he realised that he could do nothing to prevent her from pursuing her own way so it was useless to protest — nay, it was worse than useless! If he wished to remain upon good terms with Gregor Carr's heiress and continue to manage her affairs he would have to swallow her husband and pretend he liked the pill. Mr. Sloane swallowed the pill with one gulp and indeed he put such a good face upon it and became so genial and friendly that Ken decided he had misjudged the man and he was quite a good fellow after all. Certainly he seemed a good fellow today, chatting cheerfully with the other guests and drinking rather more than his fair share of the excellent champagne.

The bride and bridegroom were blissfully happy of course. They were enjoying the moment but were looking forward to better moments when they would be alone together. At first they had thought of spending their honeymoon in Greece — it was Copper's idea — but Greece would have been very hot in the middle of summer, so when "Cousin Alec" had suggested that the honeymoon be spent at Seacliff, while he and Wallace remained at Grey Gill, they had accepted the offer joyfully. At Seacliff they would be alone, with nobody to bother them, and could enjoy each other's society in peace. It would be a thousand times nicer than staying at a crowded hotel.

Soon after luncheon Anne and Ken went off together in the fine new car, which was a present from the bride to the bridegroom, and their friends came out onto the steps to wave goodbye. As Anne looked back she saw them all: Cousin Alec and Wallace, Doctor Stott and Mr. Sloane and Copper and in the window of the library she saw Mrs. Aldine and Sarah.

"Goodbye!" cried Anne, waving her handkerchief. "Goodbye, everybody!"

Then she leaned her head upon her husband's shoulder and heaved a sigh of bliss.

THE MURDER OF
ALMA ATHERTON

THEY WERE TALKING it over in the clubhouse. The afternoon round had been played for good or ill and half a dozen tumblers in different stages of emptiness were contributing to the general feeling of ease and well-being. It had been a perfect day for golf, neither too hot nor too cold; the greens were as smooth as time and labour could make them. The clubhouse, a squat white-harled building with more comfort inside than its outward appearance seemed to warrant, stood at the first tee quite near the road. An ash path and small flight of stone steps led directly to the men's smoking-room which was as usual the most comfortable room in the building. It was panelled in oak with an occasional sporting print or club notice to break the monotony of the walls. The floor was linoleum, strewn with rugs and there was a sufficiency of comfortable chairs to obviate unpleasantness between the members.

Haydon sat at the window a little apart from the others; he could see the setting sun shining upon the windows of a long low house built of grey stone with a red tiled roof. The chimneys smoked leisurely; not a breath of wind stirred the thin spirals as they rose.

It was difficult to believe that such peace and calm comfort sheltered the body of a murdered woman, difficult to feel shocked or horrified at what had occurred and yet— and yet—

The whole thing was so extraordinary, Haydon could not get over the sheer unexpectedness of it. He knew, or had known, Alma Atherton almost better than anyone. Had been almost the last person to see her alive, and knowing her as he did he was certain only of one thing; Alma could have no enemies. She was not the kind of woman to have enemies, not clever, strong nor beautiful, not even particularly charming until you got to know her. It was only when you got beneath the sweetness, the coldness, the slow sad smile that you found the real Alma whose friendship was so well worth the effort of securing.

Dear God, would he never see her again! Never again feel the cool hand in his or see the grey eyes light with friendship. There had never been anything more than sympathy and friendship between them, neither had wanted more. At thirty-two Alma had seemed older to Haydon's athletic six and twenty. He had realised her lovableness without succumbing to its lure – a state of matters not so rare as modern novels would have us believe.

In every relation of man and woman to each other it is the woman who sets the pace, draws up the rules and defines the limits. Haydon scarcely realised this, he only felt instinctively the bounds – thus far but no further. Beyond this a desert region more secure than a wall protected those things which were taboo. Yet withal Alma had no social aplomb, she was often embarrassed and shy; her unequivocal position caused her many an uncomfortable moment. She was helpless, yet incredibly strong—

Haydon turned from the window with a choked feeling in his heart.

"Reminds me of Flanders," the Colonel was saying. "Sun shining, blue skies and all that, and the ghastly thing happening. The other members of the club nodded their understanding, they had the same feeling about it.

"Incredible," Wilson murmured. He was the doctor, a Scotsman with a round red head and blue eyes. He had been telephoned for in the early morning by a terrified housemaid who had found her mistress lying on the drawing-room sofa with a bullet-hole in her heart.

Like the rest of Langhurst, Wilson had been fond of the dead woman and the scene had shocked him beyond words besides mystifying him completely. In the course of his life Wilson had come across several cases of murder and sudden death but never one where the murderer had stayed to close the eyes of his victim and fill her folded hands with late roses.

"I hope they'll catch the feller," said a tall thin youth whose handicap was plus two.

"We don't even know it was a feller," Carslake said. He leaned forward in his chair and fitted his fingers together carefully.

"Not a man?"

"Possibly not." Carslake had riveted the attention of the clubroom on himself in much the same manner as he would have done in Court for he was a rising, very nearly risen, barrister. He knew that an enigmatical statement even if entirely unsupported by evidence is the surest method of gaining a hearing in an assembly of men. "Possibly there is no murderer – I incline to a verdict of suicide."

"Impossible." Haydon cried. "Mrs Atherton – suicide – the thing is absurd on the face of it – "

"Besides," added the young man, "one looks for a cause. Mrs. Atherton had lots of money – "

"There are other troubles besides monetary ones, young man," Carslake replied. "Husbands for instance, when they have been away for years and suddenly elect to return – "

Haydon felt the hot blood rise to his forehead. "I should like to know what you are driving at," he said as quietly as he could. "Mrs. Atherton was my friend; I do not care to hear insinuations of this kind."

"Gently, my dear feller," Carslake said. "I've the greatest respect for Mrs. Atherton – we all liked her. I can't say the same for her husband – "

"A crashing cad," the Colonel volunteered.

"Listen to me," Wilson said suddenly. "I have taken no part in this discussion because I intend to keep my evidence for the inquest – daft-like thing it is but the law of the country. |Well, I'll tell ye this much and no more. It wasn't suicide. I'm willing to stake my medical reputation on that – " And it was a safe threat, for how could a woman shoot herself through the heart and then gather a bouquet of roses? "Ye might have known it wasn't suicide knowing the woman, for she was incapable of taking her own life and it did not need a psychologist, nor any other ologist to know that much."

The lawyer looked annoyed at this downright statement; he was about to reply when a welcome diversion occurred. The door of the clubroom opened and a stranger appeared upon the threshold. He was well but

172

quietly dressed in a brown suit and carried a soft hat of darker brown with a black band. There was something about him which caused Haydon to put him down as not of this country – foreign was too strong a word for the indefinable air of strangeness which surrounded him. Outwardly he was as one of themselves, his face was slightly more bronzed, perhaps, as if the sun were stronger in the land from which he came – that was all the outward difference. Haydon wondered if it were the mind rather than the body which even before he spoke produced the impression of an immense gulf between this stranger and these leisurely English gentlemen in their comfortable room, yet the voice when it came was pleasantly cultured and free from accent.

"Can one get a drink here, gentlemen?" asked the newcomer, looking round at the assembled company with an air of quiet assurance.

"If you will accept one from me, Sir," said the Colonel hospitably. Haydon pushed a chair forward; there was something attractive about this man – he wished he had been the one to stand the stranger a drink.

"That's good of you," the newcomer said as he sank into the chair and crossed his long legs. "I own I want a sundowner pretty badly. One gets into the habit easily and it is difficult to break."

"You've been abroad a lot?" suggested the plus two youth rather obviously.

The stranger seemed to take this as a hint; he produced his card-case and put a card upon the table. "Eyton's my name," he said. "If you're ever anywhere near Cape Town

173

take a run up to Edward's-land, its fine country." He enlarged for a few minutes on the amenities of South Africa in an interesting manner. Haydon, watching him, wondered what had brought him to Langhurst, he did not fit in to the suburban atmosphere yet it was difficult to say in what way he was different. Looking at his hands, always a sure guide, Haydon decided that the man had Latin blood. He did not move them much but they were alive. Long and well-shaped hands yet without any suggestion of effeminacy. The face was less easy to read but Haydon felt instinctively that it was a face to be trusted; the lean lines gave it the look of an ascetic, the dark brown eyes were piercing, the mouth large and firm.

"I suppose you have heard about the murder," said the boy who was plus two. He had hung on the stranger's every word with a dawning hero-worship in his eyes.

Eyton took a sip of the "sundowner" which had been placed at his elbow before he spoke, then he said, "It is easy to be misled by local gossip – "

It was an invitation to which nobody could fail to respond. At least four people started simultaneously to enumerate the salient points of the case; it was Carslake who emerged from the conflict, victorious by sheer weight of words.

"Mrs. Atherton," said the lawyer ponderously, "lives alone in that house over there. You can see it from the window of the clubhouse. She is married but has no children. Her husband is a big game hunter and goes away for months, sometimes years at a time, leaving his wife to her own devices. I may say that Mrs. Atherton was very popular in Langhurst – played a very pretty game of golf – in fact she was in the County team."

"Really," said Eyton politely.

Carslake nodded. "Yes, she was a very popular lady here and will be much missed – much missed. I can't say the same for her husband though. I don't think any of us were sorry that he spent so little time at Langhurst, in fact some of us have wondered how or why Mrs. Atherton brought herself to marry him."

"There are circumstances in which a girl's hand may be forced," said the stranger slowly, "especially if the man is unscrupulous."

"Atherton's unscrupulous enough," put in the Colonel with a frown. "There have been tales – "

"Tales!" echoed Carslake. "There have been more than tales about Atherton. The man leads a double or even a triple life. He returns to Langhurst today, ostensibly from Africa where he is supposed to have been shooting lions, really from Paris. I know for a fact that he has been there for the last month 'breaking his journey' – the man's a blackguard. But to return to the subject of the murder – "

"Have we digressed?" the stranger wondered. "I mean," he added as he saw the puzzled faces of his audience, "have we not been talking of this subject all the time? Can you separate the two halves; the blackguard (as this gentleman has aptly termed him) and the – the murder of his wife?"

"What could he have to do with it when he was in Paris?" asked the tall youth in a bewildered manner. He voiced the feelings of the small gathering.

"Everything or nothing," replied Eyton firmly. "In this case perhaps everything."

"My dear feller you don't insinuate," the Colonel began. "But the man was not here; only arrived this morning and knew nothing about the affair. My feller saw him come off the train – alibi and all that – what?"

The stranger shook his head. "I do not accuse Mr. Atherton of murdering his wife with his own hand – "

"You mean he – he got someone to do it for him," stuttered the Colonel.

"I do not think he hired an assassin," Eyton replied and for a moment a ghost of a smile seemed to lurk in the grave depths of his eyes.

"You're off the track altogether," Carslake announced tersely. He had held aloof from the little argument so that he might bring out his statement at the psychological moment. "I happen to know that Atherton not only gains nothing by his wife's death but actually loses a greater portion of his income."

"He gains his freedom," suggested a youth who had not yet spoken but the others shook their heads sceptically. Freedom is merely a name, to a man of Atherton's calibre. If such a man chooses freedom it is his for the taking; marriage is no bar to such pleasures as he delights in.

Haydon glanced at the South African to see how he was taking the wholesale destruction of his theory. The man looked neither surprised nor downcast; he was grave as he had been all along but there was a tense virility in his quiet pose, a conscious power seemed to emanate from him. Haydon had seen the same eager look in the face of a

176

young barrister trying to convert a dense jury to his own clear point of view. Who and what was this man? Haydon's heart missed a beat with vague excitement; there was something electric in the air . . .

"You see they have disproved your theory," Haydon said, merely to see what the stranger would reply. He had not spoken before and he wanted to see if the man would look at him – wanted a straight glance from those dark eyes. He got what he wanted instantly, for Eyton turned in his chair and their eyes met with a thrill across the room. Haydon saw that there was more than gravity beneath the piercing glance; there was pain.

"I see that they have proved that the death of Atherton's wife was of no advantage to him," Eyton said quietly.

"But rather the reverse," Carslake pushed home his advantage.

"But rather the reverse," echoed the stranger. "Still, I do not see that you thereby prove he had no hand in the matter. If I walk down my garden path and crush a beetle beneath my foot I have killed the beetle. I may not have intended to kill it – probably its death will not benefit me in any way – yet I am a murderer according to law and if the murderer of a beetle deserves death I deserve death."

There was a queer silence, embarrassing to an almost insupportable extent, even the boy who was as little psychic as most healthy youths of his age and handicap felt uncomfortable and shuffled his feet nervously. Haydon was goaded into foolish speech.

"At that rate we all deserve hanging," he burbled. "I would be afraid to say how many flies I have accounted for this afternoon."

"Ah, flies!" said the stranger lightly, "but they are pestilential."

The "but" used thus confirmed Haydon in his previous impression that Eyton was partly Latin in blood. It seemed to him that every word uttered by this queer stranger had another meaning – a deep significance which he was too dull and stupid to grasp. "If I had the key!" he thought.

Carslake's dry voice bit into his thoughts. They were straying from the subject and he did not intend to let the South African escape until he had retracted his theory of the murder. It was not that the lawyer held any brief for Atherton, it was simply the legal mind which delights in argument and contradiction.

"You practically accuse Atherton of compassing his wife's death and then say that it was unintentional. The Doctor has assured us that it was not suicide –"

"No, no" cried Eyton, roused for once from his quiet. "Certainly not suicide."

"It would therefore be interesting, supposing that it was the immorality of his life which caused her death, to know what the instrument was."

"Ah," sighed the stranger, who had recovered his calm. "Your law concerns itself with the instrument; the revolver or the hand that held it – which is guilty? Shall we punish these and leave unhung the villain who made them necessary? Listen to this, gentlemen, a man may keep his hand from killing and yet be a murderer. Another may stain his hand in blood and yet be innocent of sin – "

178

"By Gad sir!" cried the Colonel. "You're going a bit deep for me. You actually say that the man who shot Mrs. Atherton was not a murderer?"

"I did not say so, Colonel," replied Eyton. "Yet it is conceivable. You, sir, would not hesitate to shoot a white woman to save her from falling into the hands of savages. Take that case on the Indian Frontier the other day. I know nothing about India, never been there in my life, but those Afghan tribes – you would not let a woman fall into their hands alive?" Nobody spoke for a minute and after a little silence Eyton added in a low voice, "Is an Afghan savage worse than a civilised man who wallows in the filth of cities and returns to innocence when he has tired of vice?"

There were few men who could have said it without being a prig but there was no priggishness about this man, he was too earnest. His command of English was perfect yet its very purity gave Haydon the feeling that he was a foreigner. The argument seemed credible to Haydon until he saw where it was leading them and then his reason shied at the mere idea of such a thing.

"Good heavens!"

"Is it so incredible to you?" the stranger asked. "Have you tried to imagine what it would mean for a delicate refined woman to belong to a man of Atherton's stamp? To be his chattel – "

"No woman nowadays is a man's chattel." It was the Colonel who spoke, the finer nuances of the discussion had escaped him but here was something which he understood. The Colonel's lady was certainly no chattel, she carved her own path in the world with a firm hand.

179

Eyton looked at him patiently as if he would say, Your sentiments do honour to your heart if not to your head –

"No woman of strong character, perhaps, is a man's chattel. But there are women meant to be guarded and cherished, clinging, gentle gracious ladies – "

"You know her," Haydon said quickly.

"I know her," replied the man from South Africa softly, and while Haydon had used the present tense unconsciously, Eyton used it with gentle emphasis.

"I should like to know" Carslake said thoughtfully, "just what your theory is."

"I will give it to you for what it is worth, Sir," replied Eyton. "We can eliminate suicide and murder for robbery or self interest; it was none of these for obvious reasons. Mrs. Atherton had no enemies; her house was not burgled and she was temperamentally incapable of suicide. There remains the possibility that her life was taken by a friend to save her honour – to save her from a hell too fiery for her to bear."

"Things like that don't happen, my dear fellow," said Carslake aghast. He voiced the feelings of all present; the least imaginative felt a thrill of horror at the visions evoked by Eyton's theory.

The Colonel, arrived by now at the exact meaning of his guest's reference to the Indian frontier as applied to Hollingmere, found his tongue.

"Look here, if the feller felt like that why didn't he go for Atherton? That seems the obvious thing. A feller can't lay out every Afghan on the frontier, but he can do in one man."

"It would be the obvious thing," said Eyton quietly, "and I think we may take it that the man did not overlook that way out but weighed it carefully. He may have desired to save the gentle and gracious lady from the indignity and publicity of a sordid trial. He may have thought that she had borne enough in this life and believed that there are worse things than death at the hand of a friend. How can I tell what this man thought and felt and suffered before he arrived at his decision? I think he must have offered this obvious way of release to his friend but she – how could she take it?"

"They might have gone away together," whispered the long-haired youth.

"Ah" said Eyton. "So they might if she had been that sort of woman."

"And Atherton?" it was Carslake who spoke.

"Atherton is his own punishment," was the stern reply. "I don't envy Atherton; such men make their own hell."

Carslake roused himself from the dominion of the stranger's voice.

"Mind you, I don't for one instant agree with your theory," he said loudly. "Too fanciful altogether and not enough evidence to convict a fly. Then here's a point you have not considered. Atherton misses half his punishment while the thing's a mystery. The thing ought to be bruited abroad."

Wilson leaned forward to add his commonsense quota.

"He might also desire publicity to protect an innocent person from the consequences of his deed. It would not be fair to leave a mysterious crime for which an innocent person might be punished."

"That's true," admitted Eyton.

"Yet it would be a difficult thing to confide in anyone," said the young man whose handicap was plus two. "Even your best pal – might give him a bit of a shock – what?"

"Written confession," suggested Haydon who was somehow loath to see the stranger's elaborate edifice crumble to pieces.

"Won't do, Haydon," Carslake said, smiling a little in the superior manner of one in the know. "I was over at Hollingmere this afternoon; the whole place has been searched from attic to cellar. We may take it that no written confession nor statement of a startling nature has been found. Believe me sir," he added, turning to Eyton as he spoke. "You are off the track entirely."

The latter did not seem at all put about by the lawyer's incredulity.

"Well now, gentlemen," he said. "Supposing this man to be a man of words and deeds rather than letters – letters are unsatisfactory things at the best, you can never tell *how* they will be read, I mean in what light, nor by whom. Supposing this man distrusted that bit of paper, thinking that it might be trodden underfoot, or blown away, or even waved aside as the ravings of a lunatic. Supposing he preferred to leave his message some other way?"

"Yes, I quite see your point," (it was the Colonel who spoke) "but what other way is there?"

"That is just the question," said the mysterious stranger thoughtfully.

182

"He would want to leave his statement in such a way that it would be spread abroad and discussed all over Langhurst," said the Colonel. He felt rather brainy at having made that point.

Eyton agreed at once. "Yes, that would be his object," And there was for the first time, a tremble at the corners of his mouth as if he would have smiled had not life been such a serious affair.

"There is one other point," Haydon said slowly. "If your man really cared for Mrs. Atherton could he go on living when she had died by his hand?"

Eyton rose and held out his hand. There was a strange light in his eyes. "Ah," he said. "You have said what I hoped you would say – you are right."

He stood for a moment looking round the room as though he would read the thoughts behind each face. "I am very grateful for your hospitality and now I must leave you – there is someone waiting for me."

A chorus of "good-nights" followed him to the door.

"Good-night, gentlemen," he said and disappeared. They heard him run lightly down the short flight of steps.

"I wonder – " Wilson began, but his words were cut short by a sharp crack like a whip lash in the still air. They ran out and found the South African lying in the ash path with a real smile on his lips and a bullet hole in his right temple.

WHERE THE GENTIAN BLOOMS

CHAPTER 1

ONE SATURDAY MORNING towards the end of February Gerald Ferguson decided to go home for the weekend. He was a student at Glasgow University reading for a degree in Engineering and was working very hard for his exams, but two nights in the country would refresh his brain and he could easily be back in time for the lecture on Monday morning.

Home to Gerald was an old house on the hillside about four miles south of Crawbridge and, as it was on the main road from Glasgow to Carlisle, Gerald's usual manner of travelling was to get a lift upon a south-bound lorry. Why pay good money for a bus fare when you could travel free?

Gerald did not take long over his preparations. He shouted to his landlady that he was going, stowed a few necessaries into his knapsack and set forth upon his journey.

There was a great deal of traffic on the road and it was important to choose the right vehicle. Gerald had travelled in all sorts of vehicles, from private cars to fish vans; some were more comfortable than others but it was not comfort that mattered. One had to look for a conveyance that was going all the way — local traffic was useless. Today Gerald was lucky enough to thumb a lift in a furniture van which was heading for Carlisle. Nothing could have suited him better.

"Where are you off to?" asked the driver of the furniture van in cheerful tones.

"It's a house called Gowdenburn just south of Crawbridge. You pass the gates on the way to Carlisle."

"That's very convenient," said the driver of the furniture van. "I'll put you down at the gates."

The weather had been wintry, with biting winds and the ground deep in snow, but the last few days had been mild and pleasant. A warm westerly breeze had melted all the snow, and it felt like spring. It was a false spring perhaps — winter might return at any moment — but who cared? Certainly not Gerald. He was young enough to live in the present. Today the skies were blue and cloudless and the trees were like delicate etchings, their tracery of bough and twig standing out clearly in the bright sunshine Their beauty of line was more subtle than the beauty of summer foliage.

Gerald had discovered that some long distance drivers are silent individuals and others like chatting. This man was the chatty kind. He told Gerald that his name was Bob Fletcher, he was taking a lot of furniture to Carlisle and returning to Glasgow early on Monday morning. He told Gerald a good deal about himself and his affairs: about his wife and his little boy and their flat at Anniesland. Gerald listened and made suitable comments.

"And you're off home for a holiday?" asked Fletcher at last.

"Just for the weekend," replied Gerald. "I'm going to stay with my aunts, the two Miss Lilleys."

"Your aunts? I thought you were going home?"

"Gowdenburn is my home," Gerald explained. "My parents died when I was a child and my aunts brought me up."

"That's sad," said Fletcher sympathetically.

"Not really," replied Gerald. "I mean it wasn't sad for me. No parents could have been kinder than the aunts, or done more for me. For instance the other day I wrote and told them that some friends of mine were going to France at Easter for a holiday and they sent me thirty pounds and said I was to go with them and have a good time."

"They must have lots of money!"

"Well, I don't know — " said Gerald doubtfully. "They have enough to live on comfortably. Nobody has lots of money nowadays."

"What like is their house?" enquired Fletcher.

Gerald could not help smiling. The man was inquisitive, but inquisitive in such a nice way that one could not take exception to it, and as Gerald was getting a free lift to his very door the least he could do was beguile the way with conversation. This being so he explained that Gowdenburn was a small house standing upon the hillside and surrounded by a pleasant garden. It was a very old house — parts of it dated back to the sixteenth century. At the back of the house was a little wood and there was a burn which came down from the moors and provided excellent water. The place had belonged to the family for about sixty years. Gerald's grandfather, Mr. Robert Lilley, had bought it and altered it and made it into a comfortable dwelling for himself and his family. He had laid out the garden, planted shrubs and trees and had built a little bridge over the burn. At that time Mr. and Mrs. Lilley had three children: Elizabeth, Florence and Bertram. Gerald's mother, Mary was the youngest of the family and had been born at Gowdenburn.

Fletcher had been following all this very carefully. "Does your uncle live at Gowdenburn?" he enquired.

"No, just the two aunts," replied Gerald. "Uncle Bertram emigrated to Australia when he was quite young — I think he quarrelled with his father or something. At any rate he went to Australia and married and settled down. He hasn't been home for years but he sometimes writes to the aunts and sends them a card at Christmas. Sometimes he remembers their birthdays."

"Australia's a fine place for a young man. I've thought about going there and getting a good job," Fletcher declared.

"Why go to Australia when you've got a good job in Scotland?" asked Gerald with a smile.

"You wouldn't think of going out there yourself — to stay with your uncle?"

"No I wouldn't," replied Gerald. "I believe Uncle Bertie came home to Gowdenburn on a visit when I was a child but I don't remember him at all — besides I'm very fond of the aunts and they have nobody belonging to them except me. They've lived at Gowdenburn all their lives and they're getting old now. I feel sort of responsible for them. They would hate me to go to Australia and I would hate it too. Scotland is good enough for me."

Scotland certainly looked good this morning with the promise of Spring in the air.

"Och, it's not so bad today," admitted Fletcher. "Last week it was awful with all yon snow on the ground and the wind like a knife. It's no fun driving a van in those sort of conditions I can tell you."

By this time they had reached Crawbridge, a small country town amongst the bald brown Lowland Hills. Gerald knew the place well, of course, for it was only four miles from his home. It was here that his aunts went to church and did their shopping, and Gerald had gone to school here when he was a small boy. Fletcher slowed down to pass through the main street and Gerald hung out of the window and looked about eagerly hoping to see some of his friends, but the only person he saw was Mr. Bain the Minister, coming out of the Manse with a parcel under his arm and hurrying across the road. Gerald waved to him but Mr. Bain did not wave back. It was obvious that Mr. Bain did not recognise the young man in the furniture van — and who could blame him?

The gates of Gowdenburn were four miles south of Crawbridge. Gerald pointed them out and Fletcher stopped to let him off.

"It's been fine having you," said Fletcher. "It makes all the difference if you've got somebody to talk to. See here, I'll be on my way north on Monday morning if you'd like a lift back to Glasgow — but maybe it would be too airly for you. I'll be passing here at seven o'clock."

"That would suit me splendidly," Gerald told him. "I want to get back in lots of time. I'll be here at seven. Many thanks for the lift."

"Och, it's nothing, Mr Lilley," said Fletcher cheerfully.

Gerald smiled as the van moved off. His name was not Lilley — and Fletcher knew this perfectly well, for he had listened with great interest to Gerald's outline of his family history. Fletcher had called him 'Mr. Lilley' without thinking — or at any rate without thinking enough. Gerald was particularly interested in the lapse for quite recently Professor Clearthort had given his students a lecture on the subject and had ended it by saying, "If you don't possess a piece of information, that's ignorance — and very reprehensible — but if you possess a piece of information, and don't use it, that's stupidity — and stupidity is a crime." All the same, thought Gerald, there was some excuse for Fletcher's 'crime'. Gerald felt himself to be part of his mother's family (his father's family had never bothered about him). Aunt Beth and Aunt Florence were near and dear; Gowdenburn was his beloved home. The fact that his name was Ferguson, and not Lilley, seemed to Gerald purely accidental.

CHAPTER 2

GERALD SWUNG HIS KNAPSACK onto his back and set off up the drive at a good pace. He had not been home since Christmas and he was longing to see his aunts; he was longing to see their faces when he walked in unexpectedly. How pleased and excited they would be! There was no doubt in his mind about the warmth of his welcome. They would make a fuss of him and rush to air his bed — it would be extremely pleasant.

Next week was Aunt Beth's birthday and he had brought her a little gift which he knew would appeal to her. She liked unusual things; she was fond of old china and curios. This was not china but it was certainly old and unusual. It was a tiny musical box which Gerald had discovered in a second-hand shop in Argyle Street. The box was dirty and broken, so he had got it for a few shillings. Gerald carried it back to his lodgings and when he had taken it to pieces and oiled it and put it together again he found to his delight that it played a tinkling tune — a haunting little melody. The name was written on the bottom of the box: 'Where the Gentian Blooms.' Gerald mended the box and polished it and there it was — an attractive little toy! Aunt Beth would love it, and would love it all the more when he told her its history. Gerald could hardly wait to give it to Aunt Beth. Her birthday was next week but he would give her his present at once so that he could see her pleasure.

All this passed through Gerald's mind as he walked up the drive. He opened the front door and was about to call out cheerfully when suddenly he paused. The hall looked different. Where was the grandfather-clock? The old grandfather-clock which Gerald had known since he was a small child had disappeared, leaving a gap and a queer pale patch on the wall-paper.

For a moment Gerald was taken aback and then he decided that Aunt Beth must have sent it to be cleaned and repaired, but this explanation did not satisfy him completely so instead of calling to his aunts he opened the door of the drawing-room and looked in. The piano had vanished too — and not only the piano; Aunt Beth's Sheraton cabinet had gone!

Gerald was still standing, looking round, when he heard a slight noise behind him and felt a touch on his arm.

"Gerald!" cried Aunt Florence. "Oh Gerald, is this really you?" She flung her arms round him and hugged him ecstatically.

"Darling Aunt Florrie!" exclaimed Gerald. "I just had to come — I suddenly wanted to come —"

"Of course — how lovely!"

"There was no time to let you know."

"It's lovely to see you!"

As Gerald kissed her thin soft cheek and clasped her in a hug he suddenly realised how small she was — how frail! She was not really very old, just over sixty, but to him she seemed very old indeed. She seemed old and worn-thin like a silver coin that has been too long in circulation and there was a queer unearthly brightness in her face. Her eyes were still beautiful, bright blue and soft. They were very soft and full of tenderness as they looked up at Gerald.

"Aunt Florrie, where is your piano?" Gerald asked.

"We — we sent it — away."

"And the clock? And the cabinet?"

Aunt Florence hesitated.

"It's no good," said Aunt Beth who had appeared behind her sister. "We shall have to tell him."

"They were taking up a lot of room," murmured Aunt Florence. "Such a bother to clean — so we decided to sell them."

"Sell them!" exclaimed Gerald in amazement. "You sold your piano! But Aunt Florrie — "

"Taking up — a lot of room," repeated Aunt Florence in a choked voice.

There was silence for a few moments. The three of them stood and looked at each other.

Beth was older than her sister; she was the eldest of the family but she did not look it. Beth was the forceful one, the managing one. It was Beth who saw that the doors were locked at night; it was she who snibbed the windows. If there were any small repairs to be done Beth fetched her tool-basket and carried them out efficiently. She was taller than her sister, stronger and bigger in every way, but she too was very thin.

"You sold them to send me the money for my holiday!" exclaimed Gerald in dismay.

"Not really," said Beth quickly. "There were other things. The roof had to be repaired and some of the pipes were worn out. We had to have them renewed. The house is old and everything seems to be going at once."

"Why didn't you tell me?"

"You needed a holiday — " began Aunt Florence.

"We didn't want you to worry," explained Aunt Beth.

"You mustn't worry," said Aunt Florence earnestly. "There's no need to worry. The house was too full of furniture — it was just a nuisance. We're far better off without a lot of useless stuff."

Gerald now realised that there were other pieces missing. The Dresden china ornaments had gone, so also a fine old rosewood table and a couple of Queen Anne chairs. It was impossible to make an inventory, but the room looked bare. Gerald came to the conclusion that all the good things had been sold. He crossed the hall quickly and opened the dining-room door. The dining-room was empty; table, chairs, carpet, sideboard had all vanished into thin air.

"It's all right," declared Aunt Florence running after him and seizing his arm. "It's all right — really. We don't use this room, you see. We have all our meals in the kitchen. It's so much warmer and more comfortable, so much easier in every way. It's true, isn't it, Beth? Tell Gerald it's true."

"Gerald can see we don't use this room," said Aunt Beth a trifle grimly.

"What happened?" asked Gerald. "You simply must tell me. How did you lose all your money?"

"We didn't," said Aunt Florence. "We didn't lose it — at least not all at once. Our income just got smaller and smaller. Aunt Beth can explain it better than I can."

"There's nothing to explain," said Aunt Beth. "Our shares didn't pay so well —that was all. Then we had to rebuild the kitchen chimney and we had to sell some shares to pay for it, and that made our income less. Every year our

196

income seemed to get smaller and we had more expenses."

"Me!" exclaimed Gerald in distress. "My fees at the University! My digs, my books, my clothes, my holiday last year in Norway."

"You're not extravagant!" cried Aunt Florence.

This was perfectly true. Gerald was not extravagant but he did not deny himself the comforts of life. He had had no idea there was any need to practise economy. He knew now.

"If you had only told me!" he cried. "I could have cut down expenses. I could have moved into cheaper digs — "

"We didn't want you to do that," said Aunt Beth quickly. "That was the reason we didn't tell you. It's impossible to work if you aren't comfortable and well fed."

"I shall move," declared Gerald. "I can easily find a cheaper place, and — "

"No, you mustn't — it's only temporary!" cried Aunt Florence.

"Temporary?" asked Gerald, seizing on the word.

"Well, we're always hoping — things will be better — " Her voice trailed off into silence.

Gerald's heart was wrung with pity. "Look here," he said gently. "You must tell me all about it. You must tell me exactly how much you have to live on. Then we can decide what's to be done. Perhaps I could find a job — "

"You must get your degree, Gerald," interrupted Aunt Beth.

"We can last out until then," added Aunt Florence. The words were intended to be reassuring but they alarmed Gerald more than anything that had been said before. They could last out!

"You must get your degree," repeated Aunt Beth. "That's the important thing."

She was right, of course, thought Gerald. He must take his degree. After that it ought to be easy to get a good job and look after them. They would have to leave Gowdenburn, which seemed to be falling down about their ears, and come and live with him. Perhaps they could sell the place and buy a small flat in Glasgow. That would be the sensible thing to do — but how the poor darlings would hate it!

Until this moment Gerald had been a boy; he had depended upon the aunts, doing what they told him and taking what they gave him without thinking, but now quite suddenly he had become a man with a man's responsibilities on his shoulders.

"You must tell me everything," he said.

"Don't worry," said Aunt Beth. "We shall manage. It will interfere with your work if you worry."

"I shall worry much more if you don't tell me everything," declared Gerald.

"Come into the kitchen," said Aunt Beth. "It's no use standing here."

The kitchen had become the living-room. It was a large bright room with windows looking out onto the hill. There was a carpet on the floor and several shabby but comfortable chairs had been brought in, also some other pieces of furniture. Three bowls of hyacinths stood upon the windowsill in the sunshine.

They talked about their affairs off and on all day and

198

most of Sunday but Gerald could not find out the exact position. If he could have spoken to Aunt Florence by herself he could have pinned her down and got to the bottom of it but Aunt Beth was more than a match for him. Aunt Beth kept on saying he must get his degree and not worry. They would manage. He discovered that they were drawing their Old Age Pension but that did not go very far in a house like Gowdenburn. When he asked if they had tried to get a loan from the bank Aunt Florence began to say something about an 'overdraft' but Aunt Beth interrupted and declared that Mr. Wiseman was very kind and helpful, adding that Gerald was on no account to worry.

There were a few happy moments in spite of the cloud which over shadowed the party. Aunt Beth was delighted with her present and the little tinkling tune from the musical box was soothing and comforting — all the more so because Gowdenburn was now so very quiet. There was no piano for Aunt Florence to play on and there was no radio and Gerald missed the 'tick tock, tick tock' of the old grandfather clock. Afterwards when Gerald looked back at that weekend he always remembered the tinkling tune and the warm kitchen and the cold, empty, silent house.

A great deal of talk and argument produced an uneasy sort of bargain. Gerald promised not to move into cheaper lodgings and Aunt Beth consented to take back the cheque for thirty pounds which she had sent to defray the cost of Gerald's holiday. It was a compromise and neither of them was satisfied with it, but it had to do.

On Monday morning they were all up early and the two

aunts walked down to the gate with Gerald to see him off. At seven o'clock the sun had not yet risen from behind the hills and the cold grey light of dawn was very depressing. They had all made the attempt to be cheerful at breakfast but they could not keep it up and they walked down the avenue in silence.

"Don't wait," said Gerald. "It's cold, and Fletcher may be late."

"We want to see — all that we can of you," said Aunt Florence with a catch in her breath.

"I'll be back soon," Gerald told her.

"You mustn't worry," said Aunt Beth for the twentieth time. "It will interfere with your work if you worry, and there's nothing to worry about — really. We shall manage."

"I shall worry if you starve yourselves."

"We have plenty to eat," declared Aunt Florence. "You don't need so much to eat when you're old. It isn't good for you. We can use the thirty pounds to pay some of the bills and — "

"Bills!" exclaimed Gerald in alarm.

"Just a few little bills in the town," said Aunt Beth hastily. "Aunt Florence doesn't mean — "

"No, of course not," agreed Aunt Florence. "I only meant — and of course there are still some things we can sell. There's no need for you to worry."

Gerald would have liked to enquire further into the matter. This was the first time 'bills' had been mentioned and he did not like the sound of it at all, but there was no time to enquire further for at this moment the furniture van loomed out of the morning mist and drew up at the

200

gate.

"There you are — and here I am!" cried Fletcher cheerfully. "I'm a wee bit late, I'm afraid, but it's a fine morning and the roads are in grand condition so we'll easily make up the time. Nip in, Mr. Lilley!"

Gerald kissed his aunts and nipped in.

CHAPTER 3

BETH AND FLORENCE leant upon the gate and watched the van trundle off down the road.

"He's a dear good boy," said Florence in a shaky voice.

"It's a pity he came," sighed Beth. "It's a funny thing to say because it's so delightful to see him, but you know what I mean."

"He'll worry about us."

"Yes, he'll worry — and it will interfere with his work. If only we had known he was coming we might have arranged something."

"What could we have done?" asked Florence helplessly. "We couldn't have got the piano back — nor the clock — "

"I'd have turned up the whole house."

"Turned up the whole house?"

"Spring cleaning — or a burst pipe or something. We could have had the drawing room swathed in dust sheets."

Florence looked at her sister with awe. Beth was clever!

"But it's no good thinking about that now," added Beth. "The harm is done. Gerald will worry."

They were turning away when a small red post office van drew up at the gate and delivered their mail. It was mostly bills of course but there was also a parcel from Australia. It was the size of a shoe-box and was done up firmly in brown paper, sealed and registered. It was addressed to Miss Elizabeth Lilley.

"From Bertram for your birthday!" exclaimed Florence. "It's registered so it must be something valuable —

202

something we could sell."

Beth had little hope of a valuable present from Bertram but the parcel looked important so they carried it back to the house and opened it carefully on the kitchen table. When they had removed the brown paper they found a large shoe-box, full of sawdust and, nestling amongst the sawdust, four small figures in coarse pottery. The figures were intended to represent four little men; they were badly designed and crudely painted. Beth, who knew a good deal about ceramics, saw at a glance that they were worthless.

"They're dwarfs, I suppose," said Florence trying to hide her disappointment. "They're funny little things, aren't they?"

Beth had stood them upon the table and was looking at them in distaste. "Bertram always was a fool," she said.

"Oh Beth, it was kind of him to remember your birthday!"

"I didn't say he was unkind," replied Beth. "I said he was a fool — and so he is. Those horrible little figures are not worth the postage. If he had sent us a few shilling it would have been more useful."

"Let's see what he says in his letter," suggested Florence.

The letter was enclosed in the parcel.

"Dear Beth,

I am sorry not to have written to you before but I am sending you a present for your birthday with my best wishes for many happy returns. You will be amused at the contents of the parcel. I think they are valuable. As a matter of fact I picked them up myself and thought they would make an interesting addition to your cabinet of curios. Now that I have retired from the office I have more time to potter about in out of the way places and pick up little treasures. I hope you and Florence are keeping well . . ."

The rest of the letter was taken up with news about Bertram's family but as Beth and Florence had never seen Bertram's children they did not find it particularly interesting.

"I'm to put the dwarfs in my cabinet!" exclaimed Beth a trifle bitterly, and she threw the letter onto the table.

Florence said nothing. She could find nothing comforting to say. Beth's 'cabinet of curios' had been sold and although Beth had been very good about it Florence was aware that parting with her treasures had caused her a great deal of pain. The silver snuff-box had fetched quite a large sum at Christies, but the Dresden china figurines, which Beth had loved so dearly, had gone for a song. Everything in the cabinet had been beautiful or interesting or valuable and now they were all scattered and gone.

"Oh well, I wouldn't have put them in the cabinet, so it doesn't matter," said Beth with a mirthless laugh. She felt so angry with Bertram that she would have liked to the throw the parcel and its contents into the fire but that would be foolish of course. The four dwarfs would do for the White Elephant stall at the church bazaar — somebody might be idiotic enough to buy them! Thus thinking Beth wrapped the box loosely and taking it upstairs she put it on the chest of drawers which stood in her bedroom. Later, when her annoyance had worn off a little, she would have to write to Bertram and thank him for his present; it would be a difficult letter to write. If only he had sent the money! If only he had sent a few shillings with which they could have bought an extra pound of tea!

It was still quite early and as they had had their breakfast with Gerald the household duties were very soon done.

"I shall go for a walk," said Beth. "A walk over the hills will calm my mind. Tomorrow I must go to Crawbridge and pay some of the bills with Gerald's thirty pounds. It won't go far but it will be better than nothing." She sighed and added, "I used to enjoy shopping in Crawbridge but now I feel as if everybody were staring at me and I hate going into the shops where we owe money."

Florence felt the same. Shopping in Crawbridge had become an absolute purgatory.

"And there's an overdraft at the bank," continued Beth. "Mr. Wiseman is very kind but he's getting anxious about it. There's another letter from him this morning asking me to call in and see him. I shall have to go, of course, but what can I say?"

"Is there nothing else we can sell?" asked Florence, looking round in desperation. "I mean if only we could pay off the overdraft and all the bills we could manage to carry on quite well."

"If only, " agreed Beth. "Oh well, we'll have to think of something. I shall walk up the burn. I haven't been up that way since the storm. I can think better when I'm walking."

"Take a basket and get some sticks for the fire. We could do with some nice dry sticks."

By this time the sun was shining brightly; it was a beautiful morning for a walk. Florence watched from the

205

window and saw her sister striding up the path. Beth had lost weight, her clothes hung upon her tall gaunt figure, but she was wonderfully strong. It was good to be strong, thought Florence. She herself felt utterly exhausted. The weekend had been exhausting. There had been so much argument, so much discussion, and it had all led nowhere. Florence had not taken part in the argument; she had been an onlooker, putting in a few words now and then, acting as a sort of buffer, but in spite of that — or perhaps because of it — she felt exhausted. She had always known that Beth had a tremendously strong character but it had surprised her to discover that Gerald was so strong. They were alike, thought Florence, and alike not only in their strength of character but also in appearance. Gerald bore more resemblance to his Aunt Beth than to his pretty but somewhat ineffectual mother.

Florence often felt tired nowadays. Although she had assured Gerald that they had 'plenty to eat' it was not true. She and Beth were cutting down expenses in every way they could think of; they were economising in food and fuel and their clothes were almost in rags, but it was not only the lack of proper nourishment which was sapping her vitality, it was the strain. Beth was so strong that she was better able to bear it. Beth slept soundly all night and rose refreshed. Beth did not lie awake hour after hour worrying about the future.

Florence sat down by the kitchen fire and closed her eyes. I ought to have faith, she thought. "Consider the lilies of the field . . ." but the lilies of the field don't need food . . . or clothes . . .

CHAPTER 4

IT SEEMED TO FLORENCE that she had only closed her eyes for a moment when she was awakened by a tapping on the window and looking up she saw Beth standing there waiting to be let in. She rose at once and opened the back door.

"Is something wrong?" asked Florence anxiously, for so much had gone wrong in the last few months that she lived in a state of constant apprehension.

"What could be wrong?" exclaimed Beth in a queer unnatural voice.

"I just — wondered," said Florence. She glanced at the basket and added, "You didn't find any sticks."

Beth began to laugh hysterically. "Sticks!" she cried. "No, I didn't look for sticks. I never thought of looking for sticks. I found pebbles."

"Pebbles!" echoed Florence in astonishment.

"I suppose you think I'm mad!" cried Beth, still laughing in a strange excited way. "You think I'm mad to bring home a basket of pebbles — but just look at them, Florence! Look at them! They're not ordinary pebbles, are they?"

Beth's thin cheeks were flushed and her eyes were shining. It was almost as if she were feverish, thought Florence in alarm. Perhaps Beth was ill! It would be the last straw if Beth was ill! Florence was much too upset about her sister to think about the pebbles.

"You're not looking at them!" cried Beth. "Look at them! I found them in the burn. There was a pile of them underneath the bridge. The spate had brought them down. I was leaning on the bridge looking a the water when I saw something glinting — glinting in the sunshine Look, I'll show you!" She seized a handful of pebbles out of the basket and held them out. "There!" she cried. "Look at them in the sunshine! What do you see?"

Held thus, before her eyes, Florence was forced to look at the pebbles, but she still could not see anything very exciting about them.

"They're — sort of — yellow —" began Florence in bewildered tones.

"They're gold!"

"Gold?"

"Yes, gold. There are flakes of gold in them. Look at this one! Can't you see the little flakes of gold glittering in the sun?"

"It can't be gold!"

"Why not? They used to dig for gold in these hills The Scottish Regalia is made from Scottish gold. You know that as well as I do!"

Florence gasped. "You mean — you really think — but it seems — impossible."

"Why should it be impossible?"

"Gold pebbles — in our burn!"

"It was in these hills that they found the gold — "

"I know, but we've lived here for years and — "

"Don't you understand!" cried Beth impatiently. "The pebbles aren't there all the time. They were washed down by the heavy spate — it may be years before there are any more — they were washed down by the spate and piled up underneath the bridge."

"How do you know?"

"Because I found them. They weren't there the last time I looked at the burn, I'm sure of that."

"I can't believe it," declared Florence. "If there was gold in our burn it would have been discovered long ago."

"Perhaps it was," said Beth. She hesitated for a moment and then exclaimed, "Of course it was! How silly we are! Why is the place called Gowdenburn? Tell me that."

"You mean — golden burn — "

"Yes, golden burn. It's an old, old name. This place was called Gowdenburn long before Father bought it. I remember seeing the name on one of those very old maps."

Florence was still incredulous but her doubts began to vanish when Beth took up a knife and scraped round some of the pebbles.

"Beth, I believe you're right," she said in an awed voice. "It really — looks like gold."

"Of course it's gold."

"Does it — does it belong to us?"

"Of course it belongs to us. I found these pebbles in our own burn — in our own garden."

"But Beth — "

"Get your coat!" cried Beth. "I'll show you! Hurry up and get your coat. There are lots more pebbles. We must gather them all."

Florence got her coat and followed her sister up the path to the burn. Her mind was in a turmoil. At one moment she was convinced that Beth was right and the next moment she was equally certain that the whole thing was crazy and impossible. Who ever heard of such a thing? Gold pebbles in the burn! Of course it was impossible . . . but the flakes had glittered in the sun, they looked like gold, and why was the place called Gowdenburn?

When Florence reached the bridge Beth was already on her knees gathering the pebbles into a basket.

"I'll do this," said Beth. "You had better walk up the burn and see if there are any more."

Florence did as she was told. She walked on looking for the little brown pebbles and poking with her stick. Here and there she found a few but not very many for the burn ran steeply and there was nothing to hold them. Most of the little pebbles had been washed down to the bridge. She filled her pockets with those she found and, in doing so, made the discovery that they were very heavy — much heavier for their size than ordinary pebbles.

They *are* gold, thought Florence. They really are — *gold.* Metal is heavier than stone. The treasure hunt lured her on and her fatigue was forgotten.

A few minutes walk brought Florence to the spring where the water emerged from the side of the hill, trickling out from between two rocks in a small silver cascade. She knew the place well, of course — she had known it as a child — but she had not been up here for years and had forgotten it was so beautiful. A rowan had rooted itself nearby and leaned over the little fountain protectingly. There were ferns growing in the crevices and the stones were painted all colours with variegated lichens and delicately shaded mosses. There is always something mysterious about a spring, something enchanting, and

210

Florence stood there for quite a long time looking at it. Today the water was not much more than a trickle, falling into its pool with a peaceful bubbling sound but last week, with the melting of the snow, it had been a torrent, gushing out from between the rocks in a big brown wave.

Florence knew practically nothing about geology but even she realised that the water must gather inside the hill before it gushed out, and somewhere, inside the hill, there must be a hoard of golden pebbles. There they lay in the darkness waiting for an unusually heavy spate to wash them down the burn. She decided to reconnoitre and climbed on up the hill and very soon she came upon a large round depression in the ground covered with a tangle of gorse and brambles.

So it really was true! Here was the proof! Once, long ago, this had been a pit. It had been the entrance to a shaft dug in the hillside. Men had come here to dig for gold. Probably they had found some, but they had not found enough to repay them for their labour so they had filled in the workings and gone away. They had gone away and forgotten about it. Hundreds of years had passed since those days — it was in the reign of James V that gold had been found in these hills.

Florence tried to remember more about it. There had been a banquet given in honour of somebody — was it the unfortunate Mary? — and a covered dish had been put upon the table. When the dish was uncovered it was found to contain a pile of Scottish gold. Yes, she remembered that. It was the sort of thing that stuck in ones memory when dates and names had faded.

Presently she heard Beth calling to her and went back down the hill. Beth had been excited about the discovery but strangely enough Florence was not. Florence felt quite sober and her mind had steadied. The little pebbles contained gold — that was definitely established — but whether they contained enough gold to be any use remained to be proved, and before getting excited about it they would have to find out whether the gold really belonged to them.

She found Beth waiting at the bridge and told her the results of the expedition.

"There you are!" cried Beth. "What did I tell you! I knew it was gold. Whey are you so half-hearted about it, Florence? Don't you realise what it means?"

"What about mineral rights?" said Florence in doubtful tones. "There's some law about mineral rights. I don't know whether we're entitled to the gold."

"That's nonsense," declared Beth. "Of course we're entitled to it."

"We'll have to tell somebody — "

"We're not going to ask anybody. The whole thing must be a dead secret."

"But Beth — "

"We must keep it a secret," said Beth firmly. "It's the only thing to do. Surely you see that. We mustn't say a word about it to anybody."

"I don't see why — "

"You don't see why! Just think what would happen if anybody got wind that there were golden pebbles in our burn!"

"Oh, you mean boys would come and — and — "

"Every boy in the district — and not only boys. There would be an invasion," declared Beth. "People would come from near and far. The house would be besieged by newspaper reporters. Imagine the headings: TWO OLD LADIES STRIKE GOLD,' or perhaps it would be 'GOLD PEBBLES IN A SCOTTISH GARDEN.' There would be pictures of us of course: smudgy pictures in the Sunday press. There would be pictures of the house and the bridge and the garden. Hordes of sight-seers would arrive in cars or on bicycles; there would be bus-loads of people from all over the country — "

"Don't!" cried Florence. "It's too awful!"

"That's what would happen," Beth assured her. "That's what would happen in the daytime. At night there would be burglars and thieves, all the riff-raff in the district, prowling about the grounds, searching the burn with torches, breaking into the house — "

"Oh Beth, stop!" cried Florence. "I can't bear it."

Beth stopped at once. She had no wish to alarm Florence more than was absolutely necessary and now that she had made her point she could afford to be comforting and reassuring. "It's all right," she said. "I'm just telling you what would happen if the secret leaked out, but it's not going to leak out. As long as we hold our tongues about it we're perfectly safe."

Florence was silent for quite a long time and then she said. "What are we to do? How are we to find out if there's enough gold in the pebbles to make them valuable? And if they are valuable how are we going to turn them into money?"

"Yes, that's the problem," agreed Beth in a thoughtful voice. "If we can't turn them into money they're no use at all. We shall have to think about it. There must be some way round the difficulty.

CHAPTER 5

THE SISTERS discussed their problem all day and went to bed with it still unsolved. Florence lay awake for hours turning it over in her mind and getting more and more desperate. By this time she had quite come round to Beth's idea that the pebbles were valuable but however hard she tried she could think of no means of turning them into money. They might ask Gerald of course (Gerald might be able to find out how you extracted gold from pebbles) but Beth would not hear of asking Gerald. Later on when he had passed all his exams they could tell him, but not now. Gerald must not be told a word about it in case it took his mind off his work.

Florence tossed and turned and at last from sheer exhaustion she fell into an uneasy sleep. She woke at nine o'clock with a nagging headache.

There was a pleasant smell of coffee in the house when Florence went downstairs. Beth had been up for hours; the fire had been lighted, breakfast was ready and the musical box was playing its twinkling tune.

"It's a dear little tune, isn't it?" said Beth. "There's something so gay about it. I think it would sound delightful on the piano. Your could play it with variations, couldn't you?"

"If I had a piano," agreed Florence with a sigh.

"But you will," declared Beth. "The first thing we're going to buy is a piano and the first thing you're going to play on it is 'Where the Gentian Blooms'. That's settled. A piano for you and a holiday for Gerald," said Beth happily.

It was so like Beth not to think of herself at all but to take pleasure in the thought of giving pleasure.

"Yes, that would be nice," said Florence rather wearily. "But it's useless to think of pianos and holidays until we've decided what to do."

"I know what to do," replied Beth. "I've hit upon a splendid plan. I went to bed all muddled but when I woke it was as clear as crystal." She chuckled and added, "When I woke I saw Bertram's parcel standing on my chest of drawers."

"Bertram's parcel! What has that got to do with it?"

"Everything," said Beth, putting the parcel upon the table beside her sister. "Open the box and see what Bertram sent me for my birthday."

Florence knew what Bertram had sent, but she opened the box obediently and discovered that the dwarfs had vanished. The fox was full of little brown pebbles. They nestled comfortably amongst the sawdust and looked as if they had been nestling there for weeks.

"They look nice, don't they?" said Beth with satisfaction.

"But Beth — I don't understand!"

"People find gold in Australia," said Beth smiling. "You know that, don't you, Florence? Everybody knows that. Bertram picked up the pebbles himself — he says so in his letter."

"Picked them up himself!" echoed Florence in bewilderment.

"That's what he says. Don't you remember?"

"No," said Florence. "At least — "

"You had better read it again," suggested Beth, passing the letter across the table.

Florence found her spectacles and re-read Bertram's letter.

"You will be amused at the contents of the parcel. I think they are valuable. As a matter of fact I picked them up myself and thought they would make an interesting addition to your cabinet of curios. Now that I have retired from the office I have more time to potter about in out of the way places and pick up little treasures . . ."

"You see!" said Beth with a little quiver of laughter in her voice. "Bertram spends his newfound leisure pottering about in out of the way places and picking up golden pebbles. He sent me a whole box of them for my birthday, packed in sawdust. It was kind of him, wasn't it?"

"But how — how are you going to — ?" began Florence.

"That's easy. I shall take it to the bank. Mr. Wiseman will be able to tell me what to do."

"Oh Beth, I don't like it! You'll have to — to tell him — lies!"

"Not many," said Beth grimly "I may have to tell a few lies, but I don't care. We're on our beam-ends. The situation is absolutely desperate. We've tried to pretend that it isn't desperate — but we both know it is, don't we?"

"Yes," said Florence in a very low voice.

"What's going to happen to us?" cried Beth. "How are we to carry on if we don't get some money? We must have food to eat, we must have clothes! What's going to happen to Gerald if we can't scrape up enough money to pay for his lodgings?"

"Couldn't we hang on till he gets his degree? I mean — "

"And what then?" cried Beth with rising anger. "Have you thought what then? Is Gerald to support us all our lives? Are you going to be content to hang round his neck like a mill-stone? I'm not. I'd rather kill myself!" declared Beth wildly. "We're old, we don't matter. It's Gerald's future that matters — that's what I'm fighting for — Gerald's future. Nothing else matters at all — nothing! Nothing!"

Beth rose and gathered up the parcel and went off to catch the bus to Crawbridge without another word.

CHAPTER 6

FLORENCE DID NOT MIND being alone in the house; as a rule she quite enjoyed it, but today she felt restless and unsettled. Beth's outburst had alarmed her. Beth did not often lose her temper but when she did there was something elemental in her rage. It was like a thunderstorm and Florence was terrified of thunderstorms. Of course it was true. Everything Beth had said was true their situation was desperate — all those bills and nothing with which to pay them! It was true that even when Gerald had taken his degree their troubles would not be over. She and Beth would be absolutely dependent upon him — they would be mill-stones, hanging round his neck, until they died.

Although Beth was so different from herself Florence understood her very well. They both loved Gerald. Florence loved him tenderly and would have given her life for him if the need arose. Beth loved him as a tigress loves its cub and would have committed murder to save him a moment's pain. It was rather terrifying, thought Florence with an involuntary shiver.

By nature Beth was straightforward and truthful but she would plot and scheme for Gerald. She was fighting to make Gerald's future secure — nothing else mattered. The plan was clever, of course. Beth had always been the clever one of the family. She was clever and she was brave — and very obstinate. Once Beth had made up her mind to a course of action nothing daunted her or turned her from her purpose.

Every now and then as Florence swept and dusted and went about her household duties she paused and wondered what Beth was doing. What was she doing now, at this moment? Supposing something went wrong with Beth's plans! Could she be put in prison? The more Florence thought about it the more worried she became. I should have stopped her, thought Florence I should have argued with her and pointed out the dangers. I should have told her it was wicked. It is wicked to pretend the pebbles were from Australia. It's almost like stealing.

But, even as she thought this, Florence knew perfectly well that it would have been no use saying anything. Nothing she could have said would have influenced Beth in the slightest degree — and it was too late now. The die was cast. Beth had embarked upon her plan by this time and nothing could be done about it.

The day seemed terribly long. Florence had not bothered about lunch — she was too anxious and miserable — but by half past three she was hungry so she made tea and sat down to eat it at the kitchen table. There was the remains of a cake which she had made for Gerald and there were scones and biscuits. If they were not eaten they would just get stale.

Florence was in the middle of her tea, and was beginning to feel a bit better, when the door burst open and Beth rushed in. She rushed into the quiet room like a fresh breeze from the moors, her eyes shining, her cheeks, glowing.

"It's all right!" cried Beth"I ran all the way from the gate.

I could hardly wait to tell you!"

Florence could not speak. She felt quite faint.

"It's all right," repeated Beth. "Don't look like that. Everything went off splendidly. You haven't been worrying have you?"

"Worrying!" murmured Florence.

"It was quite easy," Beth assured her. "I'll tell you exactly what happened. I just walked in and put the parcel on Mr. Wiseman's desk and asked him what I should do about it. That was all."

"What did he say?"

"He said, 'Good heavens, did your brother send you these, Miss Lilley?' So then I handed him Bertram's letter. When he had read the letter he looked at me and asked what I wanted him to do and I said that you and I were both rather unhappy about it and didn't know what to do. I said, 'Are they valuable, Mr. Wiseman?' Of course he thought I was a fool — and I let him think so. It's a good plan to let people thing you're a bit half-witted, especially people who think they're very clever. It gives them a nice comfortable feeling and they're very kind to you. Mr. Wiseman was very kind indeed," added Beth giving honour where honour was due.

"He really believed the parcel had come from Australia?" asked Florence incredulously.

"Of course he did. Why shouldn't he believe his own eyes? The parcel did come from Australia, it was there for him to see."

"Are the pebbles really valuable?"

Beth nodded. "There's gold in them — and gold is very

221

valuable now — very much more valuable than it used to be. Of course Mr. Wiseman wouldn't commit himself, he's going to have them assayed and let us know the result."

"What did he say about the overdraft?"

"He isn't worrying about it," replied Beth smiling. "I mentioned it as I was coming away and he said, 'I don't think we need worry about the overdraft, Miss Lilley.'"

"So he really thinks — "

"Oh yes," said Beth cheerfully.

"Beth, I hope you told him it was a secret."

"There was no need. He told me that I mustn't say a word to anyone about Bertram's present and I must be sure to make you understand the necessity for keeping the whole thing secret. He explained that if people got to know about it there might be trouble. We were two helpless females, living by ourselves, miles from everywhere, and we might get murdered in our beds if it became know that Bertram was sending us parcels of gold. He was very serious about it — in fact he repeated it several times. Gold is dangerous stuff to have about the house."

"We've still got some," Florence reminded her.

"I know. There's a whole basketful in the coal shed." Beth laughed and added, "We'll get rid of it. I shall write to Bertram tonight and thank him for his present and ask him to send you some of those amusing little dwarfs for your birthday. You'd like that, wouldn't you?"

Florence did not reply for a few moments and then she said, "You've been very clever, Beth, but I don't like it. I can't help feeling it's dreadfully wicked."

"Wicked! What on earth do you mean?"

"It's like — stealing."

"What nonsense!" exclaimed Beth indignantly. "They're our own pebbles. We found themselves in our own garden."

"Yes, I know, but — but it feels like stealing. I mean — "

"And I didn't tell any lies at all. It wasn't necessary."

Florence was silent.

"Listen, Florence," said Beth, sitting down at the table and pouring out a cup of tea. "I've thought it all out carefully and this is how I see it. The pebbles are ours — there's no doubt about that. The problem was what to do with them. There were three things we could do. One: we could throw them back into the burn — and starve. Two: we could say where we found them and have the place besieged with all the riff-raff in the neighbourhood. Three: we could pretend the pebbles came from Australia."

Beth paused and stirred her tea. "That was our choice," she continued. "It wasn't a very pleasant outlook. I don't like secrecy and deceit any more than you do and if there had been any other way I would have taken it gladly — but there was no other way. We discussed the whole thing over and over again until we nearly went mad."

"Yes," agreed Florence with a sigh.

"As for stealing — that really is nonsense," declared Beth. "You're just being muddle-headed about it, you know. It isn't a bit like stealing. When you steal something you take it away from its owner — you're richer and they're poorer — but in this case nobody will be poorer. Tell me one single person who will lose by it," said Beth earnestly.

223

Florence could not tell her of one.

"No, you can't," said Beth nodding. "Nobody will lose a farthing; everybody will benefit. Everybody will be better off. We shall be able to pay our bills so all the people to whom we owe money will benefit; we can increase our subscription to the church; we can have more food for ourselves, more comforts, and best of all Gerald can have his holiday and stay in his comfortable lodgings with an easy mind "Isn't that true?"

"Yes," said Florence. "Yes, it's perfectly true."

"Well then, what are you worrying about?" asked Beth.

They were just finishing their tea when the door bell rang. Florence went to answer it and found Mr. Bain standing on the doorstep. Mr. Bain was the minister; he had been at Crawbridge for years and the two Miss Lilleys were his parishioners.

Gowdenburn was four miles from Crawbridge so Mr. Bain did not visit the Miss Lilleys regularly — he was a busy man — but there had been rumours. Somebody had told him that they were in trouble, that they owed money in the town. Somebody had told him that the two Miss Lilleys had lost all their money and did not have enough to eat. Mr. Bain did not believe all he heard, he had been in Crawbridge too long and was aware that a great deal of smoke might be caused by a very small fire, but now that he saw Miss Florence he began to think it might be true. She was either ill or under-nourished.

"Oh Mr. Bain!" exclaimed Florence. "How nice of you to call! We have been so busy that we haven't had time to

224

light the drawing-room fire. Do you mind coming into the kitchen? Beth and I are just having tea."

The kitchen was a pleasant place. Now that so much of the furniture had been sold it was the most pleasant room in the house. The sisters used it as a sitting room and had brought in a couple of comfortable chairs. Miss Beth was having tea; she rose and greeted him cordially.

"You must have a fresh pot of tea," she declared. "This has stood too long — "

"I'll make it!" cried Florence. "The kettle is just on the boil."

Mr. Bain sat down by the fire and watched Florence. There seemed to be no lack of food. There were scones and butter and jam and the remains of a cake. Mr. Bain could not know that these comestibles were the remains of what had been provided for Gerald's Sunday tea, and that if he had come last week he would have been offered a very much scantier meal.

"You're very comfortable here," said Mr. Bain.

"Yes, we are," agreed Florence. "We use the kitchen for meals. It's warmer than the dining room and saves making another fire. We haven't got a maid now, you see. Maids don't like being four miles from a town," she added. As she said the words she thought: I'm telling lies — or at least I'm suggesting a lie — so why should I mind Beth telling lies about the pebbles?

"Is everything all right?" asked Mr. Bain. "I mean you're all quite well? Gerald getting on with his studies?"

"Oh yes. Gerald was here for the weekend. He's getting on splendidly," said Beth. "He's very clever you know;

everybody says so, not only his adoring aunts."

Mr. Bain knew that this was true. He liked Gerald and was not in the least bored by hearing his praises sung. It was good to hear that Gerald was repaying all that that had been lavished upon him. But Mr. Bain had come for a purpose. It was a little delicate, of course. He could not ask straight out whether the Miss Lilleys needed money, whether they had enough to eat. After a few minutes he approached the subject obliquely. "How are you off for coal?" asked Mr. Bain at last. "I mean you're so far out of town that you must find it difficult to get — and it's so expensive, isn't it?"

Beth agreed. "But we manage," she said. "We burn quite a lot of wood. Gerald cuts it up for us when he comes." She laughed and added, "Sometimes I wish we had coal in our garden."

"Coal in your garden?"

"Some friends of ours who live in Lanarkshire found some coal in their garden," Beth explained. "It had been washed down their burn, so they took it and burnt it. Florence and I were wondering whether it was the right thing to do."

"What else would they do, Miss Beth," asked Mr. Bain.

"We wondered," repeated Beth. "I mean there are things called mineral rights, aren't there?"

"There are, indubitably," said Mr. Bain smiling. "But I don't think your friends need worry about mineral rights. If I found lumps of coal in my garden I should gather them up and put them in my cellar."

"You would?" asked Florence anxiously. "It wouldn't be

wrong?"

"I should have no qualms about it, none at all." Mr. Bain accepted a scone. He laughed and said, "Why not? If I found lumps of coal in my garden I should gather them up and put them into my cellar without a qualm. I should treat them as manna, Miss Beth."

"Manna," repeated Beth thoughtfully. "We never thought of that, did we Florence?"

"Manna in the wilderness," continued Mr. Bain, who liked to improve the shining hour. "You will remember how the Israelites were starving in the wilderness and manna fell from the heavens overnight. It was sent to them by God, as all good things are sent, in their time of need. Even nowadays manna is sent to those who need it — not in the same way of course but in different ways. Sometimes we do not recognise that bread has fallen from heaven, we accept it without due gratitude — "

Mr. Bain warmed to his theme; he was pleased to see the way in which his two listeners hung upon his words. He was miles away from the discovery of coal in the garden and neither Miss Beth nor Miss Florence reminded him of it.

When it was time to go the sisters went out to the door with him and watched him mount his bicycle and pedal off down the drive.

"Well, are you satisfied now?" asked Beth.

"Manna," said Florence thoughtfully.

"Yes, just when we need it — just when everything seemed hopeless."

MOIRA

THE HILLS were flooded with a misty sunshine, their purple heathery slopes looked like the richest softest velvet, their pine woods were dark and dreamy, a few big grey boulders lay scattered in stark nakedness upon the slopes. I sat there for a long time with my back against a rock drinking it in, trying to store some of the peace and beauty in my soul so that when I returned to the clash and clamour of London I could recall it all at will to

> "That inward eye,
> Which is the bliss of solitude."

A soft voice recalled me to myself:

"Are you going to paint – *that?*" it asked.

The speaker was a girl in a faded pink cotton gown, a girl with the dreamy blue eyes of the true Celt and the black, the raven black hair which holds the rainbow sheen. She might have been the spirit of the hills, just so were her eyes, brooding with memories or visions.

There was awe in the girl's voice and a faint tinge of incredulity for which I loved her.

"You think that I could not paint the hills," I said, testing her. "You think that they are too beautiful."

"I have heard that you are a very fine painter," she replied, with the evasive politeness of the Gael.

I made no answer to that; she did not seem to expect one. She sat down near me, yet not too near, with the unconscious ease and grace which were her birthright. I was in the mood to resent companionship – I had come out to be alone, for this was a luxury which was not often mine for the taking – but this woman did not disturb that sweet sense of solitude; she was one with the hills, attune with all Nature.

"You are not going to paint?" she said at last.

"I am too humble," I replied. "I have come to take a picture of the hills but not on canvas."

I could see that she understood by the sudden lightening of her eyes. Her's was a quick intelligence.

"I am not disturbing the picture?" she asked.

"You are adding to it, for you are the Spirit of the Hills."

She turned and looked at me with her quiet eyes, and I saw then that she was older than I had thought at first. She had the calm of one who has passed through storms.

"You would like to paint the Spirit of the Hills?" she said softly.

The thought had indeed passed through my mind but I had scarcely liked to suggest it, there was an aloofness about her which precluded any familiarity. I was unsure about her status – was she a peasant's daughter to whom I could offer money for the sittings? From her manner she might have been the daughter of a Lord but I knew that every Gael is born noble in pride and manner.

At her words the possibilities of the picture sprang to my mind in the sudden way that such things do, and I knew that I wanted to paint this woman more than anything on earth. I would paint her here in this very spot on the hillside with the heather and the hills and the stark rocks as a fitting background for her beauty.

"You would let me paint you just as you are in that frock?" I said eagerly.

"You are a very good painter – people go to look at your pictures?" she asked.

When I admitted that it was so, she fell into a deep reverie and I could see that she was struggling within herself. Perhaps some native prejudice, perhaps some religious scruple troubled her; I did not pretend to understand the complicated philosophy of these people.

"I would pay you well for the sittings of course. That would be only fair," I said guilefully. "I would be taking up your time you see."

"My time is my own," she replied with a touch of pride in her voice. "I don't want money, but yes, I will let you paint me – on one condition."

By this time I was so anxious to paint her that I would have agreed to anything yet her condition surprised and, I confess it, disappointed me. She wanted the picture exhibited and advertised widely, "So that everyone in London will see it."

I was used to Society ladies wanting their portraits to be exhibited, but of what use was notoriety and publicity to this Highland peasant girl? However, before we parted I had given my word that the picture would be given all the publicity possible, and she on her part had promised to be in the same spot at the same hour on the following day.

Although I was there before the appointed time Moira was waiting for me. She was sitting with her calm stillness in the same position that I had left her and her dreamy

233

blue eyes were on the hills. In her arms she held a sleeping child, a boy of perhaps six months old, a beautiful child with rounded limbs and soft downy hair.

For some moments I stood looking down at her in silence and she met my eyes with a shy pride.

"You will paint me with my son in my arms," she said at last.

I shook my head. It was a beautiful picture, a Madonna and Child, but it was not the picture that I had seen, not the picture which had started to my inward eye when I had first beheld Moira. I tried to explain this to her as tactfully as could. The boy would sleep peacefully in the shadow of the great rock – it was the Spirit of the Hills I had seen in that swift vision, not the Madonna and her Child.

Moira broke into my explanations with her soft voice.

"The hills look to the dawn as well, as to the sunset," she said persuasively. "They are the mother of our race – see how pretty he is and how good."

The child had wakened with the sound of our voices and was stretching out his little arms and laughing up into his mother's face. I hesitated for a moment and was lost. After all, what the girl said was true; the Spirit of the Hills was motherhood looking out to the future over the downy head of her child.

I set up my easel there on the hillside and started the picture. Moira was a splendid sitter; she seemed to be able to remain immobile for as long as I wanted. The child was good and lay in her lap or sprawled about amongst the heather without requiring any attention. The picture grew by leaps and bounds for I could set my whole mind to it without the need to talk to my sitter, or to remind her of her pose.

She talked so little that at the end I knew no more of her than at the beginning. Somehow I felt that there was a mystery about her; she had appeared from nowhere - out of the very ground, it seemed. Where did she go at night, what did she eat? I did not know and to tell the truth, I did not want to know – I preferred her to be all mystery. The fairylike quality of my thoughts about this woman helped me to paint her. If I had known that she lived in a prosaic cottage, or an even more prosaic house, my picture would have lost some of its glamour, some of its spiritual quality.

At the end of a week my picture was finished. I was tired with the work, physically and mentally tired, but I knew that it was incomparably the best thing I had done – perhaps the best thing that I would ever do.

Moira was sitting upright among the heather, one hand beside her on the ground, the other holding the child loosely and yet protectively. Her eyes were on the hills, her lips parted a little with wonder and longing. The child lay in her lap, a small rosy creature with one hand outstretched. It was as if he were grasping at life, asking for something.

"It is very like us both," Moira said, looking at it with a sort of tense excitement in her usually calm face.

"It is a beautiful picture," I replied.

"And very like us?" she repeated questioningly.

"And very like you," I replied.

She sighed a little as if with relief.

"I was afraid that you would make us too beautiful," she

said softly.

"That would be difficult," I told her.

She turned her calm eyes to me.

"You are laughing at me."

"Heaven forbid! It would be a bad way to repay your kindness."

"My kindness?"

"In letting me paint you," I pointed out.

This seemed a new idea to her and she thought about it for a moment without speaking.

"You have given me a great picture," I said at last. It was absurd to deny the merits of my work and I wanted to make her understand. "You have given me this, and you will take nothing from me. Won't you take something for the boy to buy him things that he needs – surely that is only fair? Let me give him a hundred pounds."

"A hundred pounds!" she cried, gazing at me with wide dark blue eyes.

"You don't think it is worth that?"

She looked again at the picture with more attention.

"It is beautiful," she breathed, "but – a hundred pounds!"

"It is worth a great deal more than that," I said, speaking to her as if she were a child. "Quite a lot of people will want to buy it when they see it – "

"But you will not sell it," said Moira, laying her little hand on my arm. "You will not sell it until it has been in those picture galleries where people will see it – "

"No, perhaps I will not sell it at all," I said thoughtfully.

Yes, I am that sort of fool – I hate to sell my pictures when I like them; to me it is almost like parting with a piece of myself.

Moira would not take the money though I could see that she was tempted by it. I did not understand her at all, but then what man, even a fashionable portrait painter, can ever hope to understand a woman's heart. Besides, in my selfishness I did not want to understand. I wanted the whole episode to remain a mystery. I wanted the Spirit of the Hills to remain a spiritual, fairy presence with no known abode, no earthly dwelling place to bind her to any fixed spot. It was perfect as it was.

I came away from the place where I had painted her, leaving her sitting there with her child, performing the sacred rites of motherhood. Her eyes were full of the mysteries of life and death.

London soon claimed me and swept me into her gay whirl of life. I did not forget Moira for I had her picture before me, but she was not a live woman in my thoughts, she was a sort of symbol – a Spirit of the Hills. The picture was even more successful than I had expected; it gained a publicity that would have satisfied the most exigent of fashionable beauties. Critics spoke of it as "the crown of a great painting career." They did more; they wrangled with bitterness as to the meaning of the picture, reading into its clear symbolism, allegories which had never crossed the mind of its creator.

I was pestered with newspaper men who wanted a story for their respective journals:

"I should be much obliged if you would tell me what it means, this wonderful picture of yours. The *Daily Dispatch* would pay . . . "

"My dear sir, it means whatever you like – everything or nothing . . . "

"But to you . . . "

"To me – everything. Good morning."

London soon tires of her playthings, and the craze for the mystery picture – which was no mystery – was dying down when one morning the bell of my studio jangled discordantly.

I was waiting for a Society woman who was too busy doing nothing from morning to night to be in time for her appointments, and quite naturally I concluded that for once she had managed not to exceed the Parliamentary quarter of an hour – but my caller was not the Hon. Mrs. Catherton Blaike. It was a young man in a well tailored blue suit and a pale grey hat. He seemed to me a perfect specimen of a young man about town but his face was slightly more bronzed than the usual run of London youth.

"Mr. Marshall?" he said interrogatingly.

I replied that it was my name.

He took a card from a crocodile skin case and I saw that it bore the name of the only son and heir of one of our great families. I noticed also that his fingers were not quite steady as he fumbled for the card, and his stick, a fine malacca cane, fell on the floor and lay there unheeded.

"I've just come from Africa – been shooting," he explained a trifle breathlessly. "Only saw the picture this morning."

"Ah – the picture."

"What will you take for it?"

238

"It is not for sale."

"Not for sale?"

"No."

"I'll give you two thousand."

"I have refused more, Mr. Darby."

"Three!"

I shook my head. I was beginning to wonder what was behind the young man's eagerness. He did not look like a buyer of pictures. He looked – Eton and Oxford and big game shooting.

"Mr. Marshall, I must have that picture – you don't understand.'"

I was suddenly sorry for the boy – he was little more. He looked pitiful – more than pitiful, he looked tragic.

"I'm afraid you must make me understand if you want the picture," I said slowly.

"That's only fair, I suppose," was the reply.

He followed me into the studio and sat down rather heavily in a long chair. I mixed him a stiff drink – he seemed to need it.

"Where did you meet her?" he said suddenly.

I might have answered the casual question if I had not seen the eagerness in his eyes that put me on my guard. After all Moira was my business; I had no right to lay her open to the persecutions of every Tom, Dick and Harry who was interested in the picture. In this case it looked as if there was more behind the interest than mere –interest.

"I thought it was you that was to do the explaining," I said quietly.

Darby sighed. "You make it horribly difficult," he said

resignedly.

I offered him a cigarette and lit one myself. What a mercy it was that Mrs. Catherton Blaike had no idea of time! If I knew her at all we were safe for another half hour at least.

"I met Moira Macdonald two years ago," said Edward Darby. "My people took a shooting box in Sutherland – she was the keeper's daughter there. I saw her first in church, and afterwards on the moors several times. We loved each other. I don't see how anyone could help loving Moira."

"Perhaps they had not seen her," I suggested helpfully.

"That was it," he replied eagerly. "They had not seen her – they *would* not see her. My mother especially – you don't know my mother, Mr. Marshall?"

I said that I had not the pleasure.

"That makes it difficult for you to understand. If you knew her you would understand at once. The family is a sort of – sort of – "

"Obsession?"

"That's it, the family is an obsession with her. She had set her heart on me marrying a girl – a frightfully nice, pretty little thing. If I had not seen Moira I'd probably have done it, but as it was, the thing was impossible. They wouldn't hear of it when I told them that I would marry Moira – you should have heard them. It was all rubbish too because Moira is fit to be anybody's wife – she has the manner of – "

"A Duchess?"

He smiled at that. "Duchesses usually have damn bad manners. They can afford to I suppose, but anyway you see

240

what I mean. Well things went on between us, and then – "

"Yes, what then?" I asked, for he had paused to light another cigarette.

"Then we were married."

I confess to being surprised.

"Then Moira is – "

"My wife – in the eyes of God and by the Scottish law."

"It was a Scottish Marriage?"

"Yes, we held each other's hands and swore before several witnesses that we were man and wife."

It was at this moment that the studio bell began to ring violently but I was not in the mood for Mrs. Catherton Blaike so I let it ring. I knew that she would soon grow tired of standing outside my door and would depart to spread abroad the report of my unbusinesslike manners and my discourtesy. But that did not trouble me at all – it is rather an asset to be considered discourteous and unbusinesslike if you are a fashionable portrait painter.

"What happened then?" I asked him when the studio bell had subsided into a blissful silence.

"There was a hell of a row," he replied succinctly.

I could well imagine it, even without the help of a bowing acquaintance with Lady Darby.

"*Her* people were just as angry as mine," he continued. "They all declared that there was no marriage. I might have stood up to them but in the middle of it all my mother was suddenly taken ill – she has a bad heart and the – er – excitement was too much for her. The doctor was quite decent, he told me to lie low and let it blow over. He warned me that any further excitement might kill her.

What could I do?"

"What *did* you do?"

"I came back to London with my people. I did not see Moira again for she had been sent away – they would not tell me where. My letters were returned to me."

"Did you go back – to Sutherlandshire?"

"Yes, later. I had an interview with Moira's father. It was pretty awful." He shivered at the recollection. "These old fellows don't mince matters you know, and they're as proud – "

Words failed him.

"What then?"

"I went big game shooting," he replied simply. "I hadn't forgotten Moira, you know, but I will say that I had got over it a little until I saw your portrait, and then it all came back and I knew from her eyes that she still loved me and was waiting for me to come."

So that was the secret of the mystery portrait, the secret that all London had been looking for and had failed to find! Here was no disembodied spirit longing for the unattainable, brooding on the mysteries of the universe. Here was merely the picture of a woman waiting for her lover. The picture was a message, a sort of love letter in oils.

"You will tell me now where you saw her – where I can find her," said young Darby, breaking into my thoughts with the impetuousness of youth.

"I will tell you where you can find your wife – and your son," I said softly.

His eyes glowed. "So it's a son! The family can't say

242

anything now, can they? Now I have got a son."

He rose to go, but I detained him for a moment.

"I hope that you will accept the picture as a – rather tardy – wedding present," I said.

Yes, I am that sort of fool.

THE MULBERRY COACH

THE RAIN HAD CEASED and a pale moon struggled through the flying clouds bathing the countryside in silver radiance. Dark trees, weighted with their summer quota of leaves bowed their heads before the strength of the wind, creaking and groaning beneath the unseen force which threatened to tear them from their roots.

Doctor Burdon drew aside the blind and watched the turmoil of nature for a few moments. He would have a dry ride home across the moor, but obviously a very windy one. His heart was so full of thankfulness, however, that the storm did not seem to matter. Nothing mattered just at the moment, except that the Angel of Death, which had spread his dark wings over the big white house upon the hill, had withdrawn them. The little life which had fluttered for some hours on the Border Land of Eternity was struggling back again up the steep and stormy path which leads at length to health.

The young doctor dropped the blind and turned back to the sick room. It was a good sized room, lighted with shaded electric lights; the side window stood open; up on the floor was an oxygen cylinder and its appurtenances; on the table was a set of medicine bottles, brandy, beef jelly, and a small hypodermic syringe – all the most modern equipment of a sick room – and pervading all was the inevitable smell of disinfectants. The patient, a child of about ten years old, lay propped up on the small white bed, breathing with difficulty.

A nurse, blue gowned and white capped, came quietly

into the room, and busied herself with some dressings on a table near the window. The young doctor smiled at her. It was quite an impersonal smile; he was pleased at the success of his treatment and of her patient care, it was that and nothing else and the nurse knew it.

"I am going home," Doctor Burdon said. "He will do now – the treatment as before – ring up if you want me."

"You will be out tomorrow?"

"Yes."

He crossed over and looked down for a few minutes at the sleeping child. A wild emotion shook him – he felt that he loved the child, though until two days ago he had never seen it. He knew that he had saved its life. "What will you make of it," he wondered.

The wind seemed to have died down a little and the room was quiet. The crackle of a pine log on the hearth was very audible.

"Oh God, thank you!" murmured the young doctor, and then, with surprise, he remembered that he did not really believe in God, he believed in serums and oxygen instead. Queer how these old superstitions cling to one, he thought as he turned and left the room.

His mood of elation persisted after he left the house, for he was very young and he had been afraid that the child was going to die. It seemed to him a horrible thing to die. You just went out like the flame of a candle – it was idle to suppose that anything vital survived – and then decay. Yes, it was all horrible; worst of all to think of death in connection with a child which had not even had a run for its money.

The rain had made the lanes very muddy, and Doctor Burdon's horse floundered through the mess like an amphibian. "By Jove," he thought. "This is pretty grim. I wonder when I shall be able to afford a small car. I might manage a motor bike, but that would be worse. Come up Dapple," he added aloud. "It will be all right when we get into the main road."

Although the moon was bright the lanes were dark in gloom from the interlacing branches of the trees. They seemed to bend down over the horseman, and once or twice his hat was nearly swept from his head.

"Curse them!" he muttered. "Why don't they cut back the trees a bit – how frightfully dangerous to let them grow wild like this!"

It was strange that, though he had been on this side road before, he had not noticed the overhanging branches until now. It was impossible that he had missed his way because there was no other road to take. Horse and rider were both glad when the corner came in sight and the main road from Guildtown to Ellerslie was reached.

It was a high corner, where four cross roads met, and from it the young doctor knew that he would have a view of the surrounding country. He drew up his horse for a breather and looked back across the dark valley for the house he had just left. It stood in a clearing high up on the opposite hills and was visible for many miles on account of its white walls. It would be pleasant to look back and see it gleaming in the moonlight; pleasanter still to see the light from his patient's room shining out across the valley showing that in this sleeping world someone

249

besides himself was awake and active.

The young doctor looked – and rubbed his eyes – and looked again. There was no lighted window; there was no white house; there was no clearing in the dark trees – they swept from the base of the hill to its crown without a break. Surely he must be dreaming – it was the hill right enough, for its queer humped shape could not be mistaken – the hill, but no white house. Was it, could it be a hallucination? He gazed across the valley with his eyes starting out of his head. Yes, it must be some strange trick of brain or eye, yet he was not given to hallucinations, he was much too materialistic. He had never suffered from any form of nerves in his life; he was as sound as a bell mentally and physically.

Dapple, who was tired of standing in the wind, moved forward along the high road, and his rider realised that, whatever the meaning of the strange phenomenon, he could do no good by standing gazing at it and had better be moving on homewards. Especially as he had a long ride before him into Ellerslie and mostly up-hill.

The road, which Burdon knew to be one of the best in England, built for motors and tarred into uniform and glassy smoothness, was unaccountably muddy and dirty. It seemed to have shrunk; the straggling hedges were nearer together; there was a deep muddy ditch on one side that he did not remember having seen there before. At first he thought that he must somehow have mistaken his way but Dapple went forward confidently; he knew his way home and was anxious to get there without further delay.

The road wound in and out, up and down. They passed

a mill where the big water-wheel was turning busily – the doctor had never noticed it before – then suddenly the road dived into a steep valley, at the bottom of which purled a stream. Dr. Burdon remembered the valley perfectly – but surely there was a high bridge which spanned it, and saved the descent. Surely there had been a bridge! Dapple splashed through a ford, swollen with the rain which had fallen in the early part of the night, and breasted the hill which rose steeply on the other side.

There should have been a cottage on the crest of the hill, a tidy, whitewashed building with a flowery garden, but the moor was bare; only a few straggling whin bushes were to be seen.

"Where on earth am I?" he wondered aloud.

Dapple still had no doubts about the way home. He pushed forward confidently into a dark still wood where the trees met overhead plunging the road in gloom.

The mud was deeper here, though Dr. Burdon would not have believed it to be possible. It splashed up to his knees.

It was so dark that he could hardly see a yard in front of him.

Presently he came to a place he knew; a high rock balanced upon another in a rather precarious manner. Yes, it was undoubtedly the rock he had seen before; there could not be two the same. The trees had been cleared a little here; some were still lying where they had been felled. The moonlight fell in a round white splash upon a cottage with a thatched roof and one tiny window. The young Doctor recognised the place, only – only he had known it as a miserable heap of broken stones.

251

"What *has* happened to me?" he demanded, and then, as his horse floundered into another black and greasy puddle, "Can this be the twentieth century? Have I gone mad?"

Dapple held on his way with a determination quite unaffected by his master's doubts, and soon they came through the wood and mounted a steep rise. Dr. Burdon looked round and saw the hills as they had always been; the humpy one behind on his right, and in front the familiar hog's back, clear and treeless in the moonlight. Below, on the right, was the river, a silver ribbon. Yes, it was all as usual, yet stay – where was the railway with its shining rails? Where was the suspension bridge which should cross the river two miles higher up? There was not a vestige of them to be seen.

The young man had just come to the conclusion that he must be drunk, although he had had nothing stronger than barley water all day, when a loud bang shattered the eerie silence of the night.

The road took a sharp turning eastwards round the shoulder of a hill. He pushed Dapple forward. He could hear loud shouts now, the scream of a wounded horse, the crashing of broken glass. "A smash," he thought, urging Dapple to a smart trot, "and no wonder. These God forsaken roads! How any motor could – " but he broke off, for, arriving at the corner, the road opened in front of him, and he saw at once that this was no ordinary smash.

A huge unwieldy coach was stuck fast in the ditch which edged the road so that it was tipped up to the last possible angle. Three horses struggled ineffectually at the traces, while a fourth lay, apparently lifeless, on the ground. A slim boy in a tight-fitting dark overcoat and high boots stood at the door of the coach, surrounded by five of the lowest and dirtiest scoundrels that Burdon had ever seen. One of them had an old pistol with which he had evidently slain the horse. The lad was keeping the five at bay with a rapier which glittered like a silver tongue in the moonlight.

One against five – no two, for, with one bound the Doctor was off his horse, another carried him into the melée.

"At 'em boys!" he shouted, laying about him scientifically. "Down with the Bosche! England for ever!"

The familiar words rose to his lips unbidden and his heart bounded with the joy of battle. Thump, thump,. thump – one rascal got the Doctor's right behind his ear, a second got a kidney punch that made him stagger, while the third, who turned to give battle, received a knockout blow on the point of his chin. He lay very still with his legs twisted beneath him and his upturned face colourless as paper in the white light of the moon. Two ruffians were now in full flight, another lay gasping on the ground with an ever widening patch of red upon his breast to show where the rapier had gone home.

The victors of the fight gazed at each other with mutual interest and respect.

"Gadzooks, Sir," said the boy, holding out his hand to the young Doctor. "It was indeed well done. On my life, three pretty blows! Sir, I am indeed your debtor. My sister and I were travelling to Guildtown when we were waylaid by these demned highwaymen. And had you not rendered us such timely assistance we should have been robbed, perchance murdered, for one against five is long odds, e'en for a Darcy."

"I'm glad I happened to be passing at the right moment," said Doctor Burdon. "But what of your sister – is she in the coach?"

"Gadzooks" cried young Darcy again. "I had forgotten her."

With some difficulty they got the door of the coach open, and between them dragged a young girl from the capacious and gloomy interior. She was a small unconscious bundle of womanhood in a dark red cloak which accentuated the dead whiteness of her face. A profusion of dark ringlets fell over Burdon's arm as he lifted her. Darcy spread a rug by the roadside and the Doctor laid the girl upon it and examined her as well as he could for injuries which she might have sustained from the upset. She had asmall cut upon her neck from the broken window and this the doctor dressed with iodine and lint.

Darcy stood by and watched him with great interest.

"I perceive that you are a surgeon sir, and a skilful one at that," he said at last. "If you are as skilful at mending pates as you are at breaking them, your services are valuable indeed."

The young Doctor looked up and smiled. "It is always easier to break a thing than to mend it, be it pate or plate," he reminded the lad.

"Touché, by my halidom!" cried Darcy delightedly. "Sir, I like your wit."

Miss Darcy now showed signs of returning consciousness and the Doctor withdrew and motioned Darcy to take his place by her side so that her first glance should light upon her brother rather than a complete stranger.

His anxiety regarding the lady at rest, Burdon was at liberty to give his attention elsewhere. Two postillions and another servant in mulberry livery now crept out from behind the hedge, where they had taken refuge at the first sight of the robbers. They looked very sheepish, as well they might, but busied themselves about the coach, cutting the dead horse out of the traces and trying to control the other three. Dapple, with commendable unconcern, was eating grass by the wayside until his master should again require his services.

Doctor Burdon stooped over the ruffian who had received Darcy's rapier through his lungs. He was beyond mortal aid. The two whom he had himself felled were still lying unconscious on the road, so, enlisting the help of one of the cowardly servants, he tied them up securely with strong cord. He felt as if he were acting in an eighteenth century play, and was enjoying himself thoroughly.

The next piece of work was obviously to get the huge unwieldy coach out of the ditch. Burdon went to the coach and examined it with great interest. It was painted a mulberry colour with black wheels and mouldings, and was lined with padded leather. It was so clumsy, with its great heavy body and huge wooden wheels rimmed with iron, that it reminded the doctor of a glorified farm-cart, and he could not help thinking what an uncomfortable journey one would have cooped up in such a primitive contrivance and jolted over the execrable roads.

Burdon was thus occupied with his own thoughts when he looked up and saw Darcy approaching.

"My sister wishes to thank you herself for your timely help," he said.

"Yes, indeed," said a soft voice. "Your assistance was most valuable. Indeed, sir, I do not know how to express my thanks to you for your gallantry in rendering us your aid."

Dawn was breaking now o'er the hog's-back hill and, in its grey light, Burdon was able to see more clearly the face and figure of the lady he had rescued. She was small and slight – he had known as much from her lightness when he had lifted her from the foundered coach – and her beautiful features were also familiar to him, for he had naturally seen her face in detail when attending to her slight wound. But, oh, the difference in them now that they were transfigured by the spirit shining through the flesh; cheeks rosy with gratitude and embarrassment, brown eyes soft yet bright with admiration for the courage which the young man had exercised on her behalf! Oh the difference in a snowy hill, when the sunrise shines upon it, changing its bleak wintry whiteness to a rosy glory of dawn, and each frozen dewdrop to a diamond of sparkling brightness!

The young doctor now really saw Joan Darcy for the first time. It was thus that he was to see her always in his "inward eye," thus that she was to remain to him to his dying day; the one perfect and exquisite embodiment of young womanhood.

For a few moments he was too shaken with a strange strong emotion to speak, and Joan Darcy held out a little ungloved hand and continued,

"May we not know the name of our gallant rescuer? I am Joan Darcy, and this is my brother, Charles."

Our hero bowed over the little hand not ungracefully.

"Henry Burdon at your service," he replied, and then added, "I am very happy to have been of some slight assistance to you and your brother, though I am sure he would have managed to drive off those villains without me. He was holding his own well when I arrived."

The boy laughed carelessly, not ill-pleased with the compliment. "Ah well!" he said. "Five to one is long odds, e'en for a Darcy. But I wager I would have given the rascals somewhat to remember before they overpowered me by their numbers."

The conceit of the words was easily forgiven when Burdon remembered the courageous and competent manner in which this gay young spark had tackled the five robbers single-handed. His youthful and confident bearing denoted pride of race and he was a worthy forbear of those second lieutenants who led their men in forlorn hopes across wire-entangled and shell-swept areas in Flanders and Gallipoli.

The morning mist was gathering now, creeping up from the river, and it was getting very cold.

"We must push on to Guildtown without more delay," Darcy said. "We should have reached there eight hours ago but have been delayed by several small accidents to the coach."

By this time the servants had got the three coach horses into position, and, with the help of the amiable Dapple, harnessed into the coach in place of the dead horse, the heavy vehicle was dragged back onto the road. It seemed none the worse for its adventure. The dead highwayman and horse were pitched into the ditch with equal unconcern – life was cheap in these people's eyes.

"What of these ruffians?" asked Henry Burdon, prodding the two live robbers with his foot. They were fully conscious now and gazed at their captors with blanched faces and staring eyes. It was evident that they were in dread of some terrible fate.

"It is a pity you did not make a better job of them, Surgeon," young Darcy said. "Odds fish, I am too squeamish to run my sword through them in cold blood, tho' it would be the easiest way for us and also for them an' I misdoubt not – "

"Set them free, Charles," begged his sister. "They have learnt a lesson not to molest honest travellers – "

"No, by my halidom!" cried the boy. "We will e'en take them with us to Guildtown and hand them over to the Mayor to deal with as he thinks fit. Ho there, my brave and valiant ones," he continued, turning to the servants. "There is room for these beauties in the rumble – lift me them in if ye are not afraid."

The three servants, whose sullen faces showed that they did not relish their master's humour, set upon the highwaymen with no gentle hands. They were not frightened of men bound and helpless, it appeared, and Darcy taunted them with their courage, crying,

"Mind there, Giles! They might bite, or scratch. Have a care to yourselves, my brave fellows!"

The wretched creatures were hoisted into a large box at the back of the coach which was evidently intended for luggage, and the lid was shut upon their shrill cries for mercy and protestations of amendment.

All was now ready for departure and there was no further excuse for delay. The young doctor had the melancholy pleasure of helping Joan Darcy to climb into the clumsy and inconvenient vehicle; of feeling for a minute her soft little hand rest upon his.

"Farewell," she whispered. "May God and his Saints protect you."

"And you, dear Lady," he replied earnestly, as he raised the little hand to his lips.

"Au revoir," Charles Darcy cried springing lightly into the vacant seat beside his sister. "If I should ever require a surgeon I'll not forget your skill in mending – and breaking – pates!"

Joan Darcy leaned forward out of the window.

"We shall meet again," she said softly and her brown eyes clung to his.

The postillions cracked their whips, and with many creakings and rattlings the mulberry coach lurched off down the road to Guildtown.

Henry Burdon stood quite still with his arm through Dapple's bridle-rein. The mist had crept up from the river to the road, and very soon the coach disappeared into its enveloping folds. For some few moments longer he could hear the creaking and groaning of the great iron-rimmed wheels upon the uneven road, and the sharp crack of the postillions' whips as they urged the overburdened horses along; but at length even that was lost to him and a chilly silence wrapped the countryside.

Dapple grew restive, with longing thoughts of his warm stable and the feed which was awaiting him there. He nudged his master's arm, and Burdon, taking the hint, mounted and went down slowly towards Ellerslie.

He was very tired and his brain refused to cope with the situation.

The sun was rising now from behind the hill, and the mist began to disperse. The road seemed to harden beneath Dapple's feet; little eddies of mist like torn cotton waste drifted past horse and rider. A morning breeze crept up the valley, thinning the mist still further, and below him the young Doctor could see something silvery-bright through its folds: it was the railway suspension bridge which spans the river two miles below Ellerslie. Burdon urged his horse forward until he was on the level with it, and could see it distinctly, its graceful network of steel-girders shining in the morning sun.

Suddenly there was a loud whistle, ear-splitting in the silence of the new-born day, and, with the drumming of many wheels, the London Express swept over the bridge. First came the great green and black engine then the carriages snaking between it, gleaming, glittering, gliding smoothly away. Away over the green smiling country it passed; over bridges and viaducts, past woods and hills and cottages, through tunnels and cuttings hewn out of the living rock.

In two hours time that train would be in London – the

Wonders of Civilization!

The Darcy's and their Mulberry Coach seemed very far away. Would he ever see her again – Joan Darcy – with her beautiful eager face and soft brown eyes? Where was she now in all the immensity of space? Had her life vanished into nothingness like the flame of a wind-blown candle? Henry Burdon found that he could not believe this. He must believe that she was somewhere, that her spirit was waiting, as his would wait, mateless and incomplete until – until someday, somewhere they would meet again.

He put Dapple to a canter and clattered into the still-sleeping town of Ellerslie as if a pack of eighteenth century highwaymen were at his heels.

THE SECRET OF THE
BLACK ROCK

JUST AT THE END of the village, where the bold black rocks began to stretch themselves out into the sea like the feet of giants there was a little white cottage with flowers in the garden. And if visitors came to the village it was always this house which caught their eyes so that they cried, "Oh what a dear little house! How white it is! Look at the little muslin curtains in the windows! Oh we *must* find out who lives there!" And if they were Americans they would stroll up to the gate and remark audibly on the whiteness of the little path which was composed entirely of sea-shells, and admire the tidy grass plots on either side. Upon the gate was a brass plate of unsurpassed brightness which boasted the word "MAINWARING" and upon the wall in spotless white was inscribed the name of the house, "ESTELLE".

There was an indefinable air of the sea about "Estelle" so that even a moderately perspicacious observer could have guessed that a sailor lived in the little house. "Why, it's just like a dinky private yacht," remarked Mrs. Vanderdecker from Boston, and her companions felt that she had "Got it slick in one".

Sometimes interested visitors would be startled by a cry of "Belay there, ye lazy varmints!" followed by a prattling stream of "Good morning all, good-morning — good evening, *poor* Polly, poor old Polly!" And looking about in surprise they would discover a grey and red parrot sitting upon the Virginia creeper which covered one corner of the house. The parrot would then scream hoarsely for

"Arethusa" and sidle along its favourite branch uttering weird nautical oaths in a breathy voice.

At the back of the house was a larger strip of garden which bordered on the cliff and here a terrace had been made from which a wide sweep of sea and rock and curving beach was visible. And here came the master of the house every morning, propelling himself in a wheel-chair.

He was about fifty years of age, broad-chested and wide-browed with a brown and silver beard which was trimmed to a sailor-like point. His blue eyes had acquired the faraway gaze of one whose life consists in thoughts rather than in deeds, but the deep wrinkles in his brown face had been traced there by sea and sun and betokened him a sailor. One saw at a glance how it was that the villagers had come to call him always "the Mate" – it was simply because no other name would have been so applicable.

From the waist upward Mainwaring was whole, as other men are whole, but downwards from the waist he was helpless as a babe, paralysed in the prime of his manhood by a falling spar which had pinned him to the deck and broken his life, as well as his body, quite neatly into two separate halves.

There was a certain pension attached to his injury, which together with his savings and the generosity of his captain enabled him to live quite comfortably with his daughter in the little house upon the cliff. If he could not be upon the sea at least he could see it swimming out before his eyes to the dim horizon where great ships passed and re-passed, on their way to lands which he knew so well. At least he could hear its voice roaring in anger, or gentle as a kitten in play upon the gleaming shore. And the ships as they went past at night winked at him in a friendly manner with their fairy-like lights, or boomed to him their frightened tale of fog-bank and Stygian gloom far out in the misty reaches of the ocean.

These things were meat and drink to the exiled man, they filled his life as the faces and voices of friends might fill the lives of most people. He was simple in many ways as all sailors are, but for all that his thoughts were long — not stretching long into the future like the thoughts of youth but straying backwards into the winding maze of the past where he had held his own with the best before that falling spar had cut short the sea-life he loved so well.

As if to compensate him for the enforced idleness of his body Mainwaring's brain was unusually active and clear, his memory unusually acute, so that hardly a detail of that full half of his life was lost to him, and he was able to wander at will in the narrow noisy streets of half a hundred ports. He could sit beneath the willow trees in bright Japan and watch the Geishas in their graceful dance; he could sail down the Red Sea in baking, roasting sunshine, or watch the surf break in snowy showers upon Pacific beaches. All the world was his for the taking as he sat in his wheeled chair, and watched the far off ships.

It was upon these ships that he journeyed to other lands. The loaded traders took him to lands where the sea of azure blue lapped snow white beaches of coral sand, and tall palm trees strayed down to the water's edge, there to stand like timid bathers wet to the ankles. Gaily coloured birds flew silently amongst the bright green verdure, and fish, scarcely less gaudy, played hide and seek in the clear lagoons which girdled the coast. Other ships there were, small and stubby, black with bad usage and worse coal, and these carried the Mate on very different voyages. Deep green the water here, and the white shore jagged with cruel ice, white and bleak as far as eye could reach; hummocks of ice and snow the only break in the dreary monotony of the scene. Mainwaring had been ice-bound upon such-like treeless wastes for seven months, and the darkness and the cold had eaten their way into his vitals. The whaler — of which he was Mate — had been caught by the sudden onslaught of Winter; for days they had striven like maniacs to hack their way out until even the most hopeful had seen the utter futility of the struggle. Fortunately there was an Esquimau village close by, and the people of it had proved friendly, providing snow huts, and sharing their food with the ice-bound mariners. It was a strange experience and one which Mainwaring had no wish to repeat in body, but it gave him real pleasure to wander amongst the ice-hummocks in imagination while he sat on his sloping terrace in the sun.

There was a great procession of men in the Mate's life, both of friends and enemies. There were men who had shared his pleasure and sorrow, sickness and health; who had saved his life, robbed him, died in his arms. Good, bad, or indifferent, Mainwaring remembered them all, and in almost every case the face and name and characteristics were clearly marked in his brain. There were women too, inevitably, amongst the sailor's memories; his Mother tall and strong with a harsh voice which belied a gentle heart; a few sweethearts in various ports of call; his wife, a gentle timid creature who had died in giving birth to his child — and last, but not least Arethusa.

Strange how at first he had resented the birth of this child, blaming the innocent babe for her Mother's death! Indeed, he had scarcely seen his daughter for the first seventeen years of her life. He had sent money regularly for her upbringing, but he had no wish to see her. Then the old active life came to an end, and the new helpless existence began, and Arethusa arrived one summer evening at the little white house upon the cliff. She turned out the incompetent old woman whom he had hired to "do for him", and rolling back her sleeves, proceeded to bring order out of chaos in a manner to delight her father's heart.

The little minx was full of spunk, thought the Mate appreciatively. He often chuckled now when he remembered how she had routed the old hag in the first skirmish. "We can't eat that," she had said calmly and emptied the contents of the soup-tureen into the refuse bucket, adding thoughtfully, "I hope it won't give the pigs indigestion."

The Mate had enjoyed the joke then, and he still enjoyed it — six years old it was and still good for a laugh. Arethusa often paused in the midst of her domestic duties to listen to that hearty deep-chested laugh, and a tender smile would play round her mobile mouth, and bring the little dimples in her peach-like cheeks.

"What a dear simple boy he is!" the smile seemed to say.

One glorious afternoon in midsummer, father and daughter were out on the terrace together. Mainwaring had just reminded his Skipper that it was six years today since she had taken command of the good ship "Estelle", and Arethusa had assured him that the important date had not been forgotten. Even now there was a surprise on the little kitchen table, a beautiful plum cake which had risen like a dream.

The six years had passed very quickly in quiet yet strangely happy companionship. The outside world scarcely existed for them save in the newspapers, yet neither of the Mainwarings had found life monotonous for they had plenty to occupy their thoughts. Many girls would have found the sequestered life insupportably dull, but Arethusa had a happy nature, she found pleasure in little things. At first Arethusa had hoped to make friends among the people of the village but she soon found that there was nobody with whom she could have anything in common amongst the girls or young men. She saw too, that her father did not care for her to be away from him for long, so the effort died a natural death. The Mainwarings kept themselves to themselves, and were judged by the villagers as "superior and unsociable".

The Mate looked at his daughter as she stood at the edge of the terrace, and he suddenly realised her beauty and her charm. She had come to him a thin slip of a girl, and now she was in the full glory of early womanhood. He noted the rounded curves of arm and hip, the soft full cheeks in which the colour came and went like the flush of dawn, deep blue eyes like his own, only less dreamy and more sparkling as befitted her age.

"You'll be leaving the ship one of these days," he told her suddenly.

"Leaving the ship!" she echoed in surprised tones.

The Mate winked solemnly and Arethusa saw that her leg was being pulled.

"One Mate's quite enough bother," she told him, her eyes full of laughter.

Mainwaring smiled tenderly and then sighed—what would happen to Arethusa when he had gone? She never met a man, her charms were hidden in this desert place. He did not want her to leave him yet he would have liked to see her married to a good husband — a sailor of course — would have liked to see her with a little child.

Arethusa was quite unconscious of her father's thoughts; her eyes had drifted seawards as they often did. She saw a small sailing yacht which fled gracefully before the wind gunwale deep in the little waves which sparkled in the sunshine. The sight gave her a feeling of sheer happiness; it was so pretty, so golden, so free.

A sudden exclamation from the Mate recalled the girl from her dreams and she saw a look of consternation grow and deepen upon her father's face. Following the direction of his look she found her eyes upon the steep and stony path which led from the shore to the terrace and coming towards them on the path was a stranger, a tall thin man in a well-fitting blue suit.

There seemed little in the stranger's appearance to account for the Mate's perturbation; he strolled along with a jaunty air of self-satisfaction, and every now and then he made a little pass with his stick and decapitated a dandelion with the precision of an artist.

"Clear the decks, my girl. Go into the house and stay there," said the Mate suddenly and fiercely.

Thus it happened that when the stranger reached the terrace overlooking the sea he found only a crippled man in a wheelchair — a crippled man who surveyed him with a pair of hard blue eyes from which the dreamy look was conspicuously absent.

"What brings you here?" asked the Mate sharply.

The stranger paused for a moment before answering and looked down at his interlocutor with a peculiarly mirthless smile. If there had been any doubt in Mainwaring's mind as to the identity of his unexpected visitor that smile would have solved it. It was a sinister smile in which insolence was blended with mock humility, the thin lips curling back from the white pointed teeth in a manner positively devilish.

"What brings you here?" the Mate repeated.

"To see an old ship-Mate."

"Your old ship-Mate can get along very well without you."

"Come come! This is not a friendly greeting."

The tone of this reproach was one of amiable banter, but there was something so deadly in the man's dark eyes that Mainwaring almost shuddered. It was like a chill wind upon a hot day. For himself, helpless as he was, he feared nothing but there was another to be considered. Arethusa was the weak joint in his armour or, as he would have put

272

it, the weak plate in his otherwise storm-worthy vessel.

"I suppose you want to borrow money," he said, trying to adopt the half-jesting tone which the other had affected. "That is what most of my old shipMates want when they come to see me."

"Do I look as if I needed to borrow money?" asked the stranger, still smiling in the sinister manner.

The Mate's fears deepened and took shape as he saw the man seat himself upon the stone bench and light a long cigarette.

In the silence which followed the sea could be heard beating monotonously upon the pebbled shore. If Henry Dutton were not here to borrow money he was here for some other purpose, and the Mate knew him well enough to be sure that it was for no good one. For the first time in his years of crippledom Mainwaring cursed his help-lessness. His hands clenched and unclenched themselves convulsively with the longing to be at Dutton's throat, with the longing to seize him and send him flying down the steep path which he had ascended so jauntily — but alas, he was as helpless as a child! He and Arethusa were in the villain's power. Dutton may or may not have been aware of the Mate's thoughts — at any rate he gave no indication of his own. His attitude was that of a friend who has gone out of his way to call upon an invalid. He talked at length, recalling old times and mutual ship-Mates, and Mainwaring realised that there was nothing for it but to take the role assigned to him in the farce of friendship.

It was all the more a farce because the two men had never been friends. Though no saint himself Mainwaring

273

had drawn the line at intimacy with men of Dutton's calibre who were not only vicious and degenerate but positively gloried in the fact.

"You are very comfortable here," said Dutton at last when he had broken the ice with his preliminary reminiscences of men and voyages. "They tell me in the village that you are a man of means and have a pretty daughter to keep house for you."

"Village folk are an idle set of gossipers," growled Mainwaring.

"Too true," returned his visitor sententiously. "Yet sometimes they supply useful information. That daughter now — I should like to meet your daughter, Mainwaring."

The Mate was about to reply with an indignant refusal but the words died on his lips. There was an undercurrent of deadly purpose beneath the man's ingratiating words.

"The girl's busy," he said, as civilly as he was able.

"No doubt," agreed Dutton amiably, but with an insolent air of power which made the Mate's blood boil. "Still she might leave her duties for a few minutes to speak to such an old friend of her father's. I am sure you must have some way of calling her if you require anything but if not I can walk up to the house and find her myself — perhaps that will be the easiest way."

He rose as he spoke, and the Mate saw at once that he was cornered. There was no means of stopping Dutton and the meeting which he dreaded so greatly was inevitable. Sea-life had rendered Mainwaring quick at decision, and finding himself once more amongst shoals and quicksands his hand grew steady upon the tiller.

"I'll call her," he said shortly, choosing the less dangerous course, and a full-throated shout of "Ship ahoy — Ahoy there Skipper!" startled the dreaming silence of the little garden.

Arethusa had been watching the two men from the attic window. Something was wrong, for her father's face had been full of trouble at the stranger's appearance, and his brief command to clear the decks had sent her heart fluttering into her throat. Never before had the Mate used such a tone to his little Skipper, her knees trembled at the mere thought of it.

For some reason she was not to meet the very personable man who carried himself with such a jaunty air. Arethusa was sorry, because people — strangers — were scarce at the Estelle, and she found them interesting. Old friends of her father's turned up very occasionally bringing with them the scent of the deep sea — different to the scent of the seashore as chalk from cheese. They brought also the glamour of the outer world and the strange sound and colour of other lands. It was therefore with pleasurable feelings that Arethusa heard her father's summons and patting her hair into order went out demurely to meet her father's guest.

The Mate's eyes were upon her as she came down the garden path, and for the second time that day he realised the sheer beauty of her. This time, however, it gave him no pleasure; nay, it was with feelings of anxiety and fear that he saw afresh her womanly charm. He could have wished her cross-eyed, hunchbacked and bow-legged rather than the vision of springtime loveliness which she was.

A glance at his visitor's face confirmed his worst-fears.

The man had gone a trifle white beneath his tan, his jaw hung open showing his pointed teeth, and his eyes were greedy.

"Arethusa," said her father, "this is a ship-Mate of mine, Henry Dutton".

They shook hands, and the Mate shuddered. That this vile thing should come in contact with his child, his innocent little Skipper was almost more than he could bear — or at least he felt it so.   Perhaps it was well for him that he could not see the future or guess how much more he must bear before he was done with Henry Dutton.

Arethusa's first impression of the stranger was very favourable; his manner was charming, courteous and restrained. He made it obvious that he admired her, and yet not too obvious. Seated beside him upon the stone bench, listening to his ripple of interesting talk, the girl could not help wondering why her father had been so upset by his sudden appearance. A dozen explanations occurred to her, but none of them was entirely satisfying. Even now the Mate seemed ill at ease, and quite unlike his usual jovial self. Dutton's reminiscences of sea-life, amusing as they were, failed to elicit the hearty laugh which Arethusa knew so well.

The afternoon shadows were lengthening upon the little garden when Dutton rose to go.

"I am staying at the Crown Inn," he said, as he held Arethusa's hand in his. "And I will look in after supper for another little talk with your father."

Arethusa looked towards the Mate for the invitation which was clearly expected, but his eyes were upon the sea.

Far in the distance a sailing vessel was beating up against the wind, and her evolutions were so interesting that he failed to observe his Skipper's signal, failed also to observe his old ship-Mate's hand when it was extended towards him. Dutton waited for a few moments, and then turned away with a little insolent laugh and disappeared over the crest of the hill still walking with the careless swagger.

The crew of "Estelle" was seated in the small dining-room (or saloon as the Mate chose to call it) having a belated tea before any mention was made of the afternoon's visitor.

"That's a bad man, Skipper," said the Mate suddenly. "Don't you have more to do with him than you can help."

A blush rose to the girl's forehead at her father's words and she replied quickly, "He seemed — nice."

"Well he's not," said Mainwaring. "There's many a ruined woman, aye and a ruined man too, who can trace their downfall to yon plausible rogue."

Arethusa was silent, but her big blue eyes were fixed upon her father's face with a look of horror and shame,

"I didn't want you to meet him," the Mate continued, "but for some reason he was determined upon it, and it was better for you to meet him out there with me at hand than for him to come up to the house. You've a helpless crock for a father, my girl — he's not good for anything."

Her woman's swift intelligence divined the meaning in his words and her heart ached with the pathos of his first and only complaint of helplessness. A small brown hand stole into the big one and rested there for a moment.

"Shall we bar the door to him?" she asked suddenly.

The Mate considered this. They might bar him out for a few days but if he meant business he could force them into a state of siege. To bar the door was a sign of weakness and fear. It might merely serve to rouse Dutton's obstinacy, might make him the more determined upon his course whatever that was. Arethusa saw the point of her father's argument, and after some deliberation they agreed to treat him with a sort of luke-warm friendliness in the hopes that he would soon become bored, and take himself off of his own accord. It seemed the only course open to them.

"But what does he want?" demanded Arethusa with a puzzled frown.

"God knows," replied Mainwaring wearily.

It soon became only too obvious what Dutton wanted at "Estelle". He came every day to the little house on the cliff, and made no secret of his passion for Arethusa. He was impervious to snubs, and oblivious to all sense of decency. Arethusa's coldness towards him seemed merely an incentive to his desire for her, and he turned a deaf ear to her father's entreaties to leave her alone. At first he had imagined it would be amusing to seduce the girl, and to blackmail her father, but her beauty grew upon him to such an extent that before many days had passed, he was willing to marry her, and share her inheritance.

Failure with the fair sex had not come his way before, and the novelty of it only added to Arethusa's charm. He was determined to have her somehow, by fair means or foul. The Mate, helpless as he was, incommoded Dutton in the pursuit of his object; he was always there destroying their tête-à-tête and interrupting Dutton's flowery periods with some downright statement or assertion. Sometimes Dutton tried to entertain his unwilling hosts with tales of his adventures, and of his prowess in battle or storms, at others he would sit silent with the sinister smile twisting his thin lips, and his dark eyes fixed gloatingly upon the terrified girl. They were never safe from him for he came at different hours. If Arethusa went to the village for a message she would find him at her elbow offering to carry her basket, and bending over her with a proprietary air which caused her sheer panic. If she were rude to him he merely smiled, if she besought him to leave her, he assured her that she was too attractive to be left without a guardian. The villagers began to nudge each other when the pair appeared, and many a nod and wink was exchanged as Arethusa and her faithful cavalier went past.

Terror took up its abode in Arethusa's eyes, she began to look over her shoulder furtively as she went about her duties, and her face lost its roundness, and became pinched and thin. The change in his little Skipper was not lost upon Mainwaring. He agonised over her like a mother, yet he was powerless in the hands of the wily Dutton, powerless to protect his child.

Would the man never tire of his hopeless pursuit? Was there no way to get rid of him? Mainwaring asked himself these questions in despair, he lay awake night after night turning over every plan which entered his mind. Alas, he could find no solution to his problem for there was always the fear of his return. The local policeman might be induced to turn the man out of the house but he could not keep him out, nor could he prevent Dutton from molesting Arethusa whenever she went out. Dutton would merely go away to return later when they were least expecting him. Their life would be one of constant dread in expectation of his return. There was nobody else, no friend or relation whose help could be procured. He might send Arethusa away, but he had nowhere to send her, no place which would be safe from the unscrupulous adventurer.

Bad as it was, Mainwaring realised that the situation might soon become infinitely worse. There were signs of impatience about Dutton. The greedy look in his eyes became more pronounced when he glanced at the girl whom he desired.

"If anything happened to me — " thought the Mate.

And he turned upon his face and beat his burning hot pillow with impotent hands.

It was long since the Mate had slept the sound health-giving sleep of freedom from care. His brain felt foggy, yet there were bright patches in it which seemed all the brighter for the surrounding dimness. He had strange visions, partly of scenes from his early youth and partly imaginary. On this particular night he could hear the sea, far in the distance, straining at its leash like an eager hound, ready to break away and race shorewards at the given signal.

In the great bay which lay in a half circle inland from the Black Rock, Mainwaring had once had a strange and alarming adventure; and tonight half in dream and half in vision he relived the episode from his past. A long shut cupboard in his brain yielded up, unasked, its long forgotten memory. Why did it do so tonight? Was it the sun, rising out of the sea like a golden coin, round and shining which opened the door?

It seemed to Mainwaring that he was out on those flats of sand and seaweed beneath the towering shadow of the Black Rock. The sea, withdrawn from the humid land, strove loudly in the grip of the unseen force which held it so securely from it's accustomed place. Village tradition averred that a Spanish ship full of gold had gone aground upon these jagged prongs, and as if to prove that the old wife's tale was true, young Mainwaring found a piece of foreign gold tightly wedged between two rocks. If there was one piece there were others, thought the boy, excited beyond all bounds by his treasure trove. He commenced a search, and in ten minutes had added another piece to the first which was reposing in his trouser pocket.

Suddenly a cold rush of water about his feet recalled him to his senses, and, realising his peril, he turned landwards stumbling amongst half covered stones and slippery seaweed. The tide rose quickly here, more quickly than a man could run, and every moment the sea grew deeper, while the strong eddies threatened to sweep him off his feet. A few moments more and the water was waist high, swirling about him muddy and dull with its swift rush over the rocks and sand.

Mainwaring struggled on towards the cliffs; he was young and very strong, and his hold on life was tenacious. By this time the bay was full of water, a seething, churning mass of foam which parted here and there upon cruel jagged rocks. Mainwaring was a powerful and confident swimmer but one glance was sufficient to show that that line of escape was closed to him; amongst that inferno of water a man would be battered to death in a few moments. He made his way as quickly as possible towards the tall cliffs which surrounded the bay. Every moment the sea rose and grew more boisterous — all his hope was upon the cliffs. If he could only reach them in time . . .

At last, after what seemed an eternity of struggle, Mainwaring reached the cliff upon which his hope was centred, but here disappointment awaited him for the sea had worn away the base until the upper part overhung the lower to such a degree that only a fly could have scaled them. He wasted a few precious moments trying vainly to find a foothold upon their crumbling flanks, but the surface was so smooth and weathered that even a goat could have found no safety there. He braced himself against the overhanging rock with the water breast high. There was no hope in him now, and scarcely fear — only a feeling of rage at the way he had allowed himself to be trapped. What a fool he had been! How futile to end one's life thus!

A seagull flew over his head with a scream of defiance at the leaping waves, and, landing gracefully upon a tiny shelf of rock, folded its wings. It had reached a place of safety above the turmoil of the water.

"If only I could reach that ledge," thought the boy.

It was one chance in a thousand, but it was the only one, and Mainwaring was not only a strong swimmer but something of a gymnast as well. He decided to risk the experiment, and leaving his position, which was quickly becoming untenable, he struck out strongly for the gull's shelf of rock. The waves and the undercurrent, pent into the bay, were so strong and boisterous that Mainwaring strong as he was, felt as helpless as a cork. Three times he had his fingers upon the ledge and three times he was torn away from it by the suction of the receding wave. The fourth time his grip held, with the strength born of desperation he dragged himself into safety. The gull flew away with a shriek of horror at this invasion of its private territory, its soft wing brushed against his face as he sank down exhausted.

Cramped and cold and drenched with spray the hours spent upon that narrow ledge seemed interminable. But at last the tide ebbed and Mainwaring descended stiffly from his refuge and made his way back to the village, a sadder and a wiser youth. So disgusted was he at his own stupidity in getting caught by the tide that he spoke of his adventure to nobody and the two gold coins had remained lost from view ever since, in the darkest corner of his sea-chest.

The sun had risen higher now and had lost its resemblance to Spanish gold. Its bright beams shone full upon the Mate's bed which was, as usual, drawn close up to the window so that his waking eyes might first behold the sea. The cheering light, which irradiated the little room, dispelled his nightmares and renewed hope in his breast. He clasped his hands like a little child and prayed that some way out of the tangle might be found.

It was still very early but Arethusa was astir. He heard

her brushing the stairs with the familiar rattle of the burnished stair-rods as accompaniment to her labour. How good she was, Mainwaring thought, what a wife she would make to some man — someone worthy of her who would bring her a clean heart, and beget healthy children to lie in her tender arms!

Presently she came in to wake her father, bringing him hot water and his morning cup of tea. The Mate saw at once that she had been weeping, for her bright beauty was blurred with tears, her small hands trembled as they placed his tray in position.

"Little Skipper!" he said pitifully.

Arethusa knelt down and flung her arms round her father's body, pressing her poor face against his breast. It was comfort to feel his strength, useless though it was. His hand, tender as a woman's, stroked her soft hair, pressing it back from the white forehead so close to his own brown and wrinkled cheek.

"He was here last night," said Arethusa at last. "I heard him in the garden, and on the roof of the shed where your chair is. He tried the door, and all the windows — "

"Good God!" said the Mate despairingly.

She gave a little sob.

"Oh Father, Oh Father!"

He had no words to comfort her.

After breakfast it was the Mate's habit to wheel himself down to the terrace, there to smoke his pipe of shag, and to watch the ships if any chanced to be in sight. If there were none he read the shipping news in the daily paper with much the same interest that a society woman would scan the court circular. On this particular morning however, he had no heart for his usual excursion; even the shipping news failed to rivet his attention. He pottered idly about the house waiting for Arethusa to finish her morning duties. The memories which had come to him so clearly during the night, or rather in the early morning, were still clear in his mind and for want of other employment he unlocked his old sea-chest, and after some trouble found the coins which had so nearly cost him his life.

Mainwaring looked at them with awakened interest as they lay in his great palm. They were dim with damp and rust, but pure gold none the less — Spanish Gold. There was something of romance about them which stirred his heart. Perhaps there were chests of these precious counters out there beyond the breakers. And then suddenly the horror of his adventure swept over him like a wave, and with a little shiver of disgust he thrust the gold into his pocket, and out of sight.

When Arethusa was ready she locked up the house securely, and they went down the garden path together. It was early October; the leaves were beginning to turn all colours and a bed of chrysanthemums smiled in the sunshine. The path was smooth and level to the edge of the terrace from where it sloped gently to the cliff. Mainwaring's chair was fitted with a strong brake so that he could stop at will half way down the terrace where the stone seat had been built into the grassy bank. Here also was a small iron table where the crew of "Estelle" occasionally took their tea.

On this particular morning Mainwaring was half way down the terrace when he suddenly realised that his brake was not acting. He struggled with it, losing a few precious seconds during which the chair gathered momentum. It was not until the chair had passed its usual resting place and was rushing headlong down the slope that Arethusa realised what had happened. She ran after it, and seizing it with all her strength dragged her father back from the cliff's edge.

For a few moments they were both speechless with horror. If Arethusa had not been there the chair and its helpless occupant would have been dashed to pieces on the rocks below, and thus ceased from troubling or being troubled with other people's affairs, but they were a plucky pair, and soon recovering from their shock, began to probe the cause of the brake's failure. It was easily solved, for the brake-rod had been neatly filed through; the two edges of the severed steel were bright from their contact with the file.

Skipper and Mate looked at each other with white faces. There was no need of words between them for each knew only too well what the other was thinking.

"Not a word of this to anyone," said the Mate, after a long and terrible silence. "You understand, girl, not a word."

"The police!" whispered the terrified Arethusa.

Mainwaring shook his head. "What proof have we that he did it? Who would believe us? Nobody."

It was only too true.

Long after Arethusa had left him to go and prepare their simple dinner, Mainwaring sat thinking. The sea retreated, curtseying as it went. It soothed him, for he felt that it was his friend, his only real friend in this careless world. The incident of the morning had not only been alarming on its own account but terrifying in that it showed how far Dutton was prepared to go to attain his ends. It showed that the man was desperate. Mainwaring knew that he was his daughter's only protector — useless and helpless, but still better than nothing, better alive than dead. Dutton had evidently realised the same truth, he would stop at nothing now. This attempt had failed but he would try some other means of putting an end to the Mate's interference with his play. The next attempt might succeed. In any case the end was inevitable and Arethusa would be left defenceless, an easy prey for the wily and unscrupulous Dutton. Was there no way out?

The Mainwarings were just starting their dinner when Dutton walked in looking very cheerful and debonair. He had made it a habit lately to turn up at this hour, partly because he appreciated Arethusa's cooking, and partly because funds were running dry, and the landlady at the inn was beginning to press him for his bill. The siege was taking longer than he had anticipated, and he was firmly convinced that this was due to the Mate's influence — that influence must be removed. It was worth a little trouble, for with Arethusa and her house and her money he would be comfortable for the rest of his life.

If Dutton were surprised to see his old shipmate alive

and looking much as usual he showed no trace of it upon his inscrutable face. If anything his smile was more in evidence than usual — more wolfish. He helped Arethusa to lay another cover and sat down to eat with the man he had tried to murder.

Mainwaring seemed in the best of spirits, laughing and joking with Dutton as if he were his best friend. To an onlooker the meal would have seemed a very friendly affair; only Arethusa sat silent and anxious for she had no clue to her father's strange behaviour. Had the shock of this morning turned his brain?

Dinner over, the Mate produced a bottle of brandy and poured out a liberal helping for himself and Dutton. The talk grew wilder and more hilarious, and presently Arethusa went out and shut the door. The sight of her father's face, flushed and excited made her sick with horror — he, the most abstemious of men, whose nightly glass of grog was his only indulgence . . .

What could be the meaning of it? She remembered the Mate saying that Dutton had ruined women and men too. Was this the beginning of it? Was his evil nature beginning to influence her father?

"She doesn't 'prove of me having a little nip," said the Mate a trifle thickly. He nodded towards the door and winked slyly. "Says it goes to my head — head's as strong's ever," he added and tossed off the remainder of his brandy to show his independence.

Dutton followed suit. "Good stuff that!" he remarked, refilling his glass with an absent-minded air.

"Y' won't find me drinking bilge," said the Mate, wagging his head from side to side knowingly. "Y'll find 'nother bottle in the cupboard, Dutton."

Dutton rose, nothing loath, but as he crossed the room his eye fell upon two gold coins which lay upon the writing table in the window. The sun shone upon them making them glitter dully. Just for a moment Dutton thought that they were sovereigns but a second glance showed him that they were larger and differently marked.

"Hulloa Mainwaring, what are these?" he asked, taking them in his hand and examining them with interest.

Mainwaring laughed unsteadily. "Spanish Gold, Spanish Gold! Y'd like to know where I got 'em — ha ha!"

Dutton's eyes sparkled at the idea of treasure, but he replied casually, "Pooh! These aren't gold, they're silver gilt medals. You got them at some Exhibition, I suppose."

"Not gold!" cried the Mate angrily. "Not gold indeed — shows all you know 'bout it. What but pure gold would have stood hundreds of years in the sea? Found these myself when I was young feller, found 'em out there in the bay at low water, sticking in holes in the Black Rock."

"I don't believe a word of it!"

"I don' care," said the Mate with difficulty. "Don' care if you don' believe it. There's Spanish Ship — treasure ship — went down out there off the Black Rock — every old wife in the village knows tale — went down with all han's — chests treasure out there — not gold indeed," he continued, seizing up the coins and growling over them like an old dog with a bone. "Not Gold! Shows all you know 'bout it."

Dutton thought hard for a few moments. The tale was

most probably true for men usually told the truth in their cups and the Mate was thoroughly ginned. The old dog must have an uncommonly weak head for a few glasses of brandy to have this effect upon him (Dutton himself felt comfortably stimulated) but perhaps the Mate had been drinking all the morning. Now that he thought of it Dutton remembered that there was an unusual air of joviality about the Mate even before the brandy had made its appearance. It was evident that he had not discovered the "accident" to his brake.

"If your tale is true it's a wonder the whole village isn't out searching for gold," he said at last, in the same tone of casual interest.

"What d'ye take me for?" chuckled Mainwaring. "There's nobody knows 'bout these two pieces of gold but me."

"You've never gone back to look for more?"

The cripple laughed bitterly. "Haven't wings!" he replied thickly, and stretching out his hand for his glass which had been filled to the brim by his attentive guest he tossed it off in one gulp.

"Spanish Gold," he murmured unintelligibly. "Spanish gold!" and sank back in a drunken stupor.

Dutton sat and watched him for a few moments, marking the sagging mouth and stertorous breathing with something akin to disgust. He himself often got drunk but he got drunk like a gentleman — or so he imagined. This man was nothing but a swine. Still, swine had their uses — dead. His fingers itched to close themselves round that unprotected throat; it would be so easy. Just one good squeeze; it would not be the first time he had done the trick . . .

And then the gold caught his eye. Spanish gold — the coins seemed to multiply, he could vision piles of them, chests of them. He could feel them running through his fingers, could hear the musical chink of one falling upon another . . .

The Black Rock rose jaggedly out of the troubled water. It spelt romance — the romance of treasure. The tide was ebbing rapidly, and the sands showed flat and shiny, the rocks bestrewn with seaweed green and brown, there was no time to be lost.

Dutton picked up his cap and stole softly out of the room.

The Mate's drunken slumber lasted until the footsteps of his guest had died away in the distance, then he wheeled himself nimbly to the window, seized his telescope which was never far from his hand, clapped it to his eye and fixed it on the shining sands and weed-strewn rocks of the Great Bay.

For a long time he remained there motionless, but at last his patience was rewarded — a tall slim figure came into view walking with a jaunty stride. Mainwaring followed it as it wound its way in and out of the boulders and weedy pools until eventually it disappeared among the dark caves and crannies of the Black Rock.